'For the Children of the Earth'

Asses in Clover

Eimar O'Duffy

Jon Carpenter

Our books may be ordered from bookshops or (post free) from
Jon Carpenter Publishing, Alder House, Market Street, Charlbury,
OX7 3PH
01608 811969

e-mail: jcp@joncarpenter.co.uk

Credit card orders should be phoned or faxed to 01689 870437 or
01608 811969

Please send for our free catalogue

Many attempts have been made, including placing an advertisement in *The Times*, to contact the estate of Eimar O'Duffy. All have failed.

First published June 1933

This edition published 2003 by
Jon Carpenter Publishing, Alder House, Market Street, Charlbury,
Oxfordshire OX7 3PH

ISBN 1 897766 86 6

Printed in England by J. W. Arrowsmith Ltd., Bristol

I thank the goodly god of Gold
Who has denied me nought,
Who has increased me fifty-fold,
Because I have not thought.

I thank the god that gave the lie
To what the Saviour quoth,
And made it possible that I
Serve God and Mammon both

I thank him yet again that he
Hath granted me this lot:
Two lands at war, yet I can be
In each a patriot.

Eimar O'Duffy, 1918
After the Easter Rising

ACKNOWLEDGEMENTS

It has only been possible to make this edition of *Asses in Clover* available through the generous work of Anne Goss, Alan Armstrong, Bryony Partridge, Keith Hutchinson and many other people. Especial thanks are due to Ken Palmerton for drawing our attention to the existence of the Cuanduine Trilogy.

PRONUNCIATION GUIDE

(*using the symbols of the Oxford Dictionary*)

Cuanduine . . Cōŏ-ŭn-dhĭn·nĕ

Mac ui Rudai . . Mŏc ē Rŏodh·ē. ('a Mhic ui Rudai' is the Vocative case, and is pronounced 'ă Vĭc ē Roŏdh·ē').

Cruaidin Cailidcheann Crōŏ·i-dhēn Cŏ·lĭd-chyown

Badb . . . . Bīv

INTRODUCTION

by Frances Hutchinson

Very little has changed since Eimar O'Duffy delivered his manuscript of *Asses in Clover* to his publisher seventy years ago. The human race is not a wit less committed to going to work and to war just as the leaders and their 'expert' financial advisors tell them to. The intervening decades have seen the rise of Hitler, the carpet bombing of civilian populations in a thousand German cities, the Holocaust, the atomic bombing of Hiroshima and Nagasaki, decades of violence against civilian populations culminating in 9/11 and the current Gulf War. The violence of man against humanity has been accompanied by the desecration of the land by agribusiness, while in the name of 'progress' social and spiritual values have been demoted to optional extras. Meanwhile Mac ui Rudai, the man-in-the-street, remains content to produce and consume the latest commercially viable fad in food, clothing, shelter, furnishings, entertainments and holidays designed by the corporate world. As debt-finance-led production and consumption devour field and forest across the globe, rendering soils, seas, lakes, rivers and the very air itself stale and unwholesome, the human race is well on its way to the end as foretold by O'Duffy early in the last century. The same sneaky ray of hope which drove O'Duffy to write his Cuanduine Trilogy impels the current editors to reprint this masterpiece of riotous anger.

Asses in Clover, the final book in the Cuanduine Trilogy, can be compared to more recent works. The zany humour in a fantasy setting was later to be echoed by Douglas Adams in *The Hitchhiker's Guide to the Galaxy*. Similarly, Tolkien's *The Lord of the Rings*, as critiqued by Patrick Curry, fanned into flames that same small spark of hope in his quest for the re-sacralization of living nature. O'Duffy's style and content is echoed in Orwell, Swift and Shaw, while Michael Moore's barely controlled rage in *Stupid White Men* continues the devastating attack on the politics of war and world order in the present day.

Born in 1893, the playwright and novelist Eimar O'Duffy succumbed to duodenal ulcers, the satirist's occupational disease, at the age of 42. He has been described as 'modern Ireland's only prose satirist'. As such, he was 'neither hanged nor drowned. He was simply ignored',* as tends to be the fate of artistic opponents of global corporatism. *King Goshawk and the Birds*, the first volume of the Cuanduine Trilogy, is set in the future, when the continued rule of the King Capitalists has further devastated the earth. Goshawk, King of the King Capitalists, is persuaded to buy up all the song birds and wild flowers (representing access to the spiritual world) for his wife, Guzzelinda. Incensed at this blatant injustice, an old

---

* Robert Hogan, *Eimar O'Duffy*. Lewisburg, Bucknell University Press (Irish Writers Series) (1972: 13).

Dublin Philosopher summons the mythical Cuchulain back to earth. After a series of droll failures, Cuchulain relinquishes the quest to Cuanduine, the son he agrees to father for the purpose of seeking justice for the common people. However, Cuanduine also fails to generate popular support for the liberation of the natural world from private ownership. The rich are content to pay for access to the theme parks created by King Goshawk, while the poor are too ground down in misery to be aware of their loss. The Swiftian sequel, *The Spacious Adventures of the Man in the Street*, follows the story of Aloysius O'Kennedy on Rathé, a semi-Utopia. *Asses in Clover* takes up the story of Cuanduine's battle to free the songbirds and wild flowers. Although O'Duffy's Cuanduine Trilogy continues to be of interest to students of Utopian literature, the full humour of the final book is lost without a grounding in the economics of social credit. While the first two books are a richly comic indictment of the political economy of the twentieth century, the final book is informed by O'Duffy's research into the teachings of Clifford Hugh Douglas and the social credit movement. Hence the present book goes beyond critique by presenting viable routes to a decentralised world order.

Published at about the same time as *Asses in Clover*, O'Duffy's *Life and Money*, a detailed summary of the basic ideas of Social Credit, ran to several editions and was warmly praised by Douglas. For O'Duffy, finance, which is privately created, has come to dominate personal and corporate decision-making, leading to social and environmental disintegration, accompanied by economic and military warfare on a global scale. The butt of his criticisms are not the leaders of corporate capitalism, who are at least honest in their self-interested quest for power, *but the ordinary person who refuses to think beyond their own immediate short-term self-interest*. Hence the blind quest for 'work', i.e. for a money income, paid by an employer, no matter what rubbish is being turned out by the financially viable economy. In both his fiction and his non-fiction O'Duffy skilfully presents the case for the ordinary person to receive a basic income as a right of citizenship. The obstacle, as he sees it, is the inertia of the brain and will of the 'man in the street'. The stark choice is between life and money. No amount of 'expert' advice can be substituted for clear thinking on the part of the individual. All have the same potential to choose between slavery and freedom. Excellent on logic, and hilariously funny, O'Duffy is low on optimism.

The work of O'Duffy and Douglas fits into a wide spectrum of political thought fundamentally opposed to the centralising of power, whether in the hands of capitalists or state monopolies. Like Douglas and O'Duffy, the vast majority of writers in this genre have been allowed to slip into virtual obscurity. H.J. Massingham, G.K. Chesterton, Hilaire Belloc and others belong to a broad church of writers sharing a common notion of the rights of the ordinary person to autonomy over their own lives. The substance of Social Credit was set out as a compact précis in Douglas' *Economic Democracy*, first published in 1919, with his subsequent publications providing amplification and elaboration of the main theme. The book lays out the basic tenets of Social Credit. Potentially, the wealth of the world is so great that competition over the existing supply is beside the point. In seeking to appropriate a greater share of the product for the worker, through securing control over administration, socialists are tilting at windmills. The root of the problem lies in the financial system, since the mechanisms whereby banks determine economic outcomes are beyond democratic control. Credit, the property of the community, should be administered by the community, and not by some centralised, unaccountable, unelected power, whether under private or state control. Instead, the community could use banks to pay a national dividend to all citizens. Observing the increasing centralisation of power following World War I and the formation of the League of Nations, Douglas predicted that financial amalgamations on the one hand and alliances of trade unions on the other heralded the crushing out of individual authority and initiative in the work place and in the civic life of the community.

A basic income or national dividend for all by right of citizenship could be introduced tomorrow with no difficulty. It is a small matter of accounting, coupled with a massive engagement of brainpower. However, recognition of the stark reality of the alternative will come just after the point of no return is reached. With debt mounting around their ears, the mass of citizens chant 'I owe, I owe, so off to work I go!' as they march like lemmings over the proverbial cliff. An Orwellian 'doublethink' has indeed taken hold (my spell-check allows the word without lighting up red). Hence individuals can shift their ethical stance according to the dictates of their current paymaster. 'Mobile truth' indeed enables us to serve both God and mammon.

The work of Douglas, O'Duffy and a host of other social credit writers contrasts sharply with the hedonism underlying modern political economy. As such, it requires detailed study, for which the texts listed below provide a starting point. Following George Orwell, we suggest that for readers more familiar with 'Newspeak', the 'Oldspeak' of Social Credit, rooted in concepts like justice and social responsibility, may initially seem incomprehensible. But it is worth the effort. The stakes are high.

Frances Hutchinson
Willow Bank, April 2003

Further Reading

Patrick Curry, *Defending Middle-Earth. Tolkien: Myth and Modernity*. London. Harper Collins (1998)

Frances Hutchinson, *What Everybody Really Wants to Know About Money*. Jon Carpenter (1998)

Frances Hutchinson, Mary Mellor and Wendy Olsen, *The Politics of Money: Towards Sustainability and Economic Democracy*. Pluto Press (2002)

Eimar O'Duffy, *Life and Money*. Putnam (1932/3)

Michael Rowbotham, The Grip of Death. Jon Carpenter (1998)

J.R.R. Tolkien, *The Lord of the Rings*. Grafton Books (1991)

CONTENTS

BOOK I

The Travels of Cuanduine

BOOK II

The Triumph of Cuanduine

BOOK III

The Passing of Cuanduine

Contents

BOOK I

The Travels of Cuanduine

CHAPTER I

How King Goshawk held a Council of State

IN my former book I told you how Cuanduine, son of Cuchulain, came down to earth to rescue the songbirds and the wildflowers from the grip of Goshawk the Wheat King; and how, for his pains, he was laughed out of his own country and frozen out of England; whereafter, for lack of something better to do, he put a laughable end to the war that had broken out between the Wolfians and the Lambians.

Now while these things were happening, King Goshawk and his liege kings were sitting in council in Manhattan, discussing the state of trade. There were assembled round the board Butterworth the Dairy King, and Tanberg the Tea King, and Ah-Sin the Rice King, and Gurgleheim the Liquor King, with his brother-in-law 'Scab' Slughorn the Crime King, who had just come from laying a million dollar wreath on the platinum coffin of his predecessor, Bud Boloni, whom he had bumped off a week before. There were also Pulpenbaum the Paper King, Gripall the Heat-Light-and-Power King, and a dozen princes of lesser commodities.

King Goshawk sat on a golden throne at the head of the table, as became the Lord and Master of all; and in a humble position behind the throne, close to the mouthpiece of the Great King's ear-trumpet, sat his secretary, Mr Slawmy Cander, whose black coat and grey trousers rendered him almost invisible among the flamboyant costumes of the kings and princes. Nevertheless he was the greatest personage in the room. Goshawk ruled the world; but Mr Slawmy Cander ruled Goshawk. Goshawk was King; but Mr Slawmy Cander was almost a god. He was director of all the banks in the world; he made credit out of nothing; and he issued that which all men worship. Nobody, however, knew that he was anything but Goshawk's secretary: for Goshawk cared nothing for the reality of power so long as he had the trappings, and Mr Slawmy Cander despised the trappings while he had the reality: therefore they kept the secret between them.

Now the matter under discussion at the meeting was a disastrous plenitude of certain crops, notably milk and rice, due to a most unfortunate succession of fine seasons over large parts of the world, whereby the profits of many princes had been seriously diminished, and large numbers of their subjects thrown out of employment, with world-wide repercussions in trade depression, bankruptcies, and distress. King Pulpenbaum denounced the selfishness, or rather inefficiency, or both, of King Butterworth and King Ah-Sin who were the cause of it all. By flooding the world with cheap dairy produce and rice they had caused universal misery and starvation, and undone all the good achieved during the past ten years by King Goshawk's policy of wheat restriction. Where was the sense of it? demanded King Pulpenbaum. What was the use of dangling vast supplies of cheap food under the noses of millions of unemployed who couldn't afford to buy it? What was the good of producing tons of butter when people had no bread to spread it on? It was enough to cause a revolution. His own industry had been hit severely by the resultant slump. The circulation of newspapers was falling off steadily, and thousands of forest-cutters had been thrown out of employment in consequence. Something, he concluded powerfully, must be done about it.

King Butterworth and King Ah-Sin pleaded that it was not their fault. They had done their best to discourage production, but the forces of nature had been against them, and they had failed.

King Goshawk scathingly reprimanded their inefficiency, and declared that he had no alternative but to order the destruction of their surplus stocks, and a reduction of thirty per cent in their output for next year.

King Ah-Sin objected that if the starving multitudes heard that vast stores of rice were being destroyed there would be trouble.

'Don't let them hear about it' said King Goshawk.

'I'll see to that' said King Pulpenbaum omnipotently.

'With the deepest respect to your serene imperiousness' said Ah-Sin, 'such doings cannot be kept dark. I would sooner distribute my stocks free to those that need them.'

At these words a violent agitation of the tube of Goshawk's ear-trumpet might have been observed. After a moment of abstraction, he said: 'There can be no tampering with the inexorable laws of economics.'

'Wal' said Butterworth, 'I don't know much about them, but I'm durned if I'm going to reduce my output thirty per cent for anybody. Why, there might be a shortage next year, and then where'd we be?'

A breath came along Goshawk's ear-trumpet.

'The alternative' said he 'is a drastic restriction of credit by the banks. They will have no choice' he added.

Butterworth went pale.

'O say!' he protested. 'Give us a chance.'

'Give us time' pleaded Ah-Sin. 'One bad season is all we need to save us, and the astrologers prophesy that it's coming along next year.'

Goshawk brightened at this good news, and his eye fell on his chaplain, the Reverend Doc. Bargold, Bishop of Broadway, who sat modestly among the minor princes, waiting till he might be wanted.

'Say, Bish' said the King, 'do you hear that? You better go right away an' order prayers for a bad harvest.'

CHAPTER II

Concerning Bish Bargold and the great Temple of Broadway

NOW Bish Bargold, by the power of Goshawk, was boss of all churches except that obstinate out-of-date church that sitteth upon seven hills. But his own temple, where he manifested his glory and drew his dividends, was in Broadway. Never in all the world was there another temple like it. The eighth wonder of the world it was, and made the other seven look silly. It was two hundred storeys high, not counting five steeples each higher than the other, and its cost was an hundred million dollars. Its walls were of jasper and jade and chalcedony, well plastered with advertisements, which brought in a revenue of five million dollars a year. Between the advertisements there were five hundred niches containing statues of successful men, with a scroll under each specifying the virtues which had enabled him to get on.

The Temple had a hundred doors, each made of one of the most expensive woods known to commerce: but the main door was of gold and ivory. On either side of this stood colossal figures representing Christ and a stockbroker clasping hands above the lintel, symbolic of the great truth that business and religion go hand in hand. Above the door was this text in illuminated letters:

THE SKY IS THE LIMIT
ANY ONE OF YOU CAN BECOME THE PRESIDENT OR A MILLIONAIRE
GET GOING
AND GO GETTING

The first floor of the Temple was a vast store fronting on Broadway; for, as Bish Bargold said, men must learn to find all they need in the Church. The store paid a 7½ per cent dividend, thus showing that it is possible to serve both God and Mammon.

Above the store was an hotel de luxe, nine storeys high, with 666 rooms, and a telephone in each: to fulfil the dictum of Bish Bargold that he who would be saved must live within the fold of the Church.

The next ten storeys of the Temple consisted of speakeasies and dope dens: for it is written, let all human activities be under the robe of religion. There was also an inner shrine of Aphrodite, served by beautiful girls who had been found not quite brainy enough for screen work. These were of great assistance to tired business men who came here to pay their devoirs to the Cyprian Goddess.

The eleventh floor consisted entirely of telephone booths; and in the middle was an altar to the virtue of telephone-consciousness: for it is well known that this virtue makes Americans what they are. No other country is so telephone-conscious as America, which has 11·9 telephones per inhabitant, as compared with 11·9 inhabitants per telephone in Europe.

The next nine storeys consisted of cafeterias, soda fountains, general stores, and movie-theatres. It was in fact a thoroughly twentieth-century cathedral, self-supporting, community-serving, with elevators flying all day from floor to floor, like the angels on Jacob's ladder, as Bish Bargold beautifully expressed it.

Above these was a vast room made to look like a grove, with imitation trees and flowers, and artificial sunlight; where various Adamite cults were permitted to assemble without clothes. For, as Bish Bargold said, our religion must be comprehensive, and surely the human body is a beautiful thing. But that was before he saw the congregation at their devotions.

Above that there was a branch of the Manhattan World Bank; and above that more than fifty floors of business offices, where the click of typewriters and calculating machines made music all day in the ear of Mammon.

Somewhere in this region, remote, mysterious, and inaccessible, were the offices of the Sacred Congregation of Sound Economics and of the Financial Inquisition. The approach to them was by a dark labyrinth of corridors, more intricate than that of Cnossos, blacker than the subterraneous channels of Acheron and Cocytus, so that none could find a way through unless provided with a clue by the proper authorities. It is said that many persons who have ventured into these arcana have been lost for ever to the memory of man, and their bones are become resting places for the blind hairless vermin that inhabit the obscurity. The Sacred Congregation was founded by Mr Slawmy Cander to inculcate in the public the spirit of faith in the mysteries of economics, and of reverence for economic laws, so necessary for the proper working of the financial system. The purpose of the Inquisition, on the other hand, is to suppress all false and unorthodox teaching by heretics and cranks. No other office of High Finance has been so grossly maligned by the enemies of the True Faith as this, and its detractors have not scrupled to conceal their malice behind specious appeals to reason and so-called freedom of opinion. But as there can be no doubt that it is the duty of Finance, as overseer and instructor of all the factors of production, to preserve sound economic doctrine, so also is she bound to restrain the malice or madness of those who would corrupt the purity of economics, and thus plunge the world into bankruptcy. This duty she carries out, not in the old-fashioned Romish way of fire and sword, but simply by a little moral pressure on newspaper editors and proprietors. It is not to be supposed, however, that further coercive powers, which she does not employ in fact, are not hers by right. In view of the disastrous consequences of unsound financial policy, there can be no doubt that she can and ought to visit with fitting punishment the heretic and the disobedient, and the time seems ripe for her to begin to do so.

We come now to the more strictly religious part of the building. First there was the chapel of St. Sisyphus and St. Procrustes, the patrons of toil and scarcity. Before the statue of St. Sisyphus—a giant in white marble, striving with cracking muscles to roll a boulder up a mountain—thousands of workless men prayed every day for employment. Before

St. Procrustes—a golden figure standing by an iron bedstead—monopolists and financiers prayed for blight and bad weather.

Next to this chapel was the shrine of St. Progressa. The figure of the great Preserver was a somewhat gaudily coloured plaster cast of the great statue in London, representing her with a scientific chaplet about her brow, and a baby beneath her feet, swaddling the orb of the world with a contraceptive appliance. Before this ikon women and girls of every degree used to pray regularly for sex knowledge and sterility. This is one of the hymns they used to sing at morning prayer in the spring of the year:

Hymn to St. Progressa

O Goddess all wise and all knowing,
  Behold us in prayer at thy fane!
Let us taste of the joys of the sowing,
  But never the garnering's pain.
Let our kisses increase and redouble;
  Let us relish the prize ere we run.
O spare us the toil and the trouble,
  And leave us the fun.

O lily-white lover of candour!
  O mine full of facts about sex!
We thank thee, celestial Pandar,
  For lifting the yoke from our necks.
Now we cherish a homely Priapus,
  To the phallus familiarly nod,
And softly and smoothly reshape us
  The grimness of God.

Thanks to thee that my claspings and kisses
  No fear of the future can foil.
Thanks to thee that my marriage-bed blisses
  Shall never bring worry or toil.
Thanks to thee that I am not as others
  Who have heeded or heard not thy lore,
The lusty lascivious mothers
  Of seven or more.

On my bosom though hot lips have lingered,
  It was not for cooling they came;
And the hands that have fondled and fingered
  Have sought but to kindle a flame.
For closed is the womb of the lover,
  Progressa, and dry is the milk,
Since thou didst the method discover
  Old Nature to bilk.

Thanks to thee we have altered the habits
  That else we had never outgrown.
Thanks to thee we can rut like the rabbits,
  And still remain sterile as stone.
Ah! founder of radiant marriage,
  'Tis to thee that we owe what we are.
Thanks to thee we've a house with a garage,
  And in it a car.

We play with light loves without peril:
  We are wild—but we take not a chance.
Loves die, and we know they are sterile:
  Naught lives but immortal romance.
Since we know there's no hell and no heaven,
  Since we know that all grain is but tares,
Our enjoyment is seventy times seven
  In suchlike affairs.

Thou art blessed by the boss and the banker
  Who hast tamed the insatiable fire,
The rage of youth baffled, the rancour
  Of lovers denied their desire.
Thanks to thee they can wed without care now,
  And the bride can remain at her post:
They can live in one room unaware now
  Of anything lost.

Thanks to thee that our children (if any)
  Shall always in prudence be got;
That we'll scrape in the very last penny
  Before we'll adventure a jot.
Thanks to thee that the heirs of the ages
  Shall never with boldness be curst,
But shall flourish the motto courageous
  Of 'safety first!'

Above the chapel of St. Progressa was the chapel of the Business Virtues, each of which was represented by an allegorical statue. There was Honesty (which, of course, is the best policy), Sobriety (coupled with self-confidence), Industry (pouring with honest sweat), Thrift (a hard-faced woman sealing up the mouth of a cornucopia), Perseverance (in getting on), Optimism (casting facts into a well), and last but most important, Faith (in oneself).

Above this was the great Church of the Modern Religion. Nobody ever prayed there, for religion consists in deeds, not words, and they were all serving the cause of true religion by making good at their jobs. But in order that the space should not be wasted, it was fitted up as an office for the Syndicate of Religious and Uplift Writers, from whose typewriters there flowed a stream of pious articles for the press of the world, which found them a very paying proposition, roping in many millions of readers not catered for in the sport, society, and sex columns. Hereunder are the titles of some of the more edifying of these features:

The Modern God, by Rev. Simon Broadhead.

The Business Man's God, by One Who Knows Him.

Let God Get You On, by Cyrus Catchum, principal of the Broadway Correspondence College.

Out of the Depths, by Maisie Goldfish, the world swimming champion.

God is my Racket, by 'Sunny' Jones, the world tennis champion.

My Racket is God, by 'Plugs' Kybosh, the famous rum-runner.

God and Economy, by an ex-Chancellor of the Exchequer.

Bring God up to Date, by Hurricane Harridge, head of the famous Store.

My Sex-Appeal is a Sacred Trust, by Undie Bareskin, Hollywood's new 'It' girl.

Prayer with a Punch, by Kid Bashville.

Debunking God, by a Plain Man.

I Believe in Love, by Gertie Slimshank, the well-known novelist.

What's Wrong with the Churches, by Popsie Tiptoes, the £1000 a night vaudeville star.

Take the Scowl off God, by Rev. Woolly Smiler.

Are Your Prayers Persuasive? by Samuel Slick, application letter specialist.

My Tip Is: Back God Both Ways, by Pete Goldberg, the Old Firm.

My Notion of Gawd, by Morgan Goldcalf.

They issued also a correspondence course on Commercial Christianity, explaining the minimum of religion necessary for a young man desiring to get on. For, as Bish Bargold said, the young man in business owes it to himself and his future to go to church occasionally. Success and a certain amount of religion seem to go hand in hand.

Above the church there were five steeples, as I have said, and on the tallest of them was an immense cross, 103 feet high, bearing in electric lights the legend:

'LET GOD GET TO BROADWAY'

Truly this Temple was a smart idea for selling salvation, and an excellent investment for its shareholders. 'Five per Cent in your Fellow-man's salvation,' as the prospectus put it. Broadway, you may be sure, was the better for so substantial a reminder of the Holy Presence. From every vantage point, by night and by day, that cross of unquenchable fire was visible, flashing its glowing testimony against the heavens, and the pious stockbroker, seeing it, murmured to himself reverently: 'The Holy Spirit bides with me wherever I may be, waking or sleeping.'

To this Temple went Bish Bargold to pray according to the command of King Goshawk.

This is the prayer of Bish Bargold:

'O God who made all things, in the name of Goshawk I beg to humbly draw thy attention to an error in thy creation, in which, despite our prayers and entreaties, thou still persistest. Lord, thou hast made Nature over-bountiful in her fruits, so that she yieldeth much in return for little toil, thereby upsetting our magnificent financial system, and casting people out of employment into starvation. Therefore we beseech thee, render our soil less fertile, our seed less potent, our labours more onerous, and their return less abundant. Send us less rain and less sunshine (except, of course, at fashionable resorts), more storms and more snow. Put forth thy creative power, and endow us with bigger and better pests, with more voracious rats and locusts. Stultify the brains of our scientists, we implore thee, that they may be less ingenious in invention. And above all things reduce our population that there may be work for all.

'In the councils of High Finance, in their efforts to cope with the present crisis: hallowed be thy name.

'In the hearts of the people, that they may cheerfully accept the burdens and sacrifices that Finance may require of them: thy kingdom come.

'In the policy of High Finance for the restoration of public credit: thy will be done.

'By the general increase of exports and surcease of imports, and by the restoration of public confidence in our magnificent economic system (not, let me repeat, by a bountiful harvest): give us this day our daily bread.

'Because the lower orders have indulged in luxury and sloth, content to draw doles instead of working; because they have been froward and discontented with our magnificent economic system: forgive them their trespasses.

'Lest we disregard the inexorable laws of political economy: lead us not into temptation.

'Because our magnificent economic system is showing signs of breaking down: deliver us from evil.

'From discontent and envy
'From the blight of leisure
'From the curse of plenty
'From unsound financial policies
'From the abomination of inflation
'From unprincipled agitators
'From theorists and dreamers
'From Utopian quackery
'From all sorts of currency cranks
} Good Lord deliver us.

'God bless the Bank of International Settlements for ever and ever, Amen.'

Bish Bargold also sang a hymn, as it is the one point on which all religions are agreed, that God likes listening to bad singing. This is the hymn sung by Bish Bargold:

'Look down, O Providence so good,
On this unhappy earth,
And, lest we die of plenitude,
Redeem us with a dearth.'

While the Bishop is singing the rest of the hymn, return we to the council chamber of King Goshawk.

CHAPTER III

The Counsel of the Kings concerning Cuanduine

WHEN the Bishop had gone out, the Kings began again to consider what was to be done about the rice plague; but presently they were interrupted by the rising of Gripall, the Heat-Light-and-Power King, who said:

'Sorry to butt in, guys, but I just gotta message of urgent public importance. The Wolfo-Lambian War is over, and all my munition workers gonna be thrown out of employment.'

'Impossible' cried King Goshawk. 'I haven't given 'em leave to break off.'

'They've done it all the same' said King Pulpenbaum omnisciently. 'I knew it an hour ago, but I didn't think it was of any importance. The papers are all featuring Frillie Lushlip's autobiography at present, and haven't room for much else.'

'I can't understand it' said Goshawk.

'I'll fetch a reporter along' said Pulpenbaum, and spoke into the telephone.

A few minutes later an alert young man salaamed before the monarchs.

'So please your Majesties' said he. 'The war has been stopped by Cuanduine.'

'Coondinner?' said Goshawk. 'Who's that guy?' and rang a bell for his Remembrancer. This was a young scholar and poet, who, having taken to himself a wife and children, and thus given hostages to fortune, as Bacon hath it, had been compelled to take to the trade of selling; and, having nothing else to sell, had sold himself to Goshawk to be his instructor and remembrancer, as men in more superstitious ages used to sell themselves to the devil.

'Cuanduine' said he 'is the alleged demigod who insulted your Majesty at Ascot last year.'

'My bucks and cents!' cried Goshawk. 'I remember him well. Tell us all about him.'

So the Remembrancer told all he knew about Cuanduine, which was not very accurate, since his information was from the newspapers. At a certain point of the narrative a tremor shook King Goshawk's ear-trumpet. 'O' said its owner. 'So that mutt, MacWhelahan, gave the fellow dough without consulting me? Very well.' Thereupon he scribbled a note, and MacWhelahan was consigned to an oubliette, and the world heard no more of him.

'Go on now' said King Goshawk; and the Remembrancer told how Cuanduine had become the lion of a London season, how he had been loved by great ladies, and made speeches to great mobs, and how he had smacked Nervolini on the breech in front of his whole people.

Goshawk's resentment vanished, and he gave a horse-laugh. 'By my bank account' said he, 'that guy's a live wire. I must buy the fellow,' and he felt for his cheque-book.

'I fear' said the Remembrancer 'he is unpurchasable.'

'I'll pay high for a guy of his sort' said Goshawk, writing a huge figure on a cheque.

'Not enough' said the Remembrancer.

Goshawk added another nought.

'No use' said the Remembrancer. 'Cash won't buy him.'

At this statement King Goshawk was seized with a sudden weakness, such as always overcame him in the presence of strange ideas; but, having sniffed the smelling-salts proferred by Mr Slawmy Cander, he regained his composure sufficiently to say: 'See here, young man. Next time you gotta canful of highball stuff like that to spill, break it to me gently. If dollars won't buy this feller, what will?'

'I don't know whether he can be bought at all' said the Remembrancer. 'But, if he has his price, it will be the fulfilment of a dream.'

'A dream?' said Goshawk.

'Your Majesty' said the Remembrancer, falling on one knee, 'lest what I am about to say may displease you, grant me now indemnity before I speak it.'

'Say on, Remembrancer' quoth the King graciously.

'Well, then, your Majesty' said the Remembrancer, 'perhaps it may be in your royal memory that once upon a time there were birds in the woods and fields, and wild flowers also grew there, and men could enjoy their song and their beauty free of charge. Then one day your Majesty took them——'

'Bought them' snapped Goshawk, looking at Mr Slawmy Cander, who had created out of nothing the credits for the transaction.

'I crave your Majesty's pardon.—Bought them for your own gardens and aviaries. Now this Cuanduine has an impracticable dream that one day they may be free again, and for the fulfilment of that dream he might enter your Majesty's service.'

'He needn't worry' said Goshawk magnanimously. 'If I take him on, he can have all the birds and flowers he wants. Send someone off at once to offer him the contract to put my advertisement on the face of the moon.'

'With the humblest respect for your Majesty's intellect' said the Remembrancer, 'you have not yet understood. Cuanduine would scorn such employment. He would say he had God's work to do.'

'Wal, let him do it. I don't wanna interfere with the guy's religion. I'm all for tolerance. He can go to any church he likes so long as he does his job right. Now just nip off and send an airman to offer him the contract.'

The other Kings had listened to this colloquy in silence so far, but now Gripall intervened.

'Say, bo' he protested, 'I don't like this at all. This feller Coondinner seems to be a dangerous sorter guy that don't oughter be encouraged.'

'O yeah!' said the other kings in chorus.

'Chief' said Pulpenbaum, 'Bud Gripall has spilt a bibful. I don't see this demigod running errands for any of us. And what's more, he seems to be a Bolshie.'

'O.K.' said a minor prince near the end of the board. 'I heard the guy speak in London, and it was all Bolsh stuff.'

'Wal, boys' said Goshawk, 'that settles it. I ain't gonna take on a guy like that. I sorter liked his pep, that's all; but if he's a Bolsh it's a wash out.'

'Wash out ain't enough, Chief' said Gripall.

'Are we kings gonna let a goldarned demigod go running round the world talking Bolsh and stopping wars? I don't believe in superstition, but this guy's got more'n human powers, and it's about time he had his wings clipped.'

'Rah! Rah! Rah!' chorussed the minor princes.

'Gripall has sound dope' commented Pulpenbaum. 'I don't wanna say too much, but a wink's as good as a bill of indictment to some folks I know, and I reckon this demigod could find easier quarters than this sordid planet.'

Here 'Scab' Slughorn, at whom Pulpenbaum's eye had been directed, began to play with his gun. Then he spoke into the telephone. 'Who's on duty?—Right. Send him up.'

A young man in airman's costume entered the room.

'Slick' said Slughorn, 'ever heard of Coondinner?'

'Yessir' said the young man.

'Very well, Slick. We don't wanna hear of him any more.'

Slick saluted, and was about to depart when Slughorn called him back.

'This is a tough job you're on,' said the Crime King. 'So no fooling about. Coondinner's a sorter demigod, you know.'

'I'll do my best, sir' said Slick. Then, turning to Goshawk with a magnificent gesture, he said: 'Ave, Cæsar, moriturus te saluto,' and marched out.

'What does that mean?' asked Goshawk.

'French for Merica specks every guy to do his duty' interpreted Butterworth, who had been to a university in his youth.

'Wal, he's paid for it, ain't he?' said Goshawk. 'And now, you guys, what about this milk and rice ramp? Are you going to cut down production or are you not?' and he scowled horribly at the Kings responsible.

'I'm willing enough' said Butterworth, 'but I daren't do it. You know your own dictum, King? You can starve all the people some of the time, and some of the people all the time, but you can't starve all the people all the time. I daren't cut down my produce unless the Tar King and the Feather King and the Hemp King will cut out their products altogether.'

'Say, bo' said Goshawk to the Science King, 'could your boys invent us a good cattle disease and a rice pest?'

'Sure' said the Science King.

'Wal, go ahead.'

'That's no good' objected Boodleguts the Tripe King, who, as he lived in the Kingdom of Kerry, had a wholesomer fear of the people than any of the others. 'If there's a milk shortage, the folks won't worry whether it's caused by a bug or a trade agreement. They'll start shooting anyway.'

At this there fell a gloom on every royal countenance, and there was a general loosening of royal guts under the strong purgation of fear. But presently King Pulpenbaum arose, and said he:

'Your Majesties, I gotta bright idea, which will both save the present situation and redound to the everlasting glory of our great and good overlord, King Goshawk. This yer overproduction ain't a genuine overproduction. There's plenty of folks in need of milk and rice, only they can't buy it. Cos why? Cos they ain't got no work to do. So what I says is this: why not *create* work for 'em? What sorter work? says you. Wal, I'll tell yer.'

King Pulpenbaum paused, while his fellow monarchs watched him impatiently.

'I was reading in a guide-book the other day' he resumed 'about the origin of them pyramids you got in your garden, King Goshawk. It says they were built in Egypt way back in history by a king called Chops to be his funeral monument. Now I guess an erection like them gave a big lot of employment, so what I say is this. Why not build a pyramid a thousand times as high, to be a gravestone for our own good King Goshawk? Not that I don't hope it'll be a long time before we stow him underneath it, but I guess it'll be a blame sight longer in the building, and if we cut out all expensive machinery and build it by hand, it'll employ half the unemployed labour in the world.'

'Brother' said Goshawk, 'you've squashed the grape-fruit,' and all the monarchs cried 'Rah! Rah! Rah!' But at the same moment the cable of Goshawk's ear-trumpet waggled like a serpent, and his face fell.

'All the same, fellers' he said, 'it won't work. We ain't got the money.'

'What are we to do then?' cried Pulpenbaum in despair.

Goshawk was silent for some moments, while a stream of wisdom flowed along his ear-trumpet.

'The fact is, boys' he said at length, 'the world is living beyond its means. We gotta economise. You boys gotta send out word to cut wages another twenty per cent, and I'm gonna instruct the governments to cut down expenditure. See?'

There was an uncomfortable silence. Then Goshawk, prompted by his ear-trumpet, spoke again:

'We gotta issue a manifesto, so's there'll be no misunderstanding. Got your notebook, sec? The worst of the depression is now over, and prosperity is just round the corner. A little more sacrifice by everybody will bring it in sight. Hard work and strict economy must be our watchwords. We must all pull together and cultivate the team spirit, and I have no doubt that sooner or later we shall win through. Got that? Now Pulpenbaum, put that on the wires. Snap in it.'

'No need' said Pulpenbaum. 'We have it all set up in stereo.'

CHAPTER IV

How Cuanduine found himself short of Cash

NOW, when the Wolfians and Lambians made peace as I have told you, both these nations begged Cuanduine to be their king and to rule over them. But the heart of Cuanduine yearned towards his own people; and he would not. Therefore they made him a Grand Commander of the Most Stupendous and Illustrious Order of the Jerusalem Artichoke, and a Knight Grand Cross of the Indomitable Order of Swashbucklers, which are the highest honours that can be accorded to foreigners by the constitutions of the states aforesaid. They also presented him with the shield with which Horatius kept the bridge, and the helmet of Perseus: as to which latter, if it had ever been able to make its wearer invisible, that virtue had now gone from it, though it was still a good warder of blows. Finally the Lambians said to him: 'Is there anything else we can give you? Whatsoever you desire, you have but to name it, and it is yours: for nothing we possess is good enough for our deliverer from slavery and death.'

Cuanduine replied that there was nothing he desired; and as for delivering them from destruction, that good deed was its own reward. 'For' said he 'there is nothing so pleasing to my eye as the sight of a free and happy people. Therefore God bless you, and farewell.' So he took the helmet and the shield, and packed them with his sword, the Cruaidin Cailidcheann, under the seat of the airplane; and he cranked up his engine on the Micropolitan Plain, where all the people of Micropolis were gathered to see him off.

At the same moment a young man stepped out from the crowd and approached Cuanduine; who received him with a handshake of welcome, for it was none other than Mr Robinson, who had come to Lambia as special correspondent for the Cumbersome papers.

'I am glad to see you' said Cuanduine to the young man. 'What is your will of me?'

'To knock around with you' said Mr Robinson. 'You are a man after my own heart, and make excellent copy.'

Cuanduine bade him step on board, and once more began to start his engine, but the engine would not budge.

'By my hand of valour' said Cuanduine, 'I have no more petrol. And by the same token, I have no money either: for I have spent every penny of what MacWhelahan gave me and what I earned from Lord Cumbersome to boot.'

'That's a nuisance' said Mr Robinson; 'and, as it happens, my pocket was picked in the crowd, so I have none either.'

'No matter' said Cuanduine. 'For this people whom I have liberated have promised me in their gratitude whatever I may desire. I will ask them for some money, and then we shall buy petrol and whatever else we need.'

So Cuanduine stepped from the plane, and going

to the people he said: 'People of Lambia, you bade me just now to ask of you anything I might desire.'

'We did, we did' said the people of Lambia.

'And thinking I wanted nothing, I asked nothing' went on Cuanduine.

'True' said the people.

'But now I find I have a most pressing need. Is it your will that I ask you to grant it?'

'You have but to name it' said the people.

'Well, then' said Cuanduine, 'I want some money.'

At that the people looked at one another in surprise and disapprobation, thinking this a most indelicate way of putting it, and hardly believing that so gallant a youth should be so mercenary. Neither were there wanting cynics to say: 'Ha! I guessed he wasn't in this business for his health,' or 'did anyone ever go into public life except for what he could get out of it?'

Seeing how matters stood, one of the Governors of the Lambians addressed Cuanduine as follows:

'Young man, I am ashamed of you. You are like all the rest of your generation, selfish, shallow, materialistic, worldly; without illusions, utterly blind to ideals, thinking only of what you can get out of life instead of what you can put into it. You want to be petted and pampered, to have all your battles fought for you, to start at the top of the ladder instead of working your way up. This is not the way the great men of the past have got on. They started without anything but their own grit and determination, and fought their way up, step by step. In the sublime words of Shakespeare:

"The heights by great men reached and kept
Were not attained by sudden flight, but they,
While their competitors were fast asleep,
Were toiling upwards in the night."

Money, in fact, is a curse. There's no greater handicap to a young man starting life. Knowing that he always has something to fall back upon, it saps his energy, curtails his initiative, and drugs his ambition. I knew a very promising young chap one time who was just beginning to make good when somebody died and left him a lot of money. From that moment he went to the bad—cards, wine, horses, women, and the devil. Years afterwards, when I met him coming out of a dopeden, a broken wreck of humanity, he told me he owed his downfall entirely to that legacy. So take my advice, young man. Make your own way in the world, and don't rely on props and crutches. And mark my words, you'll be happier eating a dry crust that you've earned yourself than the finest banquet paid for by others.

'And here's another point. These are difficult times. The pessimists have lots of bad news to gloat over. But there's a silver lining to every cloud. While some men are groaning over their losses, others are founding their careers and their fortunes. *There was never a time when the rewards of courage, enterprise, and hard work were so sure or so swift.* Difficult times are times of *opportunity*. That is being proved every day in this world of paradox.'

Another of the governors, a big fat sow of a fellow, with seven chins, and thirteen creases in the back of his neck, now came forward and spoke to Cuanduine. Said he:

'Young man, you envy the rich and think that if you had their wealth you would be happy. Nothing could be further from the truth. Money, my friend, cannot bring happiness, as I know only too well.' Here he paused to wipe away a tear. 'Money can buy none of the worthwhile things of life. Health! Beauty! Love! Goodness! Happiness! Not one of them can be bought for filthy lucre. Can you walk into a shop and order five shillingsworth of health or beauty? No. Can you telephone to a church to send up a parcel of goodness on account? No-o. Can you ask a woman to sell you a pound of love? No-ho-ho ——' Here the honest fellow began to slobber like a hippopotamus, and the thread of his argument was lost.

Next came forward the Archbishop of Micropolis, who piously admonished Cuanduine as follows:

'My son, like all the young people of this generation, you are too solicitous for the things of this world, and you lack faith in Divine Providence. Ask and you shall receive. Will not He who feeds the sparrows provide for your wants? Therefore seek not treasures of gold and silver and precious stones, for all these are but vanity: but pray for the grace of an humble and contrite heart, and resign yourself in all things to the will of heaven.'

'Amen' said the Governors in pious unison.

Then said another of the Governors: 'Besides, young man, this demand of yours is impossible. We are the trustees of the people's money, and, in any case, after their disasters, they have none to give away. And besides, you told us just now that the sight of a free and happy people was sufficient reward for you. Therefore, take your fill of it, and good luck to you.' And as it was now growing dark and the people feeling it was time for supper, they soon wandered away, leaving Cuanduine and Mr Robinson alone with the machine on the empty plain.

'Well' said Mr Robinson. 'Here's a pretty kettle of fish.'

'It is no matter' said Cuanduine. 'I am weary of greatness. Now we can wander through the world and learn the lot of common men.'

'I'm with you' said Mr Robinson. 'I believe in you, and I think you'll go far.'

Thus it was that Mr Robinson joined himself with Cuanduine and began to write him up; by which means he was destined in the fullness of time to raise himself out of the ruck of ordinary reporters and become a writer of special articles. And thus it fell out that when Slick and his air-thugs came to Micropolis they found nothing but an abandoned plane, which they took back with them to their master, Scab Slughorn, who laid it at the feet of King Goshawk. And as Cuanduine vanished altogether from human sight at this time, it was generally believed that Slick and his men had bumped him off.

CHAPTER V

Cuanduine visits a Modern Home

CUANDUINE and Mr Robinson set out on their journey, Cuanduine wearing the helmet of Perseus and the shield of Horatius, with the great sword of his father, the Cruaidin Cailidcheann, girt at his side, and Mr Robinson carrying a packet of ham sandwiches. Presently they came to a cottage, and Cuanduine said: 'Hold. Let us seek shelter here for the night.'

'Better remove those trappings first' suggested Mr Robinson, 'or the people will be frightened.'

'They must learn to be brave' answered Cuanduine, and rapped on the door.

It was opened by a comfortable buxom young fellow in a white apron, somewhat red in the cheeks, and his bare arms flecked with soap-suds, as if he had come straight from the wash-tub.

'Sir' said Cuanduine, 'we are strangers who have lost our way and crave your hospitality for the night.'

'You are welcome' replied the man with a comely smile. 'Come in, my good lads.'

He showed no sign of fear at the hero's accoutrements, which he did not appear to notice. And I may tell you now that through all their travels Mr Robinson observed that these attracted no more attention than if they had been a billycock hat and umbrella. Indeed, after a while, Mr Robinson himself ceased to notice them; which you can explain as best you can. The goodman showed them into a cosy parlour, where there was a fire burning, and a table laid for supper, and said: 'Sit down now and make yourselves comfortable. I must go and finish off my washing; but my wife will be home soon'—here he gave an eager glance at the clock on the mantelpiece—'and then we'll have a bit to eat and a chat later on.' Then he went out, and they heard him open and shut the oven door and pass a few things through the wringer.

'This is indeed passing strange' said Cuanduine, 'that the husband should keep house while the wife goes abroad.'

'O, it's natural enough' said Mr Robinson. 'He's unemployed, and the wife's out at her job.'

'But if it is necessary for the women of the country to work' said Cuanduine, 'how is it that there is no work for a man?'

'O—economic conditions, and all that sort of thing' said Mr Robinson, shrugging his shoulders easily. 'Quite the usual state of affairs now, you know, though I believe it was different fifty years ago.'

'What of the children?' asked Cuanduine.

'They haven't got any, of course,' answered Mr Robinson. 'People can't afford children nowadays unless they've *both* got jobs.'

'But if they both go out to work, who looks after the children?'

'O, they pay some unmarried woman to do that.'

'Alack, 'tis a most unnatural arrangement' said Cuanduine. 'Surely it is the man's part to provide sustenance for his family, and the woman's to tend her babies and look after the home?'

'You're out of date, my friend' said Mr Robinson. 'Sentiment's no good against hard economic facts. Besides, in these modern days women aren't going back to being men's pampered pets and their husband's chattels.'

Here there came a knock at the door, and they heard the man run out to welcome his wife home with a kiss and some soft endearments. Then the two came into the parlour. The woman of the house was very sturdily built, and clad in sober workmanlike tweeds. Greeting the visitors with a weary word of welcome, she dropped into a chair, and held out her feet to her husband; who took off her heavy boots, and put on her a pair of slippers that had been warming in the fender. Then the good houseman bustled off to the kitchen, whence he returned in a moment with a dish of canned meat and canned vegetables, nicely warmed up, on which they all fell to. When that was put away, there was brought in a bowl of most delectable canned fruit, with canned milk, and a jug of canned coffee to follow, after which they drew up their chairs to the fire (the goodman having a basket of darning in his lap) and enjoyed an hour or so of smalltalk before going to bed. Mostly it was the men that talked, for the goodman's wife, besides being of a taciturn disposition, was tired by her hard day's work, and preferred to smoke her pipe in silence; only interrupting occasionally to correct some male misconception of business or politics, which she did with the greatest gentleness and tolerance you could imagine. This, however, was not very often, for their chatter was mainly about shopping, and making ends meet, and cookery and sewing, and love; these being the subjects of greatest interest to their host, who was a thoroughly domesticated fellow, as a working woman's husband ought to be.

'And what has my little man been doing with himself all day?' asked the wife presently.

'O, he's been ever so busy' said the young fellow happily. 'And I've such a lovely surprise to tell you. I'm bringing in my own little bit of grist to the mill at last!'

'Well, that's fine!' said the woman. 'The hubby here' she explained to the others with a touch of pride, 'has been doing a bit of spare-time work lately—house-to-house selling and that sort of thing. Every little helps in these hard times.'

'You are lucky to have such a wife, sir—I mean, such a husband, madam' said Mr Robinson.

'What did you sell, dear?' asked the woman.

'Three pairs of stockings, two petticoats, and a pound of tea' said her husband proudly. 'Isn't that grand?'

'First rate' cried his wife, giving him a hug and a kiss. 'It bucks a woman up no end to know that she's got a loyal partner like you behind her. I only wish it wasn't necessary for my little hubby to work so hard' she said in a low voice. 'If times weren't so bad— But never mind. Next year I'm due for a rise, and then I won't let you do a thing.'

'You darling!' cried her husband. 'But I don't mind a bit, really. I'd do anything for you.'

'Excuse this display of sentiment, gentlemen'

said the hostess, gently disengaging herself from her husband's embrace. 'If you knew how hard the poor chappie has worked, lugging a big heavy parcel of undies from door to door, you'd understand my feelings.'

'They do you credit' said Mr Robinson. 'And I'll say again you're a jolly lucky fellow—er, girl, I mean.'

'How did you get on at the father-craft class?' was the woman's next question to her husband.

'O, splendidly. Matron says I'm getting on ever so quick.'

'The local council have started domestic classes for unemployed husbands' the woman explained to Cuanduine, 'to teach them how to mind the baby when their wives are at work, you know.'

'We hope to have a baby later on' added the husband shyly.

'Humph!' said Cuanduine.

' 'Ere, wot's wrong with you?' demanded the woman truculently. 'You've 'ad a queer mug on the 'ole blinkin' evening. Wot d'yer mean by it?'

'My friend' said Cuanduine, 'since you ask me, I will be plain with you. I would think better of you, sir, if you would put your shoulder to the wheel with sufficient vigour to afford your wife a little leisure. As for you, madam—'

' 'Ere' demanded the woman of the house, 'which of us is you addressing of——?'

'Upon my soul' said Cuanduine, looking in bewilderment from one to the other, 'I cannot tell. Your pardon, I entreat. These re-arrangements are a little puzzling to one who is unused to them.'

'Well, I suppose if you ain't modern, you can't 'elp it' said the woman. 'Now, wot about bed?'

CHAPTER VI

Cuanduine meets Mac ui Rudai

NEXT day Cuanduine and Mr Robinson, having bid farewell to their kind hosts, set out upon their travels through the world. Presently they saw a man coming towards them, trudging along wearily like one who has tramped a long way. Over his shoulder he carried a bundle, and his clothes were whitened with the dust of his journeyings.

As he was still afar off, Cuanduine said to Mr Robinson: 'I like the looks of yonder traveller, and would desire his better acquaintance, for he seems to be an honest fellow.'

'Honest enough' replied Mr Robinson, 'as the world goes: that is to say, as honest as he can afford to be.'

'No, by heaven' said Cuanduine. 'I'll vouch him honester than that, or else believe him richer than his clothes portend. He seems kindly too.'

'You would certainly say so' answered Mr Robinson 'if you saw him playing with a child, or fondling his girl by moonlight. But you would think otherwise if you saw with what gusto he would rip a man's belly with a bayonet.'

'Does he do this often?' asked Cuanduine.

'He will do it any time he is told' said Mr Robinson.

'I would have acquitted him of such folly' said Cuanduine, 'for the fellow seems intelligent.'

'No. He's not exactly brainy' said Mr Robinson; 'but he has a stock of sound common sense, which teaches him to know his place and bow to the inevitable. He takes life as he finds it, leaves well enough alone, looks before he leaps, and knows that least said is soonest mended. He thinks a bird in the hand worth two in the bush, knows that all is not gold that glitters, and that distant fields look greener than they are, believes that it's a long lane that has no turning, and is readily convinced that the darkest hour comes just before the dawn.'

'You seem well acquainted with the man' said Cuanduine.

'Well enough' replied Mr Robinson. 'His name, if I remember rightly, is Mac ui Rudai.'

Now this Mac ui Rudai was a good fellow after his fashion, but somewhat wild and barbarous and rather lewd in his habits. He would eat when he was hungry, drink when he was thirsty, and preferred wine to water when he could afford it; besides which he was of a mind to marry when he fell in love, and embrace his wife under the promptings of passion: paying no attention whatever to the advice of his betters that he should repair his waste energies with a gram or two of protein seasoned with vitamines and carbohydrates, flush his kidneys between meals, marry eugenically, and space out his children at scientific intervals of eight or ten years, or, better still, have none at all until the financial system should have room for them. This incautious improvident fellow, coming up the road as I have said, asked Cuanduine (for he feared the superior eye of Mr Robinson) how far it might be to town; which proving to be yet a stiffish number of miles, he sat down on the grass by the roadside and lit his pipe. Cuanduine sat down beside him: likewise Mr Robinson, after hitching up his trouser-legs, a thing which Cuanduine had never learnt to do in all his days on earth, to the great detriment of his bags.

Cuanduine and Mac ui Rudai then fell talking; and the man told the hero that he was one of five brothers, sons of a certain poor and hard-working man; who, when he lay dying, summoned them to his bedside, and, having no substance to bequeath them, offered them his counsel instead: as it is generally believed that when a man is come to his life's end, though eyes and ears, limbs and frame be worn out and past all service, his wits are then perfected, and his words enriched with a wisdom that comes from God knows where. This ancient toiler then, gathering his sons around him, pointed to a pile of sticks that lay at his bedside, and ordered each of the boys to take one and break it across his knee: which they did with great ease. Then the old man said to the eldest: 'Now take all the remainder of the sticks and bind them together;' and when this was done, 'see now if you can break them.' The son knew that he could not, but strained them against his knee for form's sake. 'Aha!' said the old man. 'They resist all your efforts. Learn then from this that union is strength. Stick together therefore, my boys, and you cannot be beaten.' With that he died; and, having piously buried him, the sons began to discuss their future course of action.

'First of all' said the eldest son, 'though I should be the last member of this family to show disrespect to our dear father's wishes, and though I should be the last man on earth to doubt the wisdom of the aged, or to speak ill of the dead, yet I do not consider the parable of the sticks applicable to the case. See now'—here he picked up the faggots which were still bound from the demonstration—'we cannot break this bundle: but we cannot do any mortal thing else with it either. Untied, we could use the sticks for palings, cudgels, penholders, firewood, toothpicks, and what not; but, bound up like this, they are no manner of use whatever.'

'And' said the second brother 'if they cannot be broken over the knee, a circular saw would make short work of them.'

'Precisely' said the eldest brother. 'Therefore, though union may be strength, severance is mobility: and so in God's name let us separate.'

With that they went forth severally into the world to seek their fortunes.

'We were' said Mac ui Rudai to Cuanduine 'mettlesome youths with lofty big ambitions. The eldest desired wealth above all things, and by God I think the love of money is the root of all virtue, it is so richly rewarded. This brother of mine—God bless him, I have forgotten his very name he is so high above me—vowed he would not rest until he had made a million pounds.'

'That' said Cuanduine 'was a most immodest ambition. I'll warrant he fell short of it.'

'No' said Mac ui Rudai. 'Already he has made two millions.'

Cuanduine held his peace.

'My second brother' said Mac ui Rudai 'cared

nothing for wealth, but he longed for power, and swore he would become Prime Minister.'

'He at least failed' said Mr Robinson. 'There has been no Prime Minister of your name in my memory.'

'He changed his name' replied Mac ui Rudai, 'and is already a member of the Cabinet. My third brother did not bother about power, but he yearned for fame, that his name might be on every lip, his face familiar to every eye. So he became a cinema actor, and is already featured as a star.'

'What of the fourth brother?' asked Mr Robinson; for the speaker had fallen into a silence.

'Alas' said Mac ui Rudia, 'he too has been a success, but it is a success to grieve the heart of a respectable man. He desired only to have his way with women, and he has always had it. Gentlemen, they fall to him like almond blossoms to a wind of March.'

Here Mac ui Rudai hid his face and vented an honest sigh. 'Never mind, a Mhic ui Rudai' said Cuanduine, consoling him. 'We cannot all expect to be so fascinating as that.'

'So disgustingly immoral, you mean' said Mac ui Rudai indignantly.

'O come' said Cuanduine. 'If you think him disgusting, why do you envy him?' whereat Mac ui Rudai hung his head and blushed.

'You have not yet told us of your own ambition, a Mhic ui Rudai' Mr Robinson here interposed. 'Your brothers would not seem to have left much for you.'

'Little enough' said Mac ui Rudai.

'What was it, a Mhic ui Rudai?' asked Cuanduine.

'A cottage on a hill' said Mac ui Rudai, 'and a garden round it, and a couple of fields. A wide hearth to the cottage, with red curtains to the windows, and the lamplight shining through them to welcome me home at the close of the day. A good wife on the other side of the fire, and the children playing around the floor. Work for my two hands, and enough for bite and sup and a bit over. That was the whole of my desire.'

'A modest desire indeed' said Cuanduine. 'A man would not be long in achieving that ambition.'

'Long enough' answered Mac ui Rudai. 'For look at me. I have been striving after it these twenty years, and have not achieved it yet.'

'I can only believe' said Cuanduine, 'remembering what your brothers have achieved, that you have not striven very hard.'

'Striven!' cried Mac ui Rudai. 'Wind never blew, nor frost never nipped if I have not striven. Look here, mister'—showing his horny hand—'see these muscles'—baring his right arm. 'Did these grow in idleness?'

'Then your story is incredible' said Cuanduine.

'Not a bit of it' said Mr Robinson. 'We can't all get everything we want in this world. This isn't Utopia, you know.'

'By the gods of my youth, it is not' said Cuanduine. 'A Mhic ui Rudai, you are well met. You shall have your cottage on the hill, your garden and your fields, your good wife and your scrambling babes. By my hand of valour, I will not rest until they are yours.'

'God bless your honour' said Mac ui Rudai.

'Do you want to turn society topsy-turvy?' asked Mr Robinson.

'Topsy-turvy?' said Cuanduine. 'A good word, Mr Robinson. I like topsy-turvy. A good word for a good task; and so it shall be done if there is no other way. The whole universe shall be turned topsy-turvy to provide a cottage for Mac ui Rudai.'

'Thank your honour' said Mac ui Rudai, touching his hat.

'And what would you have of me after that, a Mhic ui Rudai?' asked Cuanduine.

'Devil a bit more, God bless your honour' said Mac ui Rudai. 'If your honour will get me my wee houseen and my bean a' tighe, I will ask nothing more of God or man.'

'Is it possible you will be content with those?'

'By the hokey I will, your honour.'

'I can scarce credit such abnegation' said Cuanduine. 'Do you truly desire to live no more abundantly than this?'

'Sure what would your honour be wanting me to be wanting?' cried Mac ui Rudai. 'Isn't bite and sup and the wee houseen and the bean a' tighe, with the bit of work for my two hands, good enough for the likes of me?'

'Would you not also like flowers to look upon' said Cuanduine, 'and the songs of the birds to listen to?'

'Not I, your honour. Them things isn't for the likes of me; for it's taking my mind off my work they'd be, and putting notions into my head not suitable for my station. And wasn't it all for the best that good King Goshawk took them away from us, so as we'd have no temptation to idleness and inefficiency till we'd be earning enough to pay for enjoying them?'

'Good God, man' said Cuanduine, 'what would that aspiring protozoon, your ancestor, think of this termination to the ambition for which he first put forth a pseudopodium?'

'Alas, sir' said Mac ui Rudai, 'I cannot understand these long words. I am a simple fellow that wants only to labour and to be paid for it honestly. If you will help me to that, as I understood you to promise you would, I am ready to follow you. If you will not, why, there's an end of the matter, and I'll say good day to you and go my way.'

'Have no fear, a Mhic ui Rudai' said Cuanduine. 'You shall have your desire.'

CHAPTER VII

The pilgrimage of Mac ui Rudai

THIS is the tale of what happened to Mac ui Rudai between his parting from his brothers and his meeting with Cuanduine. Being a god-fearing decent fellow (with limitations) as we have said, he went looking for work that he might earn him the wherewithal to have the home and the wife of his desire; and he thought that having lusty muscles and a taste for sunshine and fresh air, and as there were many hungry people in the world, he could not be better employed than in the growing of wheat. Now this was in the days before the wise policy of King Goshawk had put restriction on wheat production, and the world was full to overflowing of golden grain. The growers, therefore, told Mac ui Rudai that they had no need for his services, and sent him away. After he had wandered many days in this fashion, he began to be hungry; and on being told for the hundredth time that on account of this plenitude there was no work for him to do, he asked for pity's sake for a crust of bread. But the farmer said: 'No. Why should I give you what you have not earned? Does not the scripture say: he that doth not work, neither let him eat. And between falling prices, and taxes to keep the likes of you in idleness, I can't afford it anyway. Be off out of that.' This appeared very sound to Mac ui Rudai; who thought it only fair that a man should work for his keep, and reverenced the scriptures withal. So he went his way hungrier than ever.

All this time there was a fleet of Goshawk's airplanes flying overhead, writing 'Eat More Bread' in letters of smoke upon the blue vault of the sky. After them flew another fleet equipped with loud-speakers, which all shouted in unison: 'Spread It With Butter! Spread It With Butter!' And in every tree by the roadside there was another loud-speaker that shrieked: 'Have Some Jam!' or 'Try A Spot Of Cheese!' or even 'Eggs And Bacon!' The art of publicity was at its zenith in those days, in so much that it was the boast of the trade that nobody could ever get out of sight or hearing of an advertisement of some sort; and they were even then perfecting a process by which advertisements could be conveyed to people in their dreams by means of a special sort of wireless waves.

Presently Mac ui Rudai met a bluff hearty-looking man with a round benevolent face and an air of prosperity about him, taking his ease on the King's highway. This was Professor Banger, the celebrated economist; but Mac ui Rudai, seeing how well dressed he was, and thinking that one so favoured by heaven must be fruitful in good works and kindly disposed towards the unfortunate, hailed him as a man and a brother, and having laid his case before him, begged earnestly for his advice. Professor Banger very generously tendered him a shilling and spoke in this fashion:

'My poor fellow, yours is indeed a sad case, but

you must not imagine it to be unique. There are millions of men as deserving as you—forty-nine million, nine hundred and seven according to the latest available figure—in a similar plight; and I regret to say that in the present financial condition of the world there is no hope for you. Utopian dreamers and sociological writers, whose imaginations are unchecked by knowledge of the facts, will tell you that a better distribution of the product of industry will solve your difficulties; but I have proved by indisputable figures that that is untrue. If the present annual income of society were distributed equally amongst our whole population, do you know how much would be the share of each individual?'

'No sir' said Mac ui Rudai.

'Four shillings and fourpence farthing a week' said Mr Banger. 'You couldn't live on that, my poor fellow, could you?'

'No, sir' said Mac ui Rudai.

'So you see, my poor fellow, the remedy for your troubles lies not in the redivision of the present national income, but in the whole community setting to work to increase that income.'

'Yes, sir' said Mac ui Rudai, 'and therefore I am using my best endeavours to get some work to do. Can you advise me where my work is most likely to be needed?'

The Professor shook his head gravely. Said he: 'I am afraid that in the present unfortunate condition of our magnificent economic system, there is no chance of your work being required at all.'

'I don't rightly understand that' said Mac ui

Rudai. 'You said just now that the way to put things right was for everybody to work hard.'

'True' said Professor Banger. 'But in the present unfortunate state of affairs nobody can afford to employ you. Political economy, you know, follows certain inexorable laws which it would bore you to listen to, and which you can never hope to understand. The dismal science, you know' he said gaily. 'The dismal science! Good-bye, my poor fellow. I must be going.'

So Mac ui Rudai was left standing in the King's highway, the richer by a shilling and some statistical information; but the shilling fell through a hole in his breeches pocket, and the statistics were no great consolation to a hungry man. He wandered on and on for a long time, getting hungrier and raggeder every day, till at length he met another prosperous looking man with mild eyes and a drooping moustache, to whom he addressed himself very humbly. This was none other than Mr Addled Crock, the famous economist. He listened to the tale of Mac ui Rudai with the sympathy of a statistician, nodding his head at each fact, and recording the more interesting ones in a notebook. Then he spoke in tones overflowing with sociological regret and hopelessness:

'My poor fellow, yours is indeed an unfortunate case, and illustrates one of the curious paradoxes of our magnificent economic system. It may seem strange to you that the reason why you are hungry is that there is too much wheat in the world, and that the reason why your trousers are in rags is that too many trousers are being produced. But nevertheless that is the case. Overproduction and overpopulation are the twin evils from which we are suffering—too many goods and too many people—the inevitable result of disregarding the inexorable laws of political economy.'

'I do not understand' said Mac ui Rudai stupidly.

'Well, you see' said Mr Crock, 'if fewer trousers were being produced, you would have a chance of getting a job in a trouser factory, and so could afford to buy yourself a pair of trousers; and, of course, if there were fewer people in the world, your chance of getting a job would be greater still. That's simple arithmetic.'

Mac ui Rudai, having learnt some simple arithmetic when at school, was forced to agree. Mr Crock praised his intelligence and continued:

'The truth, my poor fellow, is that you ought never to have been born. From the industrial point of view, this country requires hardly any people, for by the use of modern machinery a few hundred men can produce billions of trousers in a few weeks.'

'Who's going to wear 'em?' asked Mac ui Rudai.

'Ah!' said Mr Crock. 'There you touch on the real problem—the problem of marketing. How are we to escape from the difficulties caused by the present lack of balance between production and consumption? The answer, as I have pointed out in the press, is to develop our export trade. The potential world market for trousers is enormous. Think of the multitudes of savages in Africa and the Cannibal Islands who have no trousers. All we have to do is, by an intensive educational and publicity campaign, to make these people trouser-conscious, and so create a demand for our trousers. Then, since exports are always paid for by imports, we shall receive in return a valuable trade in cheap loincloths (carried, of course, in British bottoms) with which to clothe our own trouserless poor.'

The grandeur of this conception fairly took Mac ui Rudai's breath away. Truly it was a fine example of thinking internationally, and an excellent demonstration of the principle of the economic interdependence of nations, besides being an eloquent appeal for world unity.

'But, as I have said' Mr Crock resumed, 'our present problems are really the result of over-population. Industrially speaking, you have no possible function in society, and the real solution of your problems would have been to prevent your being born.'

'But I *am* born' said Mac ui Rudai.

'It is a disgrace to our civilisation that it should ever have happened' said Mr Crock. 'If the Government had done its duty, that terrible injustice would never have been inflicted on you. To permit the poor to breed in this reckless fashion is nothing less than national suicide.'

'My parents were not paupers, sir' said Mac ui Rudai.

'Nevertheless it is evident that they had more children than they could afford. My poor fellow, I cannot express my indignation at the injury that has been done to you. If it had not been for the improvidence of your parents and the infamous indifference of the State, you would now be enjoying the happy condition of non-existence, instead of having to tramp the earth, utterly useless, starving and ragged. Instead of being a filthy obscenity, offensive to all who meet you, and a burden to yourself, you would be a perfect ideal, a blissful nonentity, an unspoilt potentiality, a *nova tabula*, knowing nothing of pain, fear, trouble, grief, worry, or anxiety, or any other of the ills that our too too solid flesh is heir to. As the poet says:

'The man that never has been born,
Serene of soul, alike can scorn
The franchised rabble's brainless row,
Or posturing dictator's brow,

The winter sea by tempest lashed,
The thunderbolt from heaven flashed:
Nay, if the world in ruin smashed,
'Twould leave him wholly unabashed.

For him shall be no doom of death;
Nor strife of soul 'twixt doubt and faith;
Nor unrequited passion's smart,
Nor toil, nor worries of the mart.

Nor sickness, pain, nor grief shall he
Endure, nor grinding poverty;
But his the perfect bliss shall be
Of absolute nonentity.'

'Very pretty' said Mac ui Rudai.

'Of all this' said Mr Crock 'you have been

robbed by the criminal carelessness of your parents, and the still more criminal negligence of the State. It is a disgrace to our civilisation—I repeat it' said Mr Crock, his face glowing with righteous indignation. 'Henceforward I dedicate myself with renewed vigour to the cause—the sacred cause—of saving the world from the floods of unwanted babies that threaten its very existence. I shall not rest until it is the law of the land that instruction in contraception shall be an integral part of the marriage ceremony for all persons of the lower orders.'

'Thank you kindly, sir' said Mac ui Rudai. 'I'm sure your feelings does you credit. But meanwhile what's to become of me?—being, as you might say, borned already.'

'My poor fellow' said Mr Crock, 'that is indeed only too true, but of course the evil cannot now be undone. The most we can do is to prevent its recurrence. You have my heartfelt sympathy, I assure you'—here Mr Crock wiped away a tear—'and I would like to give you a penny, but that would be against my principles, and besides you would only go and spend it. But I promise you this. From this moment I dedicate myself entirely to your cause, heart, soul, and purse. I will give large and regular donations' he said, carried away by emotion, 'to the Society for the Suppression of Children among the Poor. At any rate, I will give them a guinea or so when times are better. Good morning, my poor fellow. Good morning.'

Mac ui Rudai went his way not much happier for this consolation. Presently he saw a bookish-looking gentleman pondering over world problems on a bench by the King's highway; to whom he unfolded his difficulties as before. The gentleman, who was no less a person than Professor Whipcord, the distinguished economist, listened sympathetically, for his heart was in the right place if only his head had known how to follow it. Said Mac ui Rudai, concluding his tale:

'And now, sir, I could not rightly understand these learned gentlemen, me being ignorant and stupid, and them talking such big words. But the sense I got from them is this: that whether the world is rich or poor is all the same to me. If there's scarcity, I've got to starve because there aren't enough goods to go round; and if there's plenty, I've got to starve because there isn't enough work to go round. Now that's a great hardship, isn't it? seeing how I've always believed that everything is for the best.'

Professor Whipcord answered:

'My dear fellow, those other chaps you were talking to are quite wrong. The real cause of your troubles is simply that a disequilibrium has arisen in the quantitative reciprocation between saving and investment. The prerequisites for the equilibration of the coemptive efficacy of money (that's dough) necessitate that current investment shall be equiponderantly evaluated to concurrent savings, and that the collective totality of profits, supplemental to the normal remuneration of the executant and instrumental components of productive organisation, shall be zero (nothing, you know). Now the quantum of investment is predestiterminigitated by the policy of the banks in apportioning industrial credits, whereas the quantum of saving is fortuitously effectuated by the idiosyncratic motivation and conglomerate volitional procedure of the constituent units of population; and between these there is no essential correlation. But it is only by such a correlation that the disequilibrium can be abolished and the ideal of stability attained. It may be that this correlation cannot be attained within the ambit of immemorial economic principles and precedents, but until it is attained, this phenomenon of abnormal unemployment must continue. Do I make myself clear?'

'Quite' said Mac ui Rudai. 'I understand that you have been talking the language of economics.'

'The dismal science' said Professor Whipcord. 'Ha! Ha!'

'Ha! Ha! Ha!' said Mac ui Rudai. 'And now can your honour tell me if this 'ere economics can explain 'ow I'm to be purvided with a 'ome and livelihood?'

'I'm afraid not' said Professor Whipcord. 'The science of economics explains—as I have just shown—exactly why you cannot have those things. Further than that it cannot go.'

'Lor, guvnor' said Mac ui Rudai, 'am I never going to 'ave nothing nohow?'

'I fear not' said Professor Whipcord. 'It seems hard, but there you are. Man cannot control the laws of economics. They control him. Good morning.'

Mac ui Rudai resumed his journey no wiser nor happier than before. Shortly afterwards he met one in the black attire of a priest of the Church, to whom also he told his tale, not without tears and grovellings, for he was now sick at heart and as hungry as if seven devils were eating at his vitals.

'Courage, my son' said the man of God. 'Remember that this life is but a trial for the next, and, as you have suffered more than others upon earth, so shall your reward be greater in heaven.' Then, as Mac ui Rudai would have gone his way discontented, he said: 'Perhaps you might find a job in the city.' For the man of God was a Jesuit, and knew that not by the word of God alone doth man live.

A little further on Mac ui Rudai met another clergyman, a sweet lamb-like young man, smiling like a canvasser, who, taking him in a friendly manner by the arm, said: 'My dear chappie, I can see that that old-fashioned churchman up the road has not bwightened you up very much.'

'No indeed' said Mac ui Rudai.

'It is no wonder the churches are empty' said the clergyman, 'when they fail to keep up with the changing conditions of modern life. Dark gloomy interwiors, dweawy services, lugubwious sermons, and dull monotonous chants make no appeal to the modern mind. We want our weligion to be cheewy and bwight, don't we? Well, you must come along to *my* little church, and you'll find yourself ever so bucked. We have bowls and cwoquet and tennis on the lawn, bathing in the fountain, and bwidge and tiddlywinks in the vestwy. We have wireless music on all day, and tea is served at half-past four. In the evening we sing a bwight cheerful hymn set to modern music. Now pwomise me you'll come next Sunday.'

'Well, I'd like to oblige you' said Mac ui Rudai, 'but I can't play tennis or any of them other games.'

'What? Not even tiddlywinks?'

'I never heard of it' said Mac ui Rudai.

'I'll teach you' said the young clergyman; but even so Mac ui Rudai hesitated.

'If it's the hymn you object to' said the clergyman, 'don't let that keep you away. You can leave before it begins. Most of my congwegation do, as a matter of fact. Now please say you'll come.'

Mac ui Rudai still hesitated, not, as the clergyman fancied, because he was wrestling with his indifference to religion, but because he did not like to hurt the clergyman's feelings.

'Now I tell you what I'll do' said the clergyman at last. 'We'll toss for it. Heads you come, tails you don't;' and he promptly spun a coin which, by a pious fraud, had two heads on it.

'Splendid' said the clergyman sunnily. 'I've gathered most of my congwegation in that sort of way. I play them at golf or bwidge, you know, on condition that if they win I'll dwink a glass of whiskey or say Damn, and if I win they'll come to my church. Well, ta-ta, old fruit. See you on Sunday,' and he skipped away.

Mac ui Rudai now hurried on in the direction of the city; but almost immediately he was hailed by a benevolent looking old gentleman in horn-rimmed glasses, who was sitting in the garden of a house by the wayside, writing at a table under the shade of a weeping willow, which was a source of much inspiration to him. His face was so lined and his eyes so thoughtful that Mac ui Rudai took him for some learned philosopher that might be able to give him good advice; so he entered the garden very hopefully. Now the old gentleman was a celebrated uplift-writer, by name Mr Pewling Mush, Chief Religious Editor of the Cumbersome Press; and the way he got his job was this. The great Lord Cumbersome was at one time severely tried by ill fortune, with here a million or two failing to bring in its usual twenty per cent, and there a trade union refusing to accept a wage-cut, not to mention a small newspaper that refused to be bought up at Lord Cumbersome's own terms, and also a twinge of toothache which he feared would drive him to the dentist. Altogether he was in a mood which so often impels men to doubt that the universe is ruled by a benevolent Providence. For his Lordship had never before observed that suffering existed in the world, and it seemed to him unfair that he should be singled out for these trials. Therefore he laboured in doubt; and you may be sure Heaven trembled lest it should lose the faith of one so influential. An angel was promptly dispatched to guide the hand of Lord Cumbersome so that it fell upon a newspaper by his bedside; and picking it up he read the first article he came to, an exceedingly comfortable effusion, showing in luscious meaty prose how all things are for the best, and that we should not be cast down by misfortune, but should rather welcome it, as the sunshine surely follows after rain. Lord Cumbersome was mightily cheered by this, and his faith restored; and, having noted the name of the author, who was none other than Mr Pewling Mush, then young and unknown, he gave him a permanent job, from which he worked his way up and got on splendidly. A few years afterwards Lord Cumbersome was smitten with a sickness and feared he was going to die; and having done (it must be confessed) a good deal of dirty work in piling up his millions, he began to fear that his fate in the next world might not be altogether so enviable as in this. Indeed one night he fancied he was already dead, and, detecting a smell of sulphur about, was thrown into such a panic that he sweated half his paunch away. It was only a sulphur candle the nurse had lighted in the next room; but in this salutary mood he made a solemn vow that he would give away his ill-gotten millions in charity and begin again at the bottom of the ladder. After that he got better, and you can imagine how horribly dismayed he was by the recollection of the unnecessary vow he had taken. In this difficulty he remembered Mr Mush, whom he summoned forthwith to his bedside and asked for his advice. When the matter had been fully explained to him, Mr Mush said that the sins Lord Cumbersome had committed in amassing his millions could in no way be undone by now giving the millions (and himself) away; that to give them away would cause grave scandal, upset confidence in the City, inflict loss on innocent shareholders, and throw men out of employment; that the money so distributed might fall into the hands of people who would spend or otherwise misuse it; and that so far from giving it away, he would do better to keep it and make more, thus circulating wealth and promoting employment. 'In this way' he said 'you will keep your vow in the spirit rather than in the letter; and it is the spirit that matters.' From that hour Mr Pewling Mush was made Religious Editor of the Cumbersome Press.

When Mac ui Rudai entered his garden he motioned him to a seat at his side, and said: 'Young man, I am glad to see that you wasted no time talking to that hackneyed hierophant and petrified presbyter. The time has gone by when youth could put its faith in the crumbling walls and mouldering parietes of ecclesiasticism. We must reject all the dogmas of all the churches.'

'Well, some of them anyway' Mac ui Rudai agreed.

'All of them, a Mhic ui Rudai, all of them. They are the greatest obstacle to the cause of True Religion.'

'I don't rightly understand you' said Mac ui Rudai. 'Must we reject the doctrine of Transubstantiation?'

'Certainly. That above all.'

'And also the doctrine that Transubstantiation is a vain superstition?'

'You must not interrupt me, a Mhic ui Rudai' said Mr Mush reprovingly. 'I am not accustomed to interruptions. They break the free flow of the argument. Nobody ever interrupts my articles. They must be taken as a whole, without plucking phrases out of their context.'

'I beg your honour's pardon' said Mac ui Rudai, 'and beseech your worship's continuance.'

'I was saying' proceeded the old gentleman, mollified by his submission, 'that the musty dogmas and decayed canons of the churches are the principal obstacle to the development of True Religion.'

'What is true religion?' asked Mac ui Rudai.

'I will tell you in a moment. You must know that a New Spirit has come into the world, which is struggling to shake off the putrefying corpse of the decaying Old World. Its fresh young voice is heard from Jerusalem to Geneva, from London to Los Angeles, from Galway to the Galapagos Islands, from Tokio to Tasmania, from Kamschatka to Kalamazoo, from Montana to Madagascar, from Belfast to Beluchistan, from—'

'Everywhere, in fact' said Mac ui Rudai.

'Er—yes' said Mr Mush, disturbed. 'A stupendous cataclysm of the mind and heart is awakening in the souls of the younger generation. The night of sickening cynicism and hectic hedonism is over, and a new day of fulgent faith and healthy hope is dawning. The skatological scribes and scybalous scribblers that infested with their filthy figments the lotus land of literature and the purlieus of poetry have passed away like a foul flatus, and a new generation of writers, full of sweet youthful illusions and cheery optimism has taken their place. You ask what is the True Religion. I have here on this table its Bible, and will read you some of it.'

Mr Mush took up some newspaper cuttings from the table at his elbow, and said: 'Here are a number of magnificent professions of faith by representative members of the Younger Generation, which have lately appeared in the press. The first, as you see, is entitled *What I think about God*, by the eighteen-year-old novelist, Daisy Dimnut. Just listen to this. "I believe in God, not in the anthropomorphic and short-tempered divinity worshipped within the crumbling walls of the churches, but in a supreme Spirit, the fount of wisdom and love. I am sure that such a Spirit would not want us to believe hard and fast dogmas, but would like us to believe whatever we like." Isn't that a new and original thought, so different from the dismal doctrines of crude and narrow ecclesiasticism. Then we have *God at the Wicket*, by Tommy Bails the great cricketer. "I believe that God plays with a straight bat" is his message. "In this life, as we know, the wicked sometimes prosper, and the good are occasionally unfortunate. Now that wouldn't be cricket if there wasn't a second innings in another world to put things right. Of course I don't believe in the musty dogma of eternal punishment. When the soul has taken its medicine, the Celestial Umpire will say 'over.' We may be confident that God will give us fair play. There is something essentially English about God." Can you beat that, a Mhic ui Rudai?'

'I can not' said Mac ui Rudai.

'Next we have Percy Lambkin, the Novelist of Youth. *Once More I Can Pray* is his title. "In my youth" he says "I was among the scoffers. I read a page or two of Darwin, and thought it clever to say I believed in Evolution. But now a riper wisdom has come to me. One day—in my wild hectic fashion—I put some money on a horse. It was more than I could afford, and the horse's chances, I found, were not bright. In my despair I prayed—for the first time for many years—and the horse won. I believe that was a miracle. It restored my fallen faith, and now I say my prayers regularly when I have time. I am not ashamed to say it—not a bit." There's courage for you' said Mr Mush. 'The new religion will not lack the stuff of martyrs if it needs them. He goes on: "Whenever I look upon the green grass and the blue sky and the white clouds and the wet water, I say to myself: "Surely this must be the work of a Divine Creator" and bow down in humble worship." '

Mac ui Rudai scratched his head. 'If the grass was red' said he, 'and the water dry, whose work would he think it was?'

'You must not be flippant, a Mhic ui Rudai' said Mr Mush. 'Now here is an extremely thoughtful article. *I Believe Like Anything*, by Soppy Smiler. I don't know who he is exactly, but he's young, and that's what matters. "I believe in Life" he says. "I believe in Speed. I believe in Adventure. I believe in Laughter, and Beauty, and Love. I believe in Flux as the force that brought Being out of non-existence, and will keep on getting us on in the Stream of Progress. I believe in God, and worship him in the Great Outdoor. The only thing I do not believe in is musty dogmas and moribund ritual." See, the same spirit is in all the articles. All these young people have a vivid faith in essentials, but they are repelled by the routine of ritual, and alienated by the cast-iron creeds which put swaddling-bands on the free growth of thought. It is well for them that the dominion of priests and prelates has passed away. Otherwise these priceless thoughts would never have seen the light, and their authors would have been consigned to the fires of Smithfield.'

It is to be feared that Mac ui Rudai thought that this would have been no great loss. Being now somewhat wearied of True Religion, he was of a mind to speak of his own troubles, but Mr Mush began again.

'And now' said he, 'just one more article before you go. It is called *If I Were God*, by Theodore Buncombe, and contains some really practical proposals for the improvement of the universe—'

'Excuse me' said Mac ui Rudai, 'but I am not terribly worried about the universe at the present moment, for I've got the hunger of seven devils on me, and I can't think of anything else. Could your honour tell me, since you know so much about here and hereafter, why it is that with the world full of good things, and airplanes shrieking out of the sky at me to eat more bread, and me willing and anxious to do my share of work, I can't get as much to do as will give me the price of a crust?'

'Ah!' said Mr Mush. 'There you are up against the inexorable laws of political economy. You are the victim of too great abundance. Things are so plentiful that they cannot be produced at a profit, and so nobody can afford to employ you.'

'That does not seem to me very sensible' said Mac ui Rudai.

'It is no use your trying to understand the matter'

said Mr Mush. 'The dismal science, you know. The dismal science, ha! ha! I don't profess to understand it myself. We must take it on faith from those that do.'

'Who are they?' asked Mac ui Rudai.

'The economists and bankers.'

'And is it them that says that I've got to starve in the midst of plenty?'

'O no, my good fellow. They would help you if they could, but it is impossible. These things are governed by inexorable and immutable laws.'

'Who made them?' asked Mac ui Rudai.

'They have been handed down from time immemorial, and preserved in their integrity by the Financial Hierarchy' said Mr Mush, inclining his head reverently.

'Cast-iron creeds!' said Mac ui Rudai bitterly.

'Hush, my friend!' said Mr Mush. 'You must show a more submissive spirit. You should be happy to suffer in the cause of financial orthodoxy.'

'I've suffered enough' said Mac ui Rudai. 'And what I say is, if there's a law that says I've got to starve in a world full of bread that nobody wants, that law has got to be altered.'

Mr Mush's face went pale. 'Beware!' cried he. 'This is heresy you speak. You will be refusing to prostrate yourself before a banker next.'

It happened opportunely that a banker passed along the road at that moment; whereupon Mr Mush at once fell on his knees, with his nose in the mud, dragging Mac ui Rudai down along with him: for in those days it was not lawful to look upon a banker's face, but only on his back parts. Even at the annual meetings of the banks, the directors always spoke with their backs towards the shareholders, talking, as it were, through the seat of their trousers.

When the banker had passed by, Mr Mush said: 'Be warned, young man, in time, and if you are so rash as to hold opinions of your own on this subject, have the good sense and decency to keep them to yourself. For what should we of the laity know of the laws of economics? And how can we expect to think for ourselves on such a matter without falling into error? No. There can be no economic truth outside the stout stone walls and sturdy structure of the banks; and it is our bounden duty to humble ourselves and submit our judgment to the infallible voice of the World Bank.'

'I suppose I'd better be going on my way' said Mac ui Rudai, rising.

'Good-bye, my man' said Mr Pewling Mush. 'And before you go, let me warn you against currency cranks and unorthodox economists. The Bank has very wisely closed the press and the wireless against them, but here and there their corrupting quackery occasionally creeps into print. Be sure to shun such stuff like the plague. Good-morning.'

Continuing his journey, Mac ui Rudai presently encountered a dust-cart drawn by a team of six men in harness, who were thus provided with employment under a scheme recently started by the municipality in conjunction with a local charitable organisation, and originally suggested in a letter to the press by a humane gentleman who very naturally thought it disgraceful that horses should be employed while men stood idle. You will agree, I think, that this was an eminently sane and practical way of dealing with this very difficult problem; but unfortunately, like all human contrivances, it had its drawbacks, large numbers of men engaged in the horse-fodder industry having been thrown out of employment in consequence. The problem of finding fresh employment for these men, was, however, engaging the attention of the best brains in the country.

The driver of the team, cracking his whip, called out to Mac ui Rudai that, if he were unemployed, they might be able to find him a place in the stables; but Mac ui Rudai shook his head; being, like so many of the lower orders nowadays, hopelessly unadaptable to changing conditions. He went on till he came to the city, and continued his search for work; but there was no more of that commodity to spare than in the country, and more people seeking it. One day a gentleman in a silk hat came to him and said: 'Poor fellow, I see you have no work to do. Give me your vote, and I promise that it shall be provided for you:' for, though he possessed nothing else in the world, Mac ui Rudai had a vote; which proves that we have always something to be thankful for. Next day another man in a cap came to him, and also promised him work for the same consideration. Mac ui Rudai, however, thought that the man in the silk hat would be more likely to give him work than the other; so he voted for him. But nothing came of that; so next year, when the two men again came to him for his vote, he gave it to the man with the cap, with no better result.

After that the natural good temper of Mac ui Rudai began to give way, and he lent an ear to certain orators, vile agitators that stir up discontent and class warfare. And one day, as he was standing in the street, very hungry, and with the wind whistling through the holes in his breeches, he saw a rich man coming out of a tobacconist's shop smoking a cigar as big as a torpedo. At this sight, reckoning that for the price of this bundle of burning weed he could have got him three square meals, the wrath of Mac ui Rudai boiled in his bosom, and, approaching the rich man, he said: 'You dirty dog! Why should you have everything you want, and I have nothing at all?'

Now the rich man's name was Lord Juggernaut, and he was a big man in the political world, a good fellow in his way, capable of bright ideas from time to time, and with a ready wit, all the readier from being well nourished with wine and baccy. So he said to Mac ui Rudai good-humouredly: 'What the hell? Do you think nobody ought to have a good time because you can't? Will you buy these cigars if I return them to the shop? And do you think the girl I'm going to sleep with will take you if I let her down?'

At this Mac ui Rudai forgot the voice of the agitators and said: 'No, sir. I suppose not.'

'You see, my man' Lord Juggernaut explained, 'there must be glittering prizes as an incentive to men like me to do our best. If it wasn't for that encouragement we'd do nothing. See?'

'I see' said Mac ui Rudai humbly; but it had been better if he had given the man a bit of sauce; for Lord Juggernaut, though not altogether a very admirable person, had guts, and he liked to see guts in others. The meek demeanour of Mac ui Rudai irritated him, and he said:

'Do you think that my ambitions are to be measured by yours, you clod? Do you think I must accommodate my desires to your approval, you earthworm? I want power' he said with a kick. 'I want glory' he said with another kick. 'I want cigars—and champagne—and night-clubs—and horses—and theatres—and yachts—and concubines—' With each of these words he bestowed a kick on Mac ui Rudai's stern, which Mac ui Rudai accepted very humbly, saying: 'Thank you, sir, I understand.' Then Lord Juggernaut flung him a handful of money and went his way.

CHAPTER VIII

How Mac ui Rudai was found to be entirely superfluous

BY this time the unhappy Mac ui Rudai had become as wretched looking a specimen of humanity as ever stood up in broken boots. His face was the colour of wet paper, his body bowed and shrunken, his hair matted. His clothes would have been useless to a scarecrow; for no bird could have mistaken them for human vesture. No pious person could look on him without feeling grateful to God that such a plight was not his own.

One day, as he shambled along in this condition, two gentlemen espied him from a club window, and proceeded to point appropriate morals. The one was a Scientist, the other a Dean. Said the Scientist:

'There you see the sort of thing we get by our insane policy of breeding from inferior stocks. I have no doubt that if we questioned that wretched wastrel over there, and if we could get him to tell the truth—'

'A large If' inserted the Dean.

'Quite so. Ha-ha!' said the Scientist. 'However —where was I?—O yes. He'd tell us that his father married on the dole, and his grandfather on outdoor relief. It's no wonder the race is declining. As I've said over and over again, compulsory birth-control isn't enough. These degraded creatures won't take the trouble to do it right, and while they go on breeding like lice, our best stocks—people like ourselves, you know—are simply dying out. The only remedy is sterilisation. I'd sterilise ninety per cent of the population, if I had my way.'

The Dean—who, you must note, was a Christian Dean: not an Aztec Dean, nor a Dean of Moloch or Baal, nor yet a Congo witch-finder, but a genuine Christian Dean, anointed with oil in the name of the Lord, and supposed to be preaching Christ, and him crucified—answered in this wise:

'I agree with you. The increasing numbers of these loathsome parasites on the better classes fill me with alarm. No doubt the wretched creature has a swarm of brothers and sisters as worthless and repulsive as himself. They are a plague and a pest. The disgusting hives in which they live disfigure and defile our beautiful cities, and when I see their detestable bungaloid growths spreading over the countryside like some hideous disease, and usurping the place of the beautiful mansions of the rich, I shudder with horror. The only remedy for such a state of things is an unsparing use of the knife.—Look, the wretched inefficient creature has got himself run over by a motor-car.'

The fact was that the miserable Mac ui Rudai, darting out into the gutter after a crust of bread, had been knocked down by a car which all unbiassed witnesses (that is to say, the drivers of other cars) afterwards testified was not travelling at more than sixty miles an hour. He was quickly dragged up, and duly cited before a magistrate, charged with criminal negligence and obstruction of traffic. Fortunately for the cause of justice, the magistrate was himself a motorist, and therefore able to appreciate the difficulties of the road. Having taken evidence to the effect that the driver of the car was not certifiably drunk, and that he had sounded his horn, he addressed Mac ui Rudai as follows:

'You are an idle, ignorant, stupid, and careless fellow, and your parents committed a crime against society in bringing you into the world. If they were before me now, I would sentence them to a flogging for it. The fact that you have been unemployed for so many years is sufficient proof that you are of no possible use to the state; and not content with that, you have gone out of your way to hold up the business of others—'

'I beg your pardon, sir—' began Mac ui Rudai.

'Don't be insolent, sir' roared the magistrate. 'That sort of thing will not be tolerated here. You need a sharp lesson, my man. Six months hard labour.'

Mr Buzfuz (representing the Anti-Pedestrian Association) here pointed out to his worship that the motorist's car had suffered some damage from the collision, and that the motorist himself had been much annoyed and lost five minutes of valuable time.

'He has the sympathy of the court' replied the magistrate, 'but I'm afraid this wretched inefficient creature isn't good for damages. I'll give him another three months.'

Mr Buzfuz declared himself satisfied.

Concluding, the magistrate declared: 'In my opinion, footpaths ought to be abolished. The existence of these places of refuge tends to make pedestrians careless by giving them a false sense of security, and in their own interests they should be glad to have them done away with.'

Mr Buzfuz: 'I thank your worship.'

Mac ui Rudai was then led away and cast into a dungeon.

CHAPTER IX

How Mac ui Rudai sought consolation in Religion

THUS Mac ui Rudai obtained some portion of his heart's desire, namely, work for his two hands, and food of a sort. After his release, finding himself still friendless in the world, he turned his thoughts to God, as men will when all else fails them. He therefore went into a church to pray. It was the church of the very same Dean who had witnessed his accident, and whose faith was expressed succinctly in the following Creed:

'I can see few objections to the hypothesis of a being (who may for convenience be called God), the Father (metaphorically speaking) Almighty (except that he cannot work miracles), Creator (in a sense) of heaven (if there be such a place) and (indirectly) of earth. I agree to a certain extent with some of the moral, and a few of the social, pronouncements of a (probably mythical) person who may have been called Jesus (or Joshuah), analogous to Osiris, Buddha, Mithras, Mohammed, and others, and unfortunately of Mediterranean instead of Nordic stock, which renders a good deal of his teaching inapplicable in more enlightened latitudes. Rejecting the legends which have grown up about his birth—'

But this is too long, like Polonius's beard, and you can easily guess at the rest. Mac ui Rudai, staggering wearily into the Church of this reverend gentleman, was in time to get the following sermon flung at his head:

'Dearly beloved brethren, in these days of enlightenment, when superstition finds refuge only amongst the benighted followers of the Romish faith, it is a matter of some difficulty to define what sin is. Indeed, the broader and more comprehensive our vision becomes, the less inclined do we feel to draw definitions of any sort. Just as in Science'—here the Dean bowed his head reverently—'one species of plant or animal shades imperceptibly into another, so, in the spiritual sphere, vice shades into virtue and virtue into vice, until it is impossible to distinguish between them. All is relative. Everything depends on circumstance.

'Nevertheless there is one thing which we can confidently declare to be evil, and that is the terribly increasing numbers of people of inferior stock—of the people whom, with a due sense of the gravity of the position, we may term the Devil's poor. Nobody can doubt that the first duty of the race is to breed from the best stock-brokers—I mean stocks; that is to say, from bankers, businessmen, substantial shareholders, civil servants of the higher grades, star salesmen, and so forth: instead of which we produce an ever increasing swarm of navvies, dockers, porters, carpenters, metal-workers, plumbers, ship-builders, bricklayers, spinners, weavers, dyers, mechanics, engine-drivers, miners, fishermen, and agricultural labourers, for whom no employment can be found. Now Nature — which is the modern term for God—has an inexorable way with useless people. She eliminates them:

and that elimination is attended with a considerable degree of suffering: at the present moment a hundred million superfluous people are being slowly and painfully eliminated by hunger and disease, despite all the efforts of a too humane civilisation to assist them. To make matters worse, instead of resigning themselves to their fate, these wretched beings have the presumption to defy the laws of nature, and to breed children in the midst of circumstances which inevitably condemn them to malnutrition, disease, demoralisation, and imbecility.

'That, brethren, is most certainly a sin. It is an insult to God Almighty to thus parody his image, to produce souls (if there are such things, as I see no strong reason to doubt) that are not fit material for the Kingdom of Heaven (if any). Gracious heavens, my brethren, think of the feelings of some healthy and happy stockbroker when, on entering Paradise, he finds it swarming with the same odious vermin whose presence so inconvenienced him on earth! We must at all costs prevent the eternal happiness of such desirable stocks from being polluted, and therefore we must crush out this sin of promiscuous breeding from our midst.

'There is but one remedy for such a state of things. As God authorised the Jews to smite with the sword the Hittites and the Jebusites (no doubt a metaphorical expression for the inefficients and undesirables of the day) so must we use the knife unsparingly. The country must be divided into quite small districts, each under the charge of a surgical officer, who should have power to sterilise anybody whose physical or mental condition strikes him as in any way abnormal—unless, of course, he has a sufficient income. Thus, and thus only, can the race be redeemed.'

Mac ui Rudai was not yet so confirmed in vice as not to be conscience-stricken by this harangue. Going out, he wept bitterly, beat his breast, and hid his head in an ashbin. Indeed he was in half a mind to go to a surgeon and get himself un-seminared forthwith. However, he thought better of it; and the very next day, by the greatest bit of luck in the world, he found a job.

It was in a new factory for making jim-jams, that is, ebonite golliwogs for hanging from ladies' noses, which was an adornment then in fashion. There Mac ui Rudai laboured for nearly a month; after which the factory closed down, as jim-jams had gone out of fashion in favour of flim-flams, that is, silver monkeys for hanging from ladies' ears. Mac ui Rudai was unable to obtain a place in this industry, so he took to the road again, and so fell in with Cuanduine.

CHAPTER X

Mr Robinson emphasises the superfluousness of Mac ui Rudai

WHEN Mac ui Rudai had related all his adventures, Mr Robinson said: 'In my opinion, a Mhic ui Rudai, you are a very perverse and unreasonable fellow. Admittedly it is somewhat trying to be hungry and half naked in a world full of unsaleable food and clothing, but you must recognise that the best minds of our race have been concentrated for a long time on this problem, and have been unable so far to reach a solution. It's pretty obvious, therefore, that there's no solution; so, instead of kicking up an ill-tempered shindy, you've jolly well got to resign yourself to the inevitable. The most learned economists and the most advanced churchmen of the day have given you the best possible advice under the circumstances. They've told you that you fulfil no possible function in society, and that in a properly regulated society you would never have been born. That's a pretty straight hint that, since the mischief is done, you ought to make what reparation you can for it by getting off the scene as soon as possible.'

'But damn it' said Mac ui Rudai, 'I want to live.'

'That' said Mr Robinson 'is because you will not recognise the obvious fact that your life is not worth living. What is the use of a life that is one long struggle with hunger, cold, worry, and fatigue? Its pains manifestly outnumber its pleasures, and therefore it is not worth having. Q.E.D.'

'I want to live all the same' said Mac ui Rudai obstinately.

'But surely that is not reasonable?' said Mr Robinson.

'I don't care whether it is or not' said Mac ui Rudai.

Here this philosophical discourse was interrupted by an accident. Their way led alongside a canal, and, as luck would have it, a little boy who was sailing a toy boat from the bank, overbalanced and fell in. Mac ui Rudai dived after him in a moment, and soon had him out. The boy's mother saw all this from her window near by, and, running out, she invited Mac ui Rudai and his friends into her kitchen, where she gave them a meal, dried Mac ui Rudai's clothes, and even patched them a little.

'You are a plucky fellow, a Mhic ui Rudai' said Mr Robinson later, as they continued their journey.

'I'm proud of your commendation, sir' said Mac ui Rudai ironically. 'Maybe you'll say I'm not quite so superfluous as you thought I was. If I hadn't been born, that child might have been drowned.'

'That doesn't alter my opinion' said Mr Robinson. 'The child would have been better dead, for I don't suppose there's the remotest chance of there ever being any employment for it.'

As they were thus pleasantly discoursing, the

setting sun shone out from behind a cloud, throwing long shadows before it. 'O my! What is this?' cried Mac ui Rudai in great consternation, pointing a trembling finger at his own.

'It's only your shadow, you fool' said Mr Robinson. 'Come on.'

'No, no, no. I daren't' cried Mac ui Rudai, stopping short. 'O me! O my! 'Tis the devil himself coming for me, and two others worse than himself along with him. Don't leave me, boys—' here he clutched his companions each by an arm. 'For God's sake don't leave me.'

'Let me go, you gibbering ass' said Mr Robinson.

'O, what'll I do?' blubbered Mac ui Rudai. 'Look at the horns of him. O my sainted mother and aunts, protect me! Why was I born into this world of trouble? Drive it away, Mr Man, drive it away. O, I'll go mad, so I will. This is what comes of having thoughts above my station. O lawsy me! I'll never do it again.—Ah! That's better': for another cloud had covered the sun, and the shadows disappeared.

'You are a poor fish, a Mhic ui Rudai' said Mr Robinson.

'I am not' said Mac ui Rudai. ' 'Tis you that are too brazen and rash; and maybe this is a warning to me not to entrust my affairs to such a foolhardy pair of adventurers. Stop now; for I will not go another step till I've examined your characters.'

'Well, I like your cheek' said Mr Robinson. 'Don't mind the fellow, Mr Coondinner. He isn't worth wasting time over.'

'Let us hear him notwithstanding' said Cuanduine.

CHAPTER XI

How Mac ui Rudai showed himself hostile to all manner of cranks

'WELL, sir' said Mac ui Rudai, 'that we may understand each from the start, I must tell you that I could never bring myself to follow anybody who is in any way queer or cranky. Above all things I distrust anybody who is queer about his clothes.'

Now Mac ui Rudai was wearing a pair of ancient breeches, very baggy about his nether parts, and also at the knees. He had on also a somewhat shapeless coat, open in front, and a kind of half-coat within to fill the gap. Upon his head he wore a hat shaped something like an inverted chamber-pot, which had once been black in colour, but was now a kind of unearthly green. Moreover, beneath his other garments he had a collection of shirts and things on him which, as he did not wash them too often, emitted no very fragrant perfume to mingle with the breeze.

'I know, sir' said Mac ui Rudai 'you will not take offence at what I say; for by your hat and brolly'—here he glanced at the helmet of Perseus and touched the handle of the Cruaidin Cailidcheann—'I perceive you to be most sensible in this regard. I trust, your honour, that you are equally sensible in the matter of food?'

Now Mac ui Rudai (when working) lived mainl

on meat which was brought to him in frozen lumps from distant parts of the world; on a kind of pasty bread which clung about his teeth so that they rotted in his head; on fruits canned in syrup; with, for drink, an infusion of dried leaves, sweetened and mixed with canned milk.

'Don't you worry' said Mr Robinson. 'Our friend's not a food crank, whatever else he may be.'

'That's good' said Mac ui Rudai. 'I never could abide cranks and queerities. What I say is, why should anyone want to be different from me? —me being all right, as you see, though perhaps it ain't right for me to say so, yet say it I will without any false modesty, since no one can accuse me of self-conceit, being a plain man making no pretence to cleverness, as I think your honour will agree.'

'That's all right, my man' said Mr Robinson, for Cuanduine could make nothing of this speech.

'What I say is this' said Mac ui Rudai. 'Anything that's queer or cranky is all wrong. Take these artist fellows with their new-fangled pictures —moderns, as they call themselves. Do you think I'd hang up one of them pictures in my parlour? Not me. And what's the use of painting pictures that an ordinary man wouldn't hang up in his parlour?'

'What indeed?' said Mr Robinson.

'Thank you, sir' said Mac ui Rudai. 'I am proud to find that my humble opinion meets with your distinguished support. I make no pretence to be clever, you understand. In fact, I don't *want* to be clever, seeing that cleverness only leads to conceit and bumptiousness. But I have something better to guide me, and that's common sense: the plain man's genius, as you might say. My heart is in the right place, if you understand me, and that's what really matters.'

'You've mistaken your vocation, a Mhic ui Rudai' said Mr Robinson. 'You could get three guineas an article for stuff on those lines.'

'No doubt I could' said Mac ui Rudai, 'if only I could write. I have often said to myself: "There's the makings of a born journalist in you, a Mhic ui Rudai, if you knew how to write." You see, I've got the ideas all right, but I haven't got the style; being a plain man that just says what he means straight out, without any flowers and trimmings. But, you see, flowers and trimmings is what the public wants, so it's no use sending in stuff without them.'

'You should take a correspondence course, a Mhic ui Rudai' said Mr Robinson.

'So I will, sir, so I will. And when I'm through with it, maybe the world will hear about me. But meanwhile I'm trusting to his honour here to get me an honest job of work.'

'Well, then, you will follow me?' said Cuanduine.

'If I may make so bold as to ask you one more question first' said Mac ui Rudai.

'Ask away, a Mhic ui Rudai.'

'Well, sir, I would like to be assured that your notions about the creation and structure of the universe are such as I might approve of. You must know that I was made out of nothing in the image and likeness of God, and the earth was made for me to dwell in, the sun, moon, and stars to give me light, and the animals and plants for my use and sustenance. It is true that fleas and tigers are of no great value to me, though some apologists would argue that the former serve to try me, and the latter, when in zoos, to entertain me. But on the whole, the scheme of creation satisfies me well enough, and its minor inconveniences will be amply compensated for by the eternal reward I shall obtain when I die.

'Now, sir, it would make me very unhappy if I were to be persuaded that things are not as I have said, and I desire to be assured, before giving you my valuable support, that you do not entertain any of the cranky ideas on the subject that are so prevalent in these modern days. It has been suggested, for example, by self-styled men of science, that I am descended from a monkey; which is a wicked and discomforting notion, derogatory to my dignity, disturbing to my peace of mind, and altogether offensive to religion and right thinking. You do not hold that view, sir, I trust?'

Now, as he listened to Mac ui Rudai, it seemed to Cuanduine that the fellow could not be descended from anything better than some monstrous marriage between an earth-worm and a laughing jackass; so he said very truly that he did not believe Mac ui Rudai to be the offspring of a monkey. Mac ui Rudai was much pleased thereat, and commended him as being thoroughly sensible and respectable in his views. 'But' said he 'there is another point I would also like to be assured upon, for there is an irreverent notion abroad that I shall not live for ever in bliss and glory, but shall presently go out like the flame of a candle and be heard of no more. You do not approve of that notion, do you, my man?'

Cuanduine, for his part, was well assured that Mac ui Rudai's exit would be much less agreeable than that of a candle-flame, inasmuch as he would go out with a bad smell; so he said that this notion was also none of his; whereat Mac ui Rudai's approval glowed almost into admiration.

'And now, my good fellow' said he, 'just one question more. If I may be pardoned for adverting to such a matter, do you disapprove of all immorality?'

Now Mac ui Rudai's idea of morality was this, that a man and his wife, no matter how they might have come to hate one another, should live always in amorous intercourse. But Cuanduine did not know this; therefore he assured Mac ui Rudai that he altogether disapproved of immorality.

'Heaven bless your honour' said Mac ui Rudai at this. 'I have no more doubts about entrusting my affairs to your guidance. Let us proceed at once, and the world is mine. Afterwards, perhaps, by way of reward, I may permit you to kiss my boots.'

With that he set off down the road with his head in the air and his hands in his pockets, as gay as a cock sparrow, with the others in his wake.

'You have undertaken a formidable task' said Mr Robinson to Cuanduine.

'I do not fear the difficulties' answered Cuanduine. 'But between you and me and the stars of heaven, Mac ui Rudai is not a very inspiring person to fight for.'

CHAPTER XII

How Cuanduine went in search of a Job

'AND now' said Cuanduine as they went on their way, 'as I have no money, I must even hire me out to earn some.'

'No good' said the others gloomily. 'There are no jobs going these days.'

'So long as there are wants unsatisfied' replied Cuanduine, 'there must be work to do.' For Mac ui Rudai's tale seemed to him incredible, and he believed that it was on account of his stupidity that work had been denied him. Having observed for himself on his travels that the world was full of people who were hungry and ill clad, he thought he would have no difficulty in getting something useful to do; but having inquired diligently at farm houses, at flour mills, at dairies, at sheep farms, at woollen mills, at clothing factories, at mine heads, at steel works, at brick works, at builders' yards, and a score of other places, including even shops, he learned that there was no demand for his services anywhere—so terrible was the plague of plenty that had fallen upon the earth.

At last, however, he came to a factory where, to his great joy, he saw numbers of men being enrolled for work; and, joining the queue, he presently signed on. It was a factory for making blim-blams, that is, enamelled frogs for wearing in ladies' hair, flim-flams being no longer in vogue. There he worked for a few weeks, drawing good wages; but after that the factory closed down, as blim-blams had gone out of fashion in favour of wim-wams, that is, imitation butterflies made out of stained fish-scales for glueing on the cheeks.

So Cuanduine gave up job-hunting and fell into a despond. But Mr Robinson wrote an article on How to Cure Unemployment, in which he argued very skilfully that women should wear wim-wams not only on their faces, but all over their bodies, whereby employment would be given to thousands of workers displaced from the food, clothing, and building trades. For this he received a handsome cheque, on which they all subsisted for some time. Cuanduine also earned a little money in unexpected fashion by submitting himself to be photographed as an advertisement for the body-building power of Pinkerton's Patent Pellets. In accordance with their policy of Truth in Advertising, they gave him a pellet to eat before they snapped him.

CHAPTER XIII

What they saw in the Kingdom of Assinaria

THEREAFTER they came to the frontier of the Kingdom of Assinaria, which was marked by a huge high wall, at the foot of which the road stopped short, and likewise the railway that ran beside it. At the end of the track a goods train had come to a stop, and its cargo was being handed out to a vast number of men, who were waiting, equipped with panniers, to receive it. These, as soon as they were loaded, proceeded to the foot of the wall, where each one made a cast with a rope he was carrying, so as to catch the coping stone with a hook that was on the end of it; after which they shinned up very nimbly, pack and all, and, pulling the rope up in turn, let themselves down on the other side.

Cuanduine, after watching this business for some time in enormous amazement, asked Mr Robinson the meaning of it; who explained it as follows. At one time there was free communication across the frontier both by road and rail, by means of which the Lambians and the Assinarians imported goods from one another to such an extent that both became terribly impoverished, and were finally on the verge of ruin. To check this destructive trade, the government of each country imposed heavy taxes on all goods coming from the other; but nevertheless the dreadful traffic continued, for the merchants on both sides, by bringing their prices down, persisted in the nefarious practice of selling their goods in the opposite markets. The governments thereupon imposed yet heavier taxes, but it was all to no purpose; the evil went on unchecked. At last, in despair at the total ruin that was impending, the governments ordered the roads and railways to be destroyed for a distance of one mile, and erected a wall in the gap, hoping that the expense and trouble of the journey would now be sufficient to deter the merchants from their odious courses. But even this was of no avail; not even after the governments had erected wall after wall on each side of the first. Though there were now twenty-six walls, one behind the other, the abominable process of trade still went on.

For the convenience of foot passengers there was an enclosed passage running through all the walls; but the entry to it was guarded by officers of the government to make sure that they should not impoverish the country by bringing anything into it. Cuanduine and his friends, having been duly searched, passed through, and came into the land of Assinaria, where there was another train waiting to receive the burdens of the carriers. 'By my hand of valour' said Cuanduine, 'I have seen many foolish things since I came on earth, but none the like of this.' 'At first glance' Mr Robinson replied, 'it certainly does seem rather silly; but you must admit that it gives a lot of employment.' 'By my hilt it does' said Cuanduine. 'More power to its elbow' said Mac ui Rudai.

Continuing their journey, they came to a place where there were great numbers of people employed in all sorts of strange occupations.

Some were spreading cartloads of sea sand over a field; and others were ploughing it with hand ploughs made of cardboard, and sowing it with sawdust in the hope of growing raspberry canes. To encourage this industry, a tax had been put on ordinary raspberries.

Others were drawing water out of a lake with nets, and evaporating it by standing it on ice in closed dishes. By this means they hoped to obtain salt and potash.

Others were extracting oil from bricks by squeezing them in hydraulic presses with defective valves.

Others were watering apple trees with sulphuric acid to keep up the price of fruit.

Others were massaging earthworms with lanoline in the hope of making them grow wool; while some were rubbing young lambs with depilatories to prevent overproduction of wool.

There was one man engaged in flogging a dead horse, in the hope that it might catch fire and save him the expense of burying it.

Others were building a tower to look out for invaders from Mars; there was also a huge fort being constructed to resist them, the walls of which were sheathed with asbestos for a protection against the heat-ray with which they would probably be armed.

Others were engaged in setting a forest on fire so as to give themselves employment in putting it out.

They saw one man who had bought a vast number of balloons so as to be always well supplied with air.

Others were grinding pebbles that they might never lack dust.

Others were employed in diverting the course of a

river, so that they might develop the art of irrigation in those parts; others were draining a lake in order to create a need for an aqueduct.

One man was digging sand out of a hole with a teaspoon to build a castle; and another was undigging it and carrying it back to the hole with a thimble.

Many other operations were in progress that I will not report for fear of straining your credulity. You would have thought they were trying to rival the performances of the people of Entelechy; but the truth was that they were trying to solve the unemployment problem.

Proceeding further, Cuanduine and his companions came to a pleasure park, where immense numbers of people were amusing themselves in many diverting ways.

Some were squatting on the tops of enormous great poles, not to the glory of God, but to break records. There were two old women among them who had spent most of their lives on these perches, having gone up when they were modern girls for the sake of a prize of ten pounds for whoever should stick it longest.

Others were sitting at the bottom of deep wells for the same purpose.

In one place there were a number of ancient men and women dancing; who had been so engaged longer than anyone could now remember. The promoter of the exhibition, said Mr Robinson, had died twenty years ago, and the responsibility for the payment of the prize was still being disputed in the law courts.

They saw a white-haired old lady on exhibition in

a tent, who had been the first girl to walk around the world leading a tortoise on a string.

In another tent they saw a doddering old man who had been the first baby to be born in an airplane. People paid five shillings to look at him.

They saw people getting married in great variety of places: in the sea, in treetops, in packing cases, on parachutes, on a tennis court, on the backs of hippopotamuses, in diving-bells, in the stomach of a dead whale. All these were records. For wedding rings they used a wonderful assortment of materials: one was made of the eyelashes of a film star, another of the toenails of a cricket champion, another of the carburettor of a speed car, another of the vertebra of a race-horse. One couple plighted their troth with the brass ring of the rope that had hanged a famous murderer; the bride was given away by her seventh husband, and the groom had as his best man the co-respondent in a previous divorce suit.

Such were the amusements of the Assinarians. Proceeding on their way, Cuanduine and his companions saw an empty train travelling towards the capital, the road alongside being thronged with people walking for the sake of economy.

CHAPTER XIV

What they learned at the University of Boob

CUANDUINE and his friends, shogging it afoot with the rest, came at last to the great city of Boob, the capital of Assinaria; and, walking past the stream of high-powered cars and buses, jammed tight in the roadway after the manner of the Age of Speed, they presently found a cheap hotel, where they put up for a few days, Mr Robinson having just received a cheque from his paper.

On the first day of their stay, as they were debating which of the sights they should see, Cuanduine discovered in the newspaper that there was to be a public lecture at the University by Professor Hunter Jawbone, the celebrated anthropologist, on the subject *Mankind is Approaching Perfection*. 'By my hat' said he, 'it would be worth while to hear him prove that.' Mac ui Rudai would rather have gone to the pictures; but the others persuaded him, and they went off together to the University.

Professor Jawbone addressed the gathering as follows:

'Nobody who surveys our civilisation to-day could ever imagine the condition or state in which our ancestors lived a few billion years ago. Scientific research, however, has now definitely and completely substantiated (if such substantiation be needed) the teaching of anthropologists that there was once a period when no man possessed anything but the inadequate habiliments he stood up in.'

At this information Mac ui Rudai gaped in astonishment, and immediately conceived a gigantic admiration for the anthropologists who could make such startling discoveries.

'In those bygone times' Professor Jawbone continued 'the lot of the very highest was inferior to that of the most backward and degraded savage to-day. For their food they had nothing but such fruit as they could gather from the trees, a little wild wheat which they reaped with stone sickles, or a few roots that they might grub up out of the ground. For their meat supply they depended on the chase, and if game were scarce, as it often was, they might hunt for weeks without success.'

Here Mac ui Rudai, who was a little soft-hearted, was so much affected by the abject condition of his ancestors that he began to blubber; but, on being told by an attendant to shut his trap, he restrained himself as well as he could, though he could not altogether prevent a big sob from escaping him now and then.

'For their clothing our ancestors were dependant on the same uncertain source. In short' said Professor Jawbone, smilingly condescending to slang, 'they had what we would denominate a very thin time.' Laughter. 'Worst of all' resumed the Professor, 'they had no industrial system to provide them with employment, no magnificent economic system to enable them to invest and accumulate money, and no financial system to insure the—er—efficient distribution of the products of their labour.

'Now, when we contemplate what marvels have been achieved by man in those vast æons of time, what encouragement can we gather for the endless æons ahead of us? It must not be supposed that human progress has ever followed a consistent course upwards, onwards, and forwards. Civilisation has always been characterised by cycles or waves: it is never permanent or static. The wave of progress, having attained its crest, inevitably curls over and subsides into the dark hollow of decline. Nevertheless, if our view is wide enough'—here Mac ui Rudai looked down at his trousers—'we observe that each wave in its turn has always broken down at vastly higher altitudes than its predecessors.'

'What about the hollows?' asked Mac ui Rudai, deeply interested; but he was silenced by indignant shouts of 'Hush' from the audience.

'There have been cities in the world' continued Professor Jawbone 'for six or seven thousand years; but nothing now remains of any of the great cities of antiquity—Ur, Nineveh, Babylon, for instance—but mounds of crumbling ruins, indistinguishable at first sight from the natural features of the plains that they formerly dominated. There is no reason to doubt that the affairs of these cities, and of the empires of which they were the capitals, were managed by financiers and politicians quite as efficient as any to be found in Europe or America to-day—and yet they have perished. Surely there is in this a lesson of some kind for us.'

Mac ui Rudai wondered what it was, but dared not interrupt again.

'And what will man be a trillion years hence?

Will his present upward and onward progress continue? or will he go backwards, downwards or even sideways? Hitherto he has been the unconscious puppet of circumstances. Natural forces have impelled him forward. But can he afford to be their plaything any longer? Must he now endeavour to control his own destiny? The answer, I am afraid, is in the affirmative; and the question at once arises—will conscious rationalised exertion advance him any further than blindly and passively following Nature's guidance?'

Mac ui Rudai, hitching up his trousers, waited anxiously for the answer.

'That remains to be seen' said Professor Jawbone. 'But I would venture to say this. So long as our people are willing to work full time, to co-operate with each other (preserving, of course, the competitive spirit so necessary for further progress), and to maintain a growing population (in moderation, of course), we may consider our civilisation to be on the upward slope of the wave. If anyone has any doubt on the matter, let him remember the last general election.' Cheers. 'On that occasion millions of workers voted for the reduction—nay, even the abolition—of their wages in order that the world might be restored to prosperity. So long as a civilisation can produce men and women like that, it is not only on the ascent. It is at the very crest of the wave.' Cheers.

Cuanduine and his friends left the room, much enlightened; and it cheered Mac ui Rudai no end to think that in another billion years or so people might actually be able to eat the bread they grew, and wear the trousers they manufactured. So with a stout heart he picked up a bit of string that was lying about and tied it tight round his middle, for he had lost all his buttons.

They came out now into the shady gardens of the University, where there were gathered great numbers of solemn-faced professors, some grouped together in discussion, others instructing their pupils after the manner of the Peripatetics.

One group was discussing whether, if pigs had wings, and the sky fell, and the sea was boiling hot, the world would starve for lack of boiled pork.

Another group was discussing what was to be done if, by the splitting of the atom, everybody in the world was thrown out of employment.

Another group was discussing whether an earthquake or a plague conferred the greater benefit on a community.

Another group was endeavouring to calculate the exact point at which thrift ceases to be a necessity and becomes a public danger, and likewise that at which extravagance ceases to impoverish a community and begins to enrich it.

Another group was engaged in ascertaining what degree of unemployment was an essential feature of economic health for the community.

Another group was discussing how far the incomes of the community should be reduced in order to increase its prosperity.

Another group was discussing how far the standard of living must be lowered in order to raise it.

Of those who were instructing their pupils, one was demonstrating how a dog could be fed with bits of itself. It had already consumed its tail, its ears, its legs, and the flesh of its breast and rump, and was now starting on slices of its liver. By the same experiment he also proved how little of its organism was really necessary.

Another, by excising part of the stomach of an ass, had enabled it to live on a greatly reduced diet. This operation he strongly recommended to the unemployed.

Another, by beating a dog to death, proved that contused wounds, in sufficient quantity, may be fatal to life.

Another demonstrated an ingenious method of recovering oats from the dung of horses: which he hoped would be of assistance to the poor in these hard times.

Another had very cleverly induced photophobia in a baby by beating it with a stick whenever the sun shone. By this means he proved that all our actions are automatic, and that free will is non-existent.

Another exhibited a tourniquet he had invented for the legs of sedentary workers: for he said it was unjust that while these organs were idle they should draw nutriment from the rest of the body. He showed also that by an ingenious screw arrangement a little blood could be admitted to the limbs from time to time, lest, by getting gangrenous, they might infect the general system.

Another very convincingly advocated that private practice in medicine, and all local health services, should be abolished. For, he said, disease is One Big World Problem, which cannot be solved on narrow and parochial lines, but must be left to the consideration of some future World Medical Board, after a World Conference of Experts.

Another showed them how they could always have their cake by not eating it.

Another proved that progress was inimical to progress. For he said that progress was caused by circumstantial stresses, and the effect of progress was to eliminate stresses. Therefore civilisation could only progress by returning to the Stone Age.

A distinguished economist taught that they should stint themselves in all things so that they might be able to sell their goods cheap, and thus raise their standard of living.

Another taught that it was their duty as traders to sell as much as possible, and as citizens to buy as little as possible.

Another showed them how they could afford to build stables by starving their horses.

Another demonstrated very artfully that if they were given more money they would have less money.

Another showed his pupils how to whistle for prosperity, which, he said, would set them working like the devil.

All this, though it did not comfort Mac ui Rudai enormously, nevertheless showed him exactly where he stood; and if he was not flattered that so many learned men should be at pains to explain why his belly must be empty and his breeches in rags, and why there was no work he could do to fill and mend 'em, you must put that down to his naturally wicked disposition and tendency to class hatred.

CHAPTER XV

How they went to a Party

NOW, after all this stodge, let's have a song or two. That night Mr Robinson took them all to a highball party given by some friends of his, where forbidden liquors flowed as merrily as in Mallow at its heyday, and the loveliest girls you ever saw frolicked like young calves in a meadow.

Now then, glasses all round. *Ἴτε Βάκχαι, ἴτε Βάκχαι.*

Clink a glass of cocktail:
  First a spot of gin,
Then a dash of vermouth,
  Sip of grenadine,
Touch of angostura,
  Cherry on the top,
And there's a drink to make you think
  The world is on the hop.

Here's another cocktail:
  First a spot of mint,
Next a dash of Kummel,
  Lemon juice, a hint;
Half a glass of dry gin,
  Then a dash of peach,
And there's a cup to pick you up
  Where worry cannot reach.

Here's another cocktail
To brighten up your wit:
Spot of Vermouth français,
Then a spot of It.;
One dash Absinthe,
Two of Curaçoa,
And there's a glass, my pretty lass,
To make your party go.

And it went too, like hell. In a moment they were all dancing furiously, eyes sidling, shoulders twitching, elbows jerking, bodies writhing, legs jigging, singing the joyous words of the jazz tune into one another's ears as they hugged like lovers in bed.

Blue cabbages are blooming down in Bluelick
In Kentucky.
Ain't that lucky?
So jangle all your bangles and we'll splash the ole spondulicks
In the lil home town that I was born in.
Then we'll bang the ole pianna
By the dusky Susquehanna,
Lil yaller-faced baby o' mine!
I wanna say my cutie
Has gotta bitta beauty
Whoop-ya! Whoop-ya! Whoop!
An' we gonna hang our washin' in de mornin'
On de Mason-Dixon Line.

Fill up now. Go on. Do you think this is a temperance mission? Whiskey, Gert? Over there in the coal-scuttle.

Fill your glass with old J.J.,
  Dear old Dublin's dear old whiskey.
When hearts are blue and skies are grey,
  That's the stuff to make you frisky.

Ἴτε Βάκχαι, ἴτε Βάκχαι. But what do I hail Dionysus for? ὦ Βρόμιε, thou wouldst have been sadly out of place at these revels, for there was no greatness of soul in them, nor deep-chested laughter. Though they were all plentiful drinkers, they drank not heartily but hectically, and not good red wine, but fizz and cocktails; which I would as soon drink as kiss one of these boyish girls all plastered with lipstick. Neither was their talk the tattle of generous minds set free by the Tongue-Loosener, but rather the blatherskite of silly asses. My dear, how perfectly devastating! Quite. Quite. No, he wasn't *quite* quite, you see. I believe shoulders are coming in again in the autumn. What a bore! Quite. My dear, her hat was quite too erroneous. Let me introduce you two. How're you, darling? Put it there, old top. The fellow is perfectly *eocene*—he actually *believes* in things. Yes, I shall probably remarry Bert if he's keen, but I'd just as soon go on living with him as we are now. Quite too absolutely downcasting. Quite. On the whole I rather enjoyed the war: it began to be a bore towards the end, but the first few years were quite jolly. So the priceless old relic got her face hitched up another yard or two, and she hopes it won't slip again till she's pipped him. What's wrong is that people don't *want* to work nowadays. And the poor dears are going to have a baby. My dear, how perfectly palæozoic. Quite. Put on another record, Fay.

Guess I'm in love.
Yes, I'm in love!
My sweetie is a peach,
I'll say that she's a wow,
And when she pets me
Her luscious lips are like a leech,
I feel them in my fancy now.
O gee! she gets me!

You never heard such popping of corks and such frothing of liquor as on that wild night, nor saw such bright eyes and scarlet lips, such flashing necks and backs, or such display of silken legs. I must say Fay knows how to make a party go. 'Nother spot of gin, my dear? Don't mind if I do. Fag? Thanks. Encore, Fay.

Her luscious lips are like a leech,
I feel them in my fancy now.
O gee! she gets me.

You get me too, dearie, and no mistake. What pretty knickers you've got on. Keep your hands to yourself, my lad. O well, we can only be young once.

Wonderful love!
Wonderful love!
Under the moon and star-ars.
Tum-tum-ti-tum!
Tum-tum-ti-tum!
Under the trees in car-ars.

CHAPTER XVI

What further things they observed in the City of Boob

MAC UI RUDAI had gone to the party in fancy dress, in the character of a tramp, and came back in a new pair of trousers; thus out of evil came a certain amount of good. Nevertheless he was dreadfully shocked by the whole affair, and soundly berated Mr Robinson for leading him into mischief.

Next day, continuing their peregrination of the city, they went to the Assinarian Industrial Exhibition. This enterprise had been started at the instigation of the Government in the hope of bringing about a trade revival by inducing the people to *spend more*—the people having lately cut down their expenditure as a result of their salaries being reduced in accordance with the Government's policy of economy. Cuanduine and his friends arrived just in time to hear the opening speech of Prince Katzpau, Consort of Queen Whims, who spoke these heartening words:

'People of Boob, in opening this magnificent display of Assinarian resources, it is my duty to say a few words about its purpose. Its purpose is to prove to the world that though Assinaria is going through hard times, she is not yet down and out.' Cheers. 'We may not be able to buy goods, or even to sell them: but we can still produce them. We can produce them better and cheaper than ever—'cheers

—'and so long as we can do that, we can hold up our heads above the waters of depression that are steadily rising above the heads of our rivals in the world market.

'A secondary purpose of this exhibition is to induce you to spend your money a little more freely, and thus bring about that revival of trade so necessary for world prosperity. Perhaps some of you may feel that this is a little inconsistent with the duty of economy, so rightly emphasised by the Government. Indeed our leading bankers'—here the Prince raised his hat reverently—'and also our most learned economists are divided on this point. But though I myself do not pretend to understand economics—the dismal science, ha-ha!—I do not think that the two policies are really inconsistent. They are, in fact, if I may venture to express an opinion, complementary. We have a duty to spend *and* a duty to save. We must spend all we can in the interests of employment, and save all we can in the interests of economy. As Professor Gudgeon so cleverly puts it, we spend by saving, and save by spending.' Cheers.

'In these hard times' continued the Prince after consulting his notes, 'I should like to appeal for a greater spirit of mutual helpfulness, goodwill, and all that sort of thing. The obstacles to recovery are pessimism and apathy: let us attack them with courage and good-humour. If our wages are cut, let us smile. If we lose our job, let us laugh. If our dole is cut off, let us fairly split our sides with joy; and never fear, if we take things in that spirit—the good old Assinine spirit—we shall very soon turn the corner.

'Above all things we must get together: but at the same time we must not forget that our only hope lies in preserving the competitive spirit. We must be prepared for a long spell of hard work, and to sacrifice everything, even our very jobs, without grumbling. I believe that there are many unemployed men who, sick of idleness, have offered to work without wages, and it is up to us all to give such men every possible support.' Hear, hear! 'I was told yesterday of an unemployed cobbler who has offered to cobble the boots of the unemployed for nothing.' Cheers. 'And I have also heard of an unemployed tailor who has taken on two apprentices for free training.' Shrieks of applause. 'That, ladies and gentlemen, is the spirit by which the problems of overproduction and unemployment will be solved. These men, who have risen above the mere desire for sordid gain, have given an example to us all. They have demonstrated the great truth that the acquisition of material things is nothing. Self-sacrifice is everything.' Cheers. 'Once more then, I repeat, let us get together, and if we realise that the future, if not the present, is in our own hands, we shall certainly win through.'

Hearty Assinine cheers greeted this striking speech, which was broadcast over the world, and printed beneath triumphant headlines in all the newspapers, the more telling points being emphasised with black, red, purple, or multi-coloured type. It was indeed a Rallying Call to the Assinine race, a call to rich and poor alike to give of their best in the hour of national need, and an eminently practical solution of all difficulties. Mac ui Rudai was so carried away that he ardently embraced a kind-looking Duchess who happened to be near, saying: 'Come on now, old girl, let's get together and see what we can be doing. Let us cast aside all thought of self in response to those noble words. If you are out of a job, I can introduce you to no end of good fellows who would willingly give you employment patching their breeches for nothing.'

The Duchess, however, did not notably respond to the generous fellow's enthusiasm; but told him very frigidly that if he did not keep his hands to himself she would have him arrested; at which poor Mac ui Rudai was exceedingly hurt, and crept away into a corner completely broken in spirit.

Prince Katzpau's speech stirred the Assinine nation to its depths. There was immediately formed an army of Youth, under the command of the stout veteran, General Bloodshot, to make war on Pessimism and Apathy, and a whirlwind campaign was begun. Soon the country was overrun with cheerful smiling warriors, who drove the forces of gloom in headlong rout before them. For a full account of the various happy devices they employed, I must refer you to the histories of the time; but I will tell you of a few of their merrier pranks. If a man showed himself depressed by impending bankruptcy, they sent him funny postcards, or chaffed him over the telephone. Anyone who appeared worried by business difficulties, or by inability to make ends meet, was set upon in the street by swarms of jolly fellows who tickled his ribs, or knocked his hat over his eyes, or, if this failed to cheer him, soused him in the river. There was a flying squad of frisky young girls, darling creatures, who would often descend on the labour exchanges and distribute false noses and paper caps among the unemployed. Others made war in more forthright fashion. People whose businesses had gone smash, if they did not take it with a proper levity, were visited at night by Bright Young Things, and soundly walloped. Anybody who failed to laugh when his wages were cut was tickled to death with a feather. Anybody who showed himself apathetic about his no-job was batted on the bean.

As to the beneficial effects of this campaign, I have no information.

CHAPTER XVII

How Mac ui Rudai put up a stiff line of Sales-Resistance

AFTER a tour of the Exhibition, Cuanduine and Mr Robinson went off to see the other sights of the town, but Mac ui Rudai lingered on for the pleasure of gloating over all the nice things he could not buy.

Now at one of the airplane stands there was a young salesman who was not making good. He had a pleasing manner and an expert knowledge both of planes and flying, but owing to a certain lack of push and aggressiveness, he was unable to get away with the goods, or rather, to get the goods away; which was distinctly unfortunate, as he was paid by commission only. Watching him with frightful contempt was a great six-foot-three American, smoking a cigar as long as himself, one Hiram Boloney, of Detroit, Michigan, who had come over to observe European methods of not doing business. When the young salesman had failed to sell for the thirteenth time, Mr Boloney could no longer restrain his impatience, and, striding forward, he said: 'Say, bo, you don't know as much about salesmanship as a newborn possum. Why do you think you didn't sell to any of those ginks?'

'Because they didn't want the goods, or they couldn't afford them' replied the European.

'Boloney!' said Mr Boloney. 'Ain't the whole art of salesmanship selling folks what they don't want and can't afford? Why, I've sold pictures to the blind, gramophones to the deaf, climbing outfits to cripples, and steam yachts to guys living a thousand miles from a sheet of water. I once sold the statue of Liberty to a Scotch minister, but that was for a bet, and of course I couldn't deliver the goods. Now I been watching you, buddy, and I guess your methods wouldn't sell hot coffee to a lost explorer at the North Pole. You ain't got the real telling line of salestalk. You ain't got the *intimate* touch that puts a proposition across. 'Stead o' lecturing like a school teacher about clutches and carburettors, you gotta get round your prospect's heart, and make him see that a feller that ain't soaring in the empyrean ain't half as much alive as a clam in a chowder. You gotta sell the *idea*, see? and then the machine sells itself.'

'I'd like to see you try that line on our people' said the European.

'Just you hand it to me, son, and I'll sell the whole darned outfit. See that sheep-eyed gink coming over here now?' Mr Boloney indicated Mac ui Rudai. 'I bet a five-spot I'll sell him one of your planes in ten minutes.'

'Done' said the European as Mac ui Rudai came near and stood looking admiringly at a handsome little monoplane.

'Evenin', sonny' said Mr Boloney, smiling. 'I see you got your giglamps fixed on the nicest lil line in our outfit. Like her?'

'Very much' said Mac ui Rudai.

'I guess you know a good plane when you see one, old man. Send her along?'

'No, thanks' said Mac ui Rudai. 'I'm not an airman;' and he would have moved away had not Mr Boloney put an arm affectionately about his shoulder.

'Now see here, bo, I'll tell you as a friend you're losing a good thing if you leave that machine to be snapped up by someone else. 'Sno use saying you ain't an airman. Everyone's gotta be an airman sooner or later, so why not sooner? Say, buddy, but if you ain't never soared into the blue sky on your own winged steed, you don't know what it is to live. Speedin' like a swallow, loopin', nose-divin', why, there ain't nothing like it. It's thrills all the time, and in this lil machine here, it's as safe as sittin' by the fire as well. Yes, sir. Just look at the lines of her. As graceful as a swan, and built with a single eye to stability. A gal could drive her. And say, you're the sorter guy that'll wanna take your sweetie out in something smartern a goldarned road crawler, eh? As ole man Emerson said, the way to a woman's heart is to keep slap up to date: you gotta keep surprising them all the time. Now, sirree, what d'ye say? Shall I mark her sold?'

'No thank you' said Mac ui Rudai.

'Say, bo, you don't seemter kinda got me. In these yer progressive days a plane ain't a luxury. It's a necessity. Why, over in lil old U.S. no guy with any class would be seen without a plane no moren without his pants, and you ain't gonna tell me a smart European lad like you don't wanna keep up with the times. No, sir. In these days a man without a plane don't count as much as a coon in Kentucky. But it ain't every man that's got a jim-dandy plane like this lil cutie here. This is a plane with class to it. I just sold half a dozen to one of your princesses before you came along. Now, sir, just put your name right here on the order form, and we'll deliver to your address this afternoon.'

'No thank you' said Mac ui Rudai, and went his way.

'Gee' said Mr Boloney, 'your salesmen may be saps, but I hand the goods to your buyers.'

'You mean you don't hand them' said the young salesman.

CHAPTER XVIII

Cuanduine dips into the Literature of the Period

THE same evening, Cuanduine, strolling about the city, went into a bookshop, and, having browsed around for a while, picked up a volume of poetry. The first poem in it was called Spring Song, and ran thus:

'Cuckoo!
Red is blue,
Fire is cold and water dry.
But why
Should I try
To cramp my utterance with the conventions of
rime and rythm?
My soul (if any) is impatient of all such limitations.

'O!
Let me be free of all rules and traditions.
I will sound a dozen notes together in glorious
dissonance.
Thus, and thus only, can the multitudinous
motions of my modern mind
Show.

'Ugliness is the only beauty;
Filth the only fair;
Nonsense the only sense;
Discord the only harmony.

I seek an ideology for the disintegration of the
  Unconscious.
I seek the synthesis of the artistic monad.
I will paint the gamut of sound, and twang all
  colours on my lyre,
And words shall mean exactly what I want them to,
Neither more nor less.'

Not much caring what the poet should want his words to mean, Cuanduine laid down the book and took up another, entitled 'experIment,' which opened at the poem here set down:

Nocturne.

'In the warkood
the t-t-t-t-trees
billwillowed boomcrashingly
in twombish niagaring.
mooninesslessness morribled the skoo, where
  scumbled the dunbellied sauriandclouds.
vastarkishness prevaricailed.

'But but but she came luxiferous
through through the windroar,
his wait she happinessed.
they wert wast him art she I is but you was
  mine thine us,
clingwhispered she jellytremulous.
what and what which
and and and and and and and and.'

'What language is this?' asked Cuanduine of the bookseller, who had come up expectantly.

'The New Language, sir' explained the bookseller. 'Our modern poets have found that no existing language is expressive enough to—er—express their meaning, so they've invented one of their own. Of course it's still in the transitional stage, but some of them get marvellous effects with it. That one in your hand sir, is considered one of their masterpieces.'

'Can you explain it to me?' asked Cuanduine.

'I'll try, sir. You must understand that the poet does not use words for their meaning, but for their emotive resonance. He treats language as a piano, not as a dictionary—twists words about to make them more significant, runs them together so as to blend their meaning, uses prepositions and conjunctions freely—much as a composer uses drumtaps, and cuts loose from syntax altogether. Just look at the poem before you, for instance. Note the effect of bewildered emotion produced by that marvellous line of monosyllables near the end, and the passionate questioning of that "and and and." '

'What does "warkood" mean?' asked Cuanduine.

' "Dark wood," of course.'

'And why write "t-t-t-trees?" Does the poet stammer?'

'O no, sir. That's to show what a lot of trees there were in the wood.'

''Tis marvellous ingenious' said Cuanduine. 'I suppose "mooninesslessness" means "absence of moon?" '

'Exactly. And "morribled the skoo" means "made horrible the gloomy sky." But the most ingenious word of all is that "prevaricailed." It's a mixture of "prevailed" and "prevaricated," implying that the darkness was omnipotent and deceptive.—But perhaps you don't care for poetry, sir. Here's Miss Pepstein's latest novel.'

Cuanduine took the book and read:

'MORE THAN ALL ABOUT SUSAN.

'Chapter I

'Section i

'(1)

'It is on steps that steps fail.

'It is on steps that it is on steps that steps fail.

'It is on on steps on steps steps that steps fail. Down steps and up steps and up steps and down steps steps fail that steps that steps fail fail fail.

'Steps fail up steps and down steps steps fail.

'Susan drew on her gloves on her gloves Susan drew Susan drew Susandrew Sus andrew sus Andrew. Andrew.

'She put on her hat on her hat her hat hat, and she tripped down the stairs and she tripped down the steps. It is on steps that steps fail, and on the steps her step failed, and she tripped down the steps down the steps she tripped tripped, she tripped tripped tripped tripped.'

About three chapters later Susan reached the bottom of the steps, but Cuanduine did not follow her adventures so far.

'Have you no other books?' he asked the bookseller.

'No, sir. Those are the only books that have been published for nearly twenty years.' Then, as Cuanduine glanced inquiringly at the well-stocked shelves, he added: 'I mean, of course, the only books that a gentleman like you would be bothered with. I've any amount of tripe.'

Cuanduine looked bewildered.

'Perhaps you're a bit of a recluse, sir' said the bookseller, 'so I'd better explain. Nobody can afford to publish a book nowadays unless it can carry the cost of heavy advertising—that is, unless he can be sure of selling a hundred thousand copies, which, of course, means tripe. Result of economies in education, sir, and, of course, the Depression. Novels nowadays are produced by mass production—half a dozen girls hammering at novel-machines—something like calculating machines, you know. One key for fifty words of optimism; another for a hundred words of sex-appeal; and so on. We sell 'em by the pound.'

'I'll try quarter of a pound' said Cuanduine.

CHAPTER XIX

How Mac ui Rudai went to the Pictures

ON the last day of their sojourn Cuanduine and Mr Robinson paid a visit to the Chamber of Deputies, but Mac ui Rudai, who was not interested in politics, went to the pictures. The first picture he saw was a pleasant comedy called Crepe de Chine Featuring Undie Bareskin, which I will try and reproduce for you.

Subtitle: *Mirella, only daughter of Josh Silicon, multi-millionaire, cared for nothing but clothes—*

This contention is substantiated by showing Mirella hopping about her bedroom in what looks like a pocket-handkerchief, but is really a chemise, while her maids stand by, one of them patiently holding her drawers in readiness. The gay creature at last consents a little petulantly to step into these creations, and pirouettes around some more before letting them put on her petticoat. The rest of her dressing is not sufficiently interesting to photograph, so there comes a second subtitle:

—and having a good time.

Mirella is seen dancing a *pas seul*, half drunk, at a night club, sitting on the knees of various young men, indulging in tremendous osculations, and is finally carried home dead drunk by her chauffeur.

As she is carried up the steps of the Silicon mansion, her father comes back from an all-night sitting over plans for a merger. In righteous wrath he forbids his daughter ever to go out at night again, and orders the chauffeur to refuse her the car for such purposes.

A few days later Mirella decides to wheedle the chauffeur into taking her to a night club. She finds him in the garage, lying under a car he is mending, and opens the campaign very subtly by tickling him under the chin with her toe, murmuring amorously 'Gee! I got a fearful crush on you, big boy.'

The chauffeur is coy, but after a few more maidenly blandishments, he takes her in his arms for a five-minutes kiss. Mirella then begs him to take her out that night, but he says it is as much as his place is worth, and refuses.

Mirella threatens that if he will not do as she asks she will tell her father that he has tried to seduce her, and have him sacked.

The chauffeur promises to take her to the night club if she will give herself to him for one night.

She gives herself to him for one night, with much display of underclothing.

Subtitle: *Meanwhile—*

Josh Silicon's merger fails, and he goes bust.

At the same time the chauffeur wins a sweepstake prize of a million dollars.

Mirella now discovers that she really loves the simple young fellow. She suggests that they should try a shot at marriage, and they run away together. Terrible humiliation of the proud old millionaire, who swears she shall never cross his threshold again.

Incompatibility begins to appear between the chauffeur and his bride. She spends most of his money on underclothing, till at last he refuses to foot the bill for a thousand-dollar cami-knickers. Heartbroken, the girl returns the cami-knickers to the store. The chauffeur says that in future she must be content with a dress allowance of a thousand dollars a month. The little wife brightens up. 'May I have the first month's allowance now?' The chauffeur gives her a roll of bills, and she runs out and buys the cami-knickers. She returns, wearing them. Prolonged kiss, with a close-up showing the reconciled pair fairly eating one another's faces.

Subtitle: *That night—*

Mirella and the chauffeur are seen in bed. The chauffeur says: 'I'll have to get a job again tomorrow. That was my last thousand.'

Mirella replies: 'Never mind. I'll stick to you, bo. You sure are a good spender.'

The chauffeur now realises that she really loves him, and reveals that he is really the son of a millionaire, and disguised himself as a chauffeur in order to find a woman who would really love him. Interminable kiss and fade-out.

This pretty romance was followed by the greatest of all super-films, Estelle Starshine in Shakespeare's immortal masterpiece Hamlet Prince of Denmark. This was the most expensive film that had ever been made. They had erected at Hollywood, at enormous cost, a castle exactly copied, stone by stone, from the castle of Elsinore, and every detail of dress, furniture, armour, jewellery, food, drink, and what not was as true to the times of Saxo's Amleth as the researches of a hundred scholars, hired regardless of expense, could make it. Very wisely, however, the producers had not adhered quite so closely to Shakespeare's story, which was ill suited to draw a modern audience. The play began with a bedroom scene (very sumptuous) between Gertrude and Claudius. The poisoning of the King in his garden followed; then the wedding of the guilty pair (this scene alone cost a million dollars). The only person to suspect foul play was Ophelia (Estelle Starshine), who, being in love with Hamlet, urged him to avenge his father and assert his right to the crown. Hamlet, however, hesitated to do so without sufficient evidence, and Ophelia, despising his timidity, gave him back his ring, and engaged herself to another admirer, a young courtier called Laertes.

Hamlet now fell into a mood of deep melancholy; observing which, the King and Queen began to fear that he suspected their crime. They accordingly sent for Rosita Guildenstern, a celebrated vamp, and desired her to use her arts to charm the Prince out of his ill-humour, and, if possible, discover the cause of it. Rosita at once set to work to charm him in the subtle ways characteristic of vamps, kissing and caressing him on every possible occasion, blowing smoke in his face, dancing for him, getting drunk regularly, and wearing as few clothes as possible. The Prince, however, was not in the least attracted by these wiles, but, partly because he suspected she had been set to watch him, and partly to make Ophelia jealous, he pretended to be charmed. With her assistance he got up some private theatricals to entertain the court, Rosita taking the part of a Queen who murdered her husband to marry his brother. The King was thus forced to betray himself, and Hamlet, left alone with Ophelia, told her that he now knew that she was right, and would take his revenge to-morrow. Ophelia at once promised to throw Laertes over, and threw herself into his arms. (Long close-up.)

All this was overheard by Rosita Guildenstern, who, in a fury of jealousy, informed the King. Claudius was alarmed, but dared not put Hamlet to death openly on account of his popularity with the people. In this difficulty Rosita suggested that the jilted Laertes should be incited to challenge Hamlet to a fencing match, in which Laertes should use a poisoned sword. Ophelia, however, overheard the plot and warned Hamlet; who took care, when the foils were offered him, to pick the poisoned one. Laertes, in a panic, confessed everything, and, after a general slaughter, the play closed with Hamlet and Ophelia locked tight in each other's arms.

Mac ui Rudai, who had been a little shocked by Crepe de Chine, enjoyed this play immensely, and said that Shakespeare was not so highbrow as he had been led to believe.

CHAPTER XX

How Assinaria went to War

MEANWHILE Cuanduine and Mr Robinson, sitting in the Strangers' Gallery of the Parliament House, heard the Prime Minister move a vote of credit for a thousand million pounds for the war against Faraway. The cause of the war was this. Faraway was at one time a backward undeveloped country, without banks or buses or picture houses, or any others of the essentials of civilisation. A few years ago it had been provided with these appurtenances by the enterprise of Assinine capitalists who thought that if it were properly developed it would provide them with a market for the goods which their own people were unable to buy. All these investments were now imperilled by a civil war which had broken out in Faraway between the Thingumajigs and the Thingumabobs, as the local factions were called; for as these were now well furnished with civilised weapons, there was danger that the railways and factories might be damaged. It was feared also that the receipts of the picture houses might be affected. An expeditionary force had accordingly been despatched, and had already established itself on the soil of Faraway.

'In taking this step' said the Prime Minister, 'we have acted in defence both of our honour and our safety and of our legitimate interests. The lack of central authority in Faraway made it impossible for us to negotiate, and the chaotic conditions which jeopardised our investments compelled us to intervene for the restoration of law and order, not merely in our own interests, but in the interests of the Faraway people themselves.' Cheers. 'Critics of the Government have said that this action is a violation of the Treaty for the Renunciation of War; but let me tell them that it is nothing of the sort. By that treaty we promised "to renounce war as an instrument of national policy." Let our critics note the exact wording of this document on which they rely in their nefarious purpose of defaming their own country in the eyes of the world. In the first place, this action of ours is not war at all. We have never declared war on the Farawavian nation. We have merely despatched what might be called a force of armed guardians of the peace to protect our legitimate interests. It is true that these guardians of the peace have bombarded several towns and routed several Farawavian armies, but that was because their purely pacific intentions were met by violent resistance.

'In the second place, this war (if it is a war) is not being used as an instrument of national policy. Our national policy is one of peace, and such a policy could not possibly be served by recourse to war. Finally, I do not think that anyone can contend that it was the intention of the signatories of the treaty, in outlawing war, to outlaw any use whatever of armed force to settle political questions. Such an interpretation would have made agreement among the nations that signed it impossible, and would have rendered nugatory any progress in the direction of true peace. I repeat, therefore, that neither the spirit nor the letter of the treaty has been infringed in the remotest degree by this action of ours.'

At this point a Socialist member interrupted, and pointed out that by the second clause of the treaty the nations had agreed 'that the settlement of all disputes, of whatever nature or whatever origin, which may arise among them, shall never be sought except by pacific means.'

'That' replied the Prime Minister 'is exactly what we have done. We have sought the solution of this difficulty by pacific means, and the responsibility for violence rests on the Farawavians.' Cheers.

The vote of credit was carried almost unanimously, and the great Assinarian nation girt itself for war. From that moment there was employment for everybody. Mac ui Rudai got a job in a munition factory, and forthwith bought himself a new suit of clothes, and ate all day like a cow. Mr Robinson was sent by his paper to the front, but before he went he used his good offices to secure a post for Cuanduine in the Propaganda Department. 'It's not altogether a job suited to a demigod' he said apologetically, 'but it'll keep the wolf from the door anyway.'

'I am much obliged to you' said Cuanduine, 'though I have here a weapon'—putting his hand on the Cruaidin Cailidcheann—'that an army of wolves could not withstand.'

'I meant hunger' said Mr Robinson, who was not naturally a poet, but used imagery because he had never learnt how to talk. He then went on to explain the duties that would be required of Cuanduine in his new post: how he would have to write up the justice of the Assinarian cause and the wickedness of their adversaries, and tell the world what an entirely base and worthless people the Farawavians were, and how their soldiers were contemptible cowards, so that one Assinarian was a match for ten of them.

'If that is so' said Cuanduine, 'the Assinarians will have no great honour in overcoming them.'

'Don't you worry about metaphysical questions like that' said Mr Robinson. 'All you've got to do is to write the stuff and draw your pay.'

Cuanduine was well contented to do this, remembering that the children of this world are wiser in their generation than the children of light. So he hired himself out to the Propaganda Department, and wrote whatever he was commanded. And now Cuanduine had reason to be thankful for the gift of unscrupulousness that had been bestowed on him in the Fourth Heaven. For he had to tell the world that the Farawavians were the most abominable race that ever was spawned, unclean, uncivilised, cruel, treacherous, haughty, overbearing, mean, cringing, slavish, irreligious, blasphemous, superstitious, given to adulteries, fornications, and unnameable vices; that the rich among them oppressed the poor, and the poor, without reason or excuse, detested the rich; that the nation in its policy was rapacious and tyrannical, hating freedom, and aspiring to world domination; and that the Assinarians were fighting purely and unselfishly for truth, justice, freedom, and religion, and for the real benefit of the Farawavian people themselves; but that nevertheless the rights and interests of Assinaria, nay, her very existence, were at stake. He told also that the ferocious Farawavian soldiery used weapons that grievously hurt the gentle Assinarian warriors, who, for their part, always wrapped their bullets and bayonets in cotton wool; that the Farawavian troops always ran away, or surrendered in multitudes, the moment an Assinarian soldier looked crossly at them; and that the Assinarian troops fought with a gallantry unparalleled in the world's history, enduring the most horrible slaughter, and winning victory after victory against the most obstinate resistance and the most overwhelming odds.

In writing all this Cuanduine enjoyed himself immensely; but he enjoyed still more the faces of the public as they swallowed it all down to feed the stomach of their righteousness and wamble in the guts of their hatred. It moved him to exquisite laughter to watch their goggling eyes and gaping mouths as they poisoned their souls with the stuff they paid him to write and would have hanged him for refusing to believe if it had been written by someone else. In a very ecstasy of mendacity he poured out more and more of it into their insatiable maws until even his supporters remonstrated that if he laid it on so thick he would spoil the effect. They need have had no such fear, however, for the credulity of the Assinarians was so inexhaustible that when presently he fabricated a story that the ordinary drink of the Farawavians was the blood of Assinarian babies served up in the skulls of their fathers, they believed him more firmly than ever.

The happiest of his inventions was his announcement that this was a War to End War, and that when it was over all poverty and injustice would disappear from the earth; for by this bait all the Socialist leaders and advanced thinkers, who had formerly held discreetly aloof, were now induced to give it their support; not however by fighting in it, but by writing about it; and these writings gave Cuanduine the most rapturous amusement. For his services he was very well paid, and, as he did not eat so much as a mortal man, he was able to put some money by, so that when the war was ended by the conquest of Faraway, he was no longer a slave to necessity.

CHAPTER XXI

How Mac ui Rudai made good; how he married a modern girl; and how he went to the bad

MAC UI RUDAI showed himself cleverer than you would expect in his job at the munitions factory. It was said of him by his superiors that he could beat anyone at a routine task; he had a remarkable flair for thinking of new weapons; and if he was incapable of working them out, that was of no consequence, as they had plenty of scientists well able to do so. His brightest idea was for a bomb filled with a gas that drove people mad, which, being dropped on the towns of the enemy, set them all slaughtering one another, and this brought the war suddenly to an end; for which reason Mac ui Rudai is to be counted among the great humanitarians and benefactors of mankind, as having made a really practical contribution to the difficult and almost insoluble problem of how to limit or reduce the admitted horrors of war.

By suchlike inventions he made a good deal of money, and, had he been wiser, he might have lived happily ever after. But alas! his appetites had grown with his income, and he no longer desired the little houseen and the bean a' tighe that were once the goal of his ambition. It is to be feared that the pictures were partly responsible for his downfall; for, having seen several hundred filmstars in their cami-knickers, he could not help feeling that it would be more enjoyable to possess a girl so prettily undressed than to tie himself to a bean a' tighe who—now he came to think of it—would be wearing good stout bloomers with double gusset and reinforced seat. At first he tried to banish these desires, which he believed to be the temptations of the Devil; but they were really prompted by the impletion of his seminal vesicles under the recurrent stimulus of innumerable undressing scenes, and they soon became so overwhelming that at last, becoming acquainted with a slim, slinky, silk-legged modern girl, he told her his passion and begged her to be his. I will tell you this love-story from the woman's point of view, as love and romance are pre-eminently woman's business.

Kathrynne was a typical modern girl, delightfully frank and unsentimental, a good sport, and thoroughly boyish. Indeed, if she had not worn petticoats and silk stockings, painted her lips, powdered her cheeks, shaved her armpits, permed her hair, giggled a great deal, thought and talked chiefly about clothes, practised coquetry on men, and performed her toilet in restaurants and public places, she would have been as like a boy as one pea to another. Originally she was rather plain, for Nature does not seem to understand that beauty and romance are a woman's birthright. However, after treatment by a beauty specialist, she managed, by means of creams, paints, powders, and massage, and by wearing a face-improver at night, to look much the same as other girls. She had three faces: a pinky-white face for day wear, a slightly bronzed face for sports wear, and a sex-appeal face for evening wear, or when she wanted to get something out of somebody. She was seventeen, and lived with her parents, who were too old-fashioned to realise that freedom to do what she likes is a woman's birthright. Chafing under the restraints they put on her, she listened favourably to Mac ui Rudai's advances, thinking that marriage would mean a better time and more fun.

Disillusionment came only too soon. When the first rapture had died down—that is to say, on the Tuesday after the wedding—she realised that she did not love her husband. What she had taken for love was only physical attraction. She was in love with love rather than with the man. Moreover, man-like, he did not understand her. He did not seem to know that romance and happiness are a woman's birthright. The insensible fellow did not appreciate how much a woman's happiness depends on little things—on frequent compliments and caresses, on little attentions and services, on never neglecting to notice a new hat or frock, on subtle adaptations to her varying moods, on unfailing patience with her little contrarinesses, on the instantaneous gratification of her lightest whim, on the complete self-effacement of her husband, and so on—mere trifles, it might seem to the crude male mind, yet on them it depends whether a marriage shall ripen into an enduring passion (say, for six months or so), or end prematurely in bitter disillusion and misery.

Mac ui Rudai was either too blind or too selfish to realise this; and perhaps circumstances were against him. He was working all day, and Kathrynne was dancing all night, so that they saw little of each other, and from the first, almost unconsciously, they drifted apart. Vaguely Kathrynne sensed that something was amiss. No matter how much she danced, nor how many cocktails she drank, she could not rid herself of an undefined sensation of dissatisfaction. She felt that she was being cheated by Fate, which apparently is unaware that having everything her own way is a woman's birthright.

Then one day a friend in whom she confided suggested that things would be better if they had a baby. 'Babies bring love and happiness into the most unsatisfactory homes' she said.

So they had a baby; but after the first few days' excitement disillusion came again. There was a certain monotony about the little creature. The same demands recurred day after day, and gave little scope for originality in satisfying them. Soon Kathrynne sensed the old boredom creeping into her heart once more.

To her friend she said: 'A girl doesn't need motherhood until she has tasted every other experience that life has to offer. Maternity should not be thrust upon her till she is capable of getting the most out of it.'

A few days later Kathrynne went to a cocktail party and then on to a dance, and forgot all about the baby. When she got back she found that it had fallen off the window-sill on which she had left it, and broken its neck.

'Perhaps it was better so' she said, recognising, with the courage characteristic of the modern girl, that it is no use crying over spilt milk. A woman of any other generation would have sat down helplessly and cried.

After that Kathrynne and her husband drifted

further apart than ever. There was a chasm between them that could never be bridged. Both felt somehow that there was something wrong with their marriage, but what it was they could not guess. The man, blind and selfish as all men are, laid the blame on Kathrynne. She, with the unerring instinct and the candour that are the unique gifts of woman, would have told him that it was his, only that they were never together long enough to allow her the opportunity. The gap between them widened day by day. His masculine insensibility and self-sufficiency, his callous indifference to her need for the joy and laughter that are a woman's birthright, irritated, exasperated, almost maddened her. The faster she spent his money, the further they drifted apart. 'Can he not *see?*' she asked herself desperately.

At last a comforter made his appearance. At a night-club she met a handsome young man called Peregrine with the sort of crinkly hair that she adored. He charmed her by his unselfish attentions. He fetched cocktails for her, he never failed to notice when she was wearing a new frock, his compliments were too divine. Joy entered once more into poor Kathrynne's life. Half unconsciously she allowed him to take her into his arms. He kissed her mouth, her neck, her eyes. He understood her. Perfectly.

'You do not love your husband' he whispered.

'He does not understand me' Kathrynne replied.

Peregrine kissed her again.

'We have absolutely nothing in common' moaned Kathrynne. 'I never loved him *really*. It was a silly girlish infatuation on my part. Physical pash, you know. He swept me off my feet and all that.'

Peregrine kissed her ear.

'He doesn't want his wife as a companion, but a chattel,' said Kathrynne. 'Once he asked me to sew a button on his coat.'

'The brute!' cried Peregrine with a shudder, and kissed her nose.

'How well you understand me—dear' breathed Kathrynne.

Peregrine kissed her whole face.

Presently, when they were calmer, he said:

'Understanding and sympathy, happiness and romance, these and anything else she fancies, are a woman's birthright.'

Kathrynne began to feel happy again. Disillusionment vanished. All men, she realised, were not like her husband.

'Take me away with you' she cried, abandoning all thought of self in the rapture of reawakened love. Women are like that. However modern they may pretend to be, they are thoroughly romantic and sentimental at heart.

Peregrine, however, did not rise to the occasion. A complete cynic, he had been merely playing with her, as he had played with many another trusting woman. 'What about a spot of cocktail?' he said, and vanished out of her life.

Kathrynne saw him now in his true colours, and realised that she had never loved him. What she had taken for love was merely physical attraction, a temporary passion, a passing infatuation. Turning her back on the gay party, she went home to her husband.

'Let us begin all over again' she said. 'Romance

and happiness and a few other things are a woman's birthright. Give me those, and I am ready to forget the past.'

Her husband looked at her with a strange look in his eyes.

'We ought to share each other's interests, dear' said Kathrynne, laying her soft cheek against his. 'You must give up all that horrid work of yours, and come with me to dances and night clubs. Let our life be one long cocktail party together.'

At last her husband understood her.

'Don't you know I've gone bust?' he said.

Kathrynne caught her breath on a sob. She could see that the chasm between them was unbridgeable. This man would never understand her. Gathering her expensive cloak about her with a gesture of scorn, she went out of his life for ever.

Mac ui Rudai thought himself well rid of her, but it must be confessed that he was a contributor to his own ruination. He had spent whatever money she left him on finery and amusement, and, having got the sack at the conclusion of peace, he was now without a penny or the prospect of earning one. He became soured and disgruntled. He declaimed bitterly against the ingratitude of the Assinarians, and declared himself disillusioned about the glory of war, which he affirmed to be a foolish and wasteful method of settling international disputes.

He had to sell his cars and his wireless sets and his fine clothes to buy food, and, at last, being entirely on the rocks, he presented himself again to Cuanduine in the same pitiable plight as on their first meeting, and urged him to take up his cause with more vigour than he had shown hitherto. Cuanduine admired his cheek, but Mr Robinson, who had come back from the seat of war, eyed him sourly, for he wanted Cuanduine to undertake some notable stunt, worthy of being written up in the papers.

Cuanduine, having listened to both pleas, said: 'Do you think either of you can turn me from what I have a mind to? I have my own destiny to follow. If you will follow it too, well and good; if not, 'tis no matter. We shall none of us die of grief.'

With these words he set forth. Mac ui Rudai hung back, unable to make up what he called his mind, and Mr Robinson promptly went after Cuanduine, thinking that, once rid of this nuisance, he would be able to prevail on the hero to do as he wished. However, they had not gone far before Mac ui Rudai went shambling after them; and in this manner they left the city and the cultivated lands around it, and came into the hill country where men no longer dwelt.

CHAPTER XXII

How Cuanduine fell in love

CUANDUINE and his companions, pursuing their journey, came one day to a pleasant valley, where there were trees and flowers and running streams, and the spirit of peace dwelt among sweet odours and quiet sounds. As they looked upon this scene they saw the figure of a young girl afar off; and Cuanduine said: 'This is the vision of my heart's desire. Here will I stay till I have enjoyed her.'

'What?' cried Mac ui Rudai, shocked. 'Would you desert my cause, that you have sworn to champion, for dalliance and flirtation?'

'Your cause can wait' said Cuanduine.

'Not an instant' said Mac ui Rudai. 'Mine is the cause of justice and humanity, and he who would desert it is a dirty dog and I won't give him my vote.'

'O, cheese it' said Mr Robinson, who thought he would have a spicier story to write if Cuanduine were to pursue the young girl than if he were to champion the cause of Mac ui Rudai.

'Begone, you slug' said Cuanduine to Mac ui Rudai, 'for I have a mind to follow my own desires rather than to serve your necessities.'

'What, you conceited upstart' cried Mac ui Rudai in a rage. 'You highbrow! You self-styled intellectual! Do you think yourself better than I am? Do you not know that better men than you have been content to be my servants, outbidding one another with promises if only they might obtain the position.'

'They do not seem to have served you very well' said Cuanduine, looking at his trousers.

Mac ui Rudai then began to upbraid Cuanduine, heaping reproaches and evil names upon him. But now the Gods were weary of Mac ui Rudai, and they had other work for Cuanduine to do: therefore they cast a deep mist about the place, so that the others saw him not, and, wandering about, they presently found themselves far removed from the valley, nor could they remember in which direction it lay. So Mac ui Rudai went on looking for work, and Mr Robinson returned to London.

But Cuanduine went up into the valley, and in the middle of it he met the girl he had seen from afar. She was the fairest thing he had yet seen among the fields and cities of earth. She had hair like ripe corn, and eyes as blue as the cornflower, lips red as poppies, and cheeks blushing from the kisses of the sun. Her body was strong and lissom, with proud shapely breasts and rounded limbs, and hips worthy of a strong man's hopes; all which was very pleasing to Cuanduine, who was rather old-fashioned in his tastes, and, having met no proper woman in his walks on earth, but only imitation boys and demi-strumpets, was yet a virgin. Addressing her with modest courtesy, he said: 'Gentle and fair, you are my heart's desire. I give you my love, if you will take it, and would have you to my life's partner in the work of God.'

The girl smiled upon Cuanduine, and put her hand into his; but she said nothing, being rapt with the beauty of the grandson of Lugh.

'Who are you, my beloved?' said Cuanduine, 'for truly I can think of no name to match your loveliness.'

'I am what you have said' answered the girl. 'Have you not called me your heart's desire? And what matters beyond that? Your love I take, and I give myself to you to be your life's partner in the work of God.'

After that they wasted no more time, but there in the sunlight, upon the green floor of the valley, by the side of a laughing stream, under the benison of the sky, amid the hum of bees and the odour of many blossoms, they took their pleasure. The girl gave Cuanduine the seven pleasures of woman. The pleasure of kissing; for which her lips were as fragrant as flowers, and her cheeks like ripe fruit, and behind her ears and beneath her hair it was like cool grottoes where violets blow. The pleasure of shy unveiling: for there is nothing sweeter than shyness, and no triumph like its conquest by the arms of love. In her gown the girl was like a queen, and like a comrade, and like a nosegay of many flowers; in her undergarment of green silk she was like a daffodil and like a wanton mistress; and in her naked beauty she was like a lily and the desire of all desiring. The pleasure of beauty revealed in the shamelessness of perfect joy. The pleasure of the breasts, which were like warm hives full of honey. The pleasure of the body, which her lover took as one grasping the golden apples. The pleasure of the kiss of the bodies in the ecstasy of self-forgetfulness.

So Cuanduine entered into the body of his love, into the womb of his bride, into the heart of life.

CHAPTER XXIII

Cuanduine at the heart of life

O LOVE, my love,
My heart's desire!
All loveliness in one bright form embodied:
My own, all mine.
All mine: yet mine is nothing, and I no more.
All's one.

Life within me, what's your will?
One more frame to test and kill?
One more taste of joy and pain?
One more chance to seek in vain?
Laugh—and see the fools surviving?
Love—and know the rage deriving?
Then breed your kind for further striving?
Have it so.
Restless seeker, 'gainst all reason,
Have it so.
The great engines crash through the night:
The self-devouring stars roar in their courses:
And nowhere is there rest beneath the heavens,
No rest but death, but have it so.
Grim *ΑΝΑΓΚΗ*, God-compelling,
Since it must be, have it so.
Life and all the toil of it,
Joy and all the pain of it,
Love and all the rage of it,

Laughter and the sting of it,
Have it so.

Pitiless *ΑΝΑΓΚΗ*, defiance in thy teeth.
Live, Life, and die, and live, and die, and live
Ever for ever.
O my love, my love!

CHAPTER XXIV

How Cuanduine begot sons and daughters

SO Cuanduine slept upon the breast of his love; and as it was the first time he had slept since his coming on earth, his sleep was long and deep. When his bride awoke, she laid him gently on the grass, and when she had bathed in the stream she brought him fruits she had gathered that they might break their fast together. But Cuanduine still slept, and, looking up, she beheld a young man, fairer than the sun, standing over him, who said: 'Let him be: let him sleep his fill: for he shall not sleep again in this foolish world till he has done the work that the Gods have appointed.' With these words the young man vanished, and she knew then that it was Angus Og that had spoken, and she kept his commands.

Now from thenceforward the Gods put their blessing on that valley, so that it was always summer there. At the prayer of Lugh, Demeter took her curse from it, and even dark Hades consented that his bride should walk there at her pleasure. Beneath the feet of Persephone the floor of the valley flowered with profusion of immortal blossoms, and the trees brought forth fruit a hundredfold in the light of her smile. Apollo shone there with double splendour. Selene lingered there by night, and the rest of the world saw only the flash of her feet as she hurried home to Endymion. Artemis, the chaste huntress, mounted ward over the encircling hills, lest any from the outer world should intrude; and grey-eyed Pallas Athene came, and of her wisdom and prudence tempered the exuberance of Gaia, so that she engendered no hurtful or monstrous thing. Neither did she permit Pan to enter till he had purged himself of his grosser qualities that he learned when he left the pastures of Arcadia to be worshipped in cities: thereafter his pipes were heard in the valley, now here and now there, like the cry of the cuckoo. Under the ægis of Pallas there were generated from the foam and spray of the river a multitude of fair nymphs, and the sunrays begat dryads of the shadows of the forest. Here indeed, in this one spot of earth, there was such peace and plenty and beauty as the world has not known since first men used gold for coin instead of the adornment of their loves.

In this abode, while Cuanduine slept, his wife travailed and bore twin boys, strong lusty little fellows, the one fair with the curls of the sun-god, the other dark after the manner of the men of Eirinn. As befits the offspring of heroes, they grew as much in a week as common children do in a year; so that when Cuanduine awoke they were as fine a pair of seven-year-olds as you would wish to see: for so long was Cuanduine's great sleep.

Now he took the boys and trained them in all manly feats, in wisdom and knowledge, in music and all accomplishments. The heroes also came down from Tir na nOg to assist in their education. Their grandfather Cuchulain taught them his seven feats of arms and to be modest towards women. Sencha taught them sweet speech, and Bricriu the jest that discomfiteth fools and economists. Cathbad the Druid taught them cunning and unscrupulousness. Ferdiad taught them how to take a beating in good part. Naoise taught them to be generous in victory, and Ainnle and Ardan to cast envy out of their souls. Grave Fergus instructed them in kingliness of spirit: for, having been first a king, afterwards he became a subject, and, after many years of faithful service, in the end he became a rebel, in the cause of justice and in fulfilment of his plighted word. 'For' said he 'it has been falsely related of me by poets and historians that I counted my kingship well lost for love, which would be the part of a pleasure-drunken fool. But truly I counted it well lost for this reason, that no man is fit to be a king, for in trying to rule others he forgets how to rule himself. O it sickened me sometimes to see myself in the throne of judgment pretending to administer what the wisest man born cannot rightly understand, and leading others by the guidance of my own folly. Therefore, my boys, do not seek to rule; and if kingship be thrust upon you, as fools will always seek to be governed by someone, give them the answer that Pantagruel gave to the Parisians when they would have made him their governor: "that there is too much slavery in these offices, but if you have any hogsheads of good wine, I will willingly accept a present of that." And if thereafter they insist that you shall govern them, then you may do so without further misgiving, for they had better be governed by you than by anyone else.'

Such was the training and education of the sons of Cuanduine. Afterwards Cuanduine embraced his wife again, and she bore twin girls, the loveliest little creatures that ever brought joy to a father's heart. They had fair rosy cheeks, and curls golden and brown, and soft fat dimpled legs, and little plump bellies like young puppies. They were wilful, spirited, careless little things, coquetting even with their Daddy, and as good as all young things are and they were never crossed in anything, so that the valley was filled with their laughter. They sported with Cuanduine in the sunshine, climbing on his shoulders, pulling his hair, and chasing each other round his legs; and they were for ever calling for stories, and asking questions, and dragging him off to show him the wonderful new things there were in the world. In all this Cuanduine took great delight; for there is no pleasanter possession for man or demigod than a little daughter, and two little daughters are better still.

CHAPTER XXV

How Cuanduine took counsel upon certain very delicate matters

CUANDUINE himself trained his boys as to the right use and care of the body and all its parts. As to one part, however, he was in a little doubt how to proceed; for he himself, on account of his heavenly ancestry, had no such difficulties as fall to the lot of mortals, since his reason reigned supreme over all his appetites; but he knew that his sons, being three parts human, would not be altogether so fortunate. As he pondered over the question, there came to him a vision from heaven in the shape of a lean hollow-eyed man in a brown robe girt with a knotted cord. This was the holy Saint Maceratus, of whom you will read in the Acta Sanctorum that he spent his whole life in the rigid mortification of the flesh for the subjugation of unclean desires: for so he called the pretty games of love. To this end, when he was seven years old, he took a vow never to look upon the face of woman, and, if ever he was compelled to be in the presence of one, he cast his eyes modestly downwards, for skirts were long in those days. He took a vow also never to look upon his own body, fulfilling it so well, if the hagiographers are to be trusted, that his skin became like the bark of a tree for want of washing. He also scourged himself three times a day, and wore a thick rope about his body under his clothes, which ulcerated his flesh so that he stank like corruption; whereby he became so unpopular even among his brother ascetics that he was forced to withdraw into the uninhabited wilderness, and there died in the odour of sanctity.

This apparition said to Cuanduine: 'Rash man! It has become known to me in heaven that you contemplate instructing your innocent sons in the secrets of the devil. Forbear, I command you: for if once they know what horrible carnal delights are in store for them, they will never be satisfied till they have enjoyed them, and so put themselves in peril of eternal damnation.'

'How then' said Cuanduine 'shall they be fortified against the pricking of bodily desire? For you know that with the rest of the body the implements of love grow too, so that when the containers become filled with the stuff of life, in the absence of knowledge there arise grave perturbations to the detriment of mind and body.'

'Speak not so grossly' commanded Saint Maceratus. 'These promptings you speak of come from the devil, and are to be subdued by prayer and fasting, and by contemplation of the sufferings of our Redeemer and the blessed martyrs.'

At this point intervened Bricriu of the Bitter Tongue, who had been instructing the boys in repartee, and having seen Saint Maceratus from afar, and guessed what his mission was, came over to the help of Cuanduine.

'This is nonsense' said he. 'For it is well known that the contemplation of suffering is itself pleasurable to the senses, as Kraft Ebing and Havelock Ellis testify, converting the appetite for the female into a desire either to inflict or to suffer pain according to the character of the individual. Which puts me in mind of a good story I heard once of a young lad, who, upon reading some of this pious matter that you command, was so inflamed that he ran out at once to perform some naughtiness that might earn him a whipping from his governess. It happened that the governess also, by the advice of her confessor, had been indulging in pious meditation, which so much affected her that she laid on to the youngster with a passionate zeal that made him howl for mercy. You must know that in such cases only the early blows are pleasurable. After the first sensuous warming of the posterior, the remainder of the thrashing is not quite so voluptuous, your masochist being no fonder of weals and contusions than your normal subject. Our young hero, therefore, began to kick and to struggle, but the governess, being young and sturdy, only lambasted him the harder, till at length in his agony he caught hold of her dress and nearly pulled it off her. In that moment he discovered what he really wanted, and the governess, seeing that he was sorry for his fault, made haste to console him.'

'I know not' said Maceratus 'whether this is a bawdy story or a scientific investigation into what is best left unknown. Either way, 'tis prompted by the devil. But if supernatural aids to chastity will not content you, there remain the natural courses of hard study and physical exercise whereby the attention of the mind is diverted from fleshly curiosities, and the nutriment that might otherwise flow to the lower parts of the body is totally absorbed by the brain and musculature. Much may also be done by means of cold baths, to reduce the bodily heats that engenerate sensual lusts, providing always that a becoming modesty be observed, so that the nakedness of the body be not exposed in these lustrations. To these must be added a rigid restriction of the diet, eschewing all such gross inflammatory foods as eggs, butter, meat, fish, fruit, sugar, and so forth, that tend to puff up the flesh and exalt the lower members, and confining oneself to harsh and stringy substances, like roots, grass, or perhaps a little stale bread and dry cheese, whereby the digestion is so taxed that the controlling centres of the brain are altogether distracted from generative purposes. Wine too must be avoided, being a wicked prompter to lechery, and even water should be taken in moderation, for if the baser parts be deprived of moisture, the secretion of disturbing humours will be impeded. It is also a wise precaution to spend as little time as may be lying sluggishly abed, for the devil is never so active as at night, ranging from pillow to pillow, whispering thoughts of a dear companion to frolic with; on which account the pious hermits of the desert would rise from bed in the small hours and cast themselves naked into the snow, or into thorns and nettles, to tame the raging heats of sensuality. But above all things it is necessary to avoid the reading of books that have any tendency to stir the erotic imagination; and to shun all pictures and statues of subjects in the nude, than which nothing is more certain to arouse the prickings of lascivious desires. Finally the eyes of the youths must be trained so that the sight of a young woman shall at once inspire them with horror and repulsion, and move them to fly from her presence; for, as St. Boniface says, likewise St. Skinniface, St. Prurita, St. John Flagellarius, St. Sallacious, and others, from temptations to impurity there is no safety but in immediate flight. By these means, Cuanduine, and by no others, you may hope, with God's aid, to keep your sons chastely innocent till the time comes for them to be joined in holy matrimony to whatever prudent, pious, submissive, dutiful, homely spouses you may choose for them.'

'Why, you withered nut, you squeezed orange' cried Bricriu, 'you macerated leaf, you sapless mummy, do you think the world is to be saved by fellows bred in this fashion?'

'I think, sir pagan' replied Maceratus, 'that he who would save the world must first preserve his own soul from the snares of the flesh and the devil.'

Here their discourse was interrupted by the appearance of another vision in their midst, no less than the holy Saint Progressa herself, who, addressing Cuanduine, said: 'Do not heed this ancient out-of-date unprogressive old prurient prude, who can think of nothing but sin and shame—'

'That is false' interrupted Maceratus. 'For though it is sinful before marriage even to look at a woman lustfully, after you are joined in holy wedlock you may do as you please, since she is your lawful wife, and she may refuse you nothing under pain of mortal sin.'

'Disgusting' said Progressa, turning away from him. 'But this fellow's views are quite out of date. It is now agreed that sex is the most beautiful, the most ennobling, the most radiant, the most spiritual, the most gloriously saccharine of all the wonders created by God; and it is therefore contrary both to nature and to divine ordinance to put any restraint upon it whatever. It is above all things necessary that the young people should come to it joyously and without fear or shame, as a rapturous and spontaneous expression of mutual love. You should therefore instruct them as early as possible, frankly, and without any false modesty that may lead them to associate the act with sin or wrong-doing. I know that many people find this difficult, owing to the sense of shame fostered by conventional morality. My advice in these cases is to make the revelation gradually, beginning with the lovely illustration of the flowers, the reproductive organs of which can be examined and dissected without embarrassment, while the process of pollenation cannot shock the most sensitive imagination. I must admit, however, that all authorities are not agreed on this point—'

'I'm not surprised to hear it' said Bricriu. 'For I heard a story of a young lad who was instructed in this botanical fashion, and at the end of the allegory, "Mummy" says he, "where are my stamens?" '

Progressa blushed. 'No hard and fast rules can be laid down' she said hurriedly. 'Some authorities recommend that children should be allowed to observe the courtships of animals, but preferably not earthworms. These creatures are hermaphrodites, and in their couplings each enjoys the sensations of both sexes; which, it is feared, might inspire envy in the little human observer, and possibly produce an inferiority complex. By one or other of these methods the necessary knowledge will be acquired naturally and beautifully. Afterwards the parent's sole duty is to abstain from all interference whatever, any repression of this heavenly instinct being contrary to nature and to the ordinances of God as revealed to me.'

'Alack!' said Cuanduine. 'Between the two of you I am altogether flummoxed, bewildered, and put to a *non plus*. There seems to be but one point on which you are agreed, namely, that this one organ is of more importance than all the rest of the body put together: so much so that one's whole life should be devoted either to exercising it or to keeping it in subjection. This seems to me to be a little disproportionate. For on the one hand men are afflicted with many truly evil passions—such as pride, covetousness, anger, envy, and cowardice—which they will need some part of their energies to subdue; and on the other hand, this organ which you, madam, belaud so extravagantly, is but a thing we have in common with goats and monkeys. Surely we should take more pride and joy in those features we have which are unique, as the hand and the brain, with its powers almost worthy of a god.'

At this point the discussion was interrupted

by the arrival of another spirit, fat, smiling, and a little suggestive of a eunuch, who said: 'Hello, everybody. I'm Mr Jolliboy. At least I *was* before my translation to a happier world. I just dropped in because I thought the conversation was becoming a trifle—shall we say?—morbid. Let's have a little fresh air on the subject. What I say is this. Cannot men and women be good pals and jolly sports together, living in free and equal association, unconscious of any difference between them? Clean healthy-minded youngsters is what we want. Jolly boy-and-girl friendships, you know, without any nonsense about—er—sexandthatsortofthing, eh? what! I could always trust *my* boy, by jove. Jolly kid! Girls were *safe* with him—absolutely. He could spend a whole summer's day with the prettiest girl on earth and never give a thought to any of thatsortofthing. Not a spark of sentimentality in him, you know. Hardly knew whether a girl was pretty or not, the healthy young dog, God bless him!—O yes. He married at last, when he was about fifty—girl he'd known since childhood. Happiest couple you ever saw.—No. No children, but I always think childless marriages are the happiest, don't you? More time to devote to *each other*, don't you know?'

'Pish, you sapless ninny!' cried Bricriu.

'Patience, brother' said Cuanduine. 'It takes all sorts to unmake a world. I thank you for your counsel, Mr Jolliboy, but it is something detached from realities, and helps me very little—'

'To follow it is to rush unarmed into temptation' said Maceratus.

'It is rather to run away from life' said Progressa. 'Come, Cuanduine, be modern, and try my way.'

'Madam' said Cuanduine, 'part of your counsel is good. But as to the other part, has it occurred to you that if my lads run as free as you propose, they will soon be so saddled and bridled with family cares that they will have no time for the performance of noble deeds?'

'Never fear' said Progressa. 'There is no danger nowadays of such a calamity; for I have myself provided against it by the cleverest and most beautiful of human inventions—'

'I am aware of that' said Cuanduine.

'Then you need have no further anxiety. For by this means, if your boys should unfortunately misconduct themselves with young women, as mettlesome lads are apt to do when their spirits are hot and the spring is in their veins, they can do so with perfect safety; on the other hand this same contrivance may save them from such temptations by enabling them to marry early, since it secures them against the danger of having children before they can afford them.'

To this discourse, which was delivered with as much modesty as sweetness, and as much reason as eloquence, Cuanduine made answer: 'By Ares and Aphrodite, fair lady, I can see that by this assistance my boys will grow into very hardy and valiant warriors.'

'And prudent withal' said Progressa.

'Truly' said Cuanduine. 'Nevertheless it seems to me that these preparations and adjustments must detract not a little from the beauty and spirituality of the conjugal embrace on which you have so eloquently descanted.'

'It is to be feared' said Progressa, 'that in some small degree they do. But on the other hand, the beauty of conjugal love is utterly destroyed by the breeding of swarms of unwanted brats. You know, of course, that a normal woman can have a child every year from the age of fifteen to forty-five. That would mean thirty children in her lifetime; or sixty if they were all twins, ninety if they were triplets, and, if they were quadruplets, a hundred and twenty. The imagination reels before such figures.'

'Yet I have seen very few women with a hundred and twenty children' said Cuanduine.

'That, of course, is exceptional. But if we strike an average, and say sixty, the imagination still reels. Anyway, large families are destructive of conjugal love and married happiness. Just try for a moment to look at this question from the *woman's point of view*, forgetting your antiquated masculine prejudices, which are the product of male selfishness and sensuality, fostered by the superstitious sentimentality of so-called religion. Forget also your brutal desire to have plenty of cannon-fodder for future wars, and your materialistic anxiety to have large numbers of underpaid robots engaged in industry. Consider how the health and appearance of the wife are ruined, and her freedom curtailed, by the necessity of caring for a lot of squalling little wretches, who make her existence a perpetual slavery; how her tremendous powers of loving (surely a woman's noblest quality) are dissipated among a horde of egotistical rivals. True happiness is impossible in such a home, where there is nothing for each love-starved little mite but a hasty kiss and a "run away and play, darling: mummy's busy," and the unfortunate husband is neglected entirely. Compare such a noisy barrack with the blissful love-nest of the small family, in which wife and husband can be all in all to each other, their life one long caress, one perpetual wooing, and the one or two well-spaced, well cared-for, and adored little darlings can blossom like flowers in the honeyed atmosphere of all-embracing tenderness.'

Progressa paused for a moment, but neither Cuanduine nor Bricriu could venture to speak, being on the verge of vomiting.

'Come' said Progressa, 'let us be practical and face the facts. Consider the case of an unfortunate woman in the slums, who has already borne seventeen sickly imbecile children to her drunken syphilitic mentally-deficient husband, and is faced with the prospect of bearing a dozen more. What is the poor creature to do?' cried Progressa, bursting into tears. 'Is she to be left a helpless victim to her fate? Must she remain the miserable slave of her husband's brutal lust? bearing one unwanted child after another till she goes exhausted to the grave? Would you deny this poor woman the same rights as her richer sisters?' she demanded demagogically.

'Madam' said Cuanduine, 'though I have observed that the people of this world are neither very beautiful, not very healthy, nor very sensible,

I cannot believe that a huge proportion of them consists of drunken syphilitic imbeciles with seventeen children. Nevertheless I will not leave these to their fate; but will rescue them, when my time is come, not with contraceptive appliances, but with this good sword of mine—' tapping the hilt of the Cruaidin Cailidcheann. 'However, let us now return, by your leave, to these boys of mine, who are neither drunken, nor feeble-minded, nor syphilitic, nor married to women with seventeen children. You say that they should be free of repression and the sense of shame, and should consummate their love beautifully and without fear?'

'Certainly.'

'And that the clasp of love should be a spontaneous act of careless joy, a fiery and rapturous impulse, born of a mutual passion in the lovers for perfect union?'

'Yes.'

'But how in the name of God can it be such an act if they go to it in a coward fear of fruition, first poking and fiddling about with your damned apparatus like plumbers at a sinkhole? By the high dignity of man I swear this is folly and abomination. 'Tis blasphemy against love, degradation of the body, and abdication of the sovereignty of the soul.'

'By the gods of my people' said Bricrui, ''twould make a tomcat laugh to see them at their preparations. Prithee, mistress, would it not make a fine subject for a realist painting—Bride Preparing for her Nuptial Night? The poets shall do justice to it too, singing:

'My love, my love, come to my arms,
If everything is safe—'

And we shall have fine arias and serenades expressing the rapture of the lover who has perfect confidence in his preventive.'

'You are a lewd ribald fellow' said Progressa, 'and I will not stay here to be insulted.'

'Neither will I listen any longer to this pagan exaltation of carnal lust' said Maceratus, who all this while had been standing in the background, blushing at the freedom of language used by both parties to the discussion. 'Though your principles in this matter are orthodox, Cuanduine, the arguments by which you support them are both heretical and lascivious, and I gravely fear you will come to a bad end.' With that he gathered his cloak about him, and departed in high dudgeon for Paradise.

'Unreasonable as your arguments are' said Progressa, 'it is at least something that you are not influenced by the musty dogmas of the churches. I begin to think that your opposition to my ideas is due rather to misunderstanding than to religious and narrow-minded objections. Your love of life is up in arms against what you conceive to be a gospel of death. You must understand, therefore, that we do not propose to abolish mankind altogether—'

'What a pity' said Cuanduine. 'I sometimes think that would be a very good idea.'

'O come, sir' said Progressa. 'That surely is inconsistent.'

'Not a whit. For it is only natural to wish that this pitiable squinting race of self-complacent vermin, so riddled with superstition and disease, so stupid, so selfish, so covetous, so ferocious, so lecherous, so much addicted to hypocrisy and cant, so wasteful and destructive, so blind to reality, might be wiped out of existence and the earth left clean for some better breed. Nevertheless, as we are brethren, and as we know that the Gods had some high purpose in starting the experiment, we put the wish away as unkind and unreasonable.'

'Still, you might agree to a moderate reduction of their numbers to accommodate them to the resources of the earth.'

'Why, madam? How can anyone in the present know what numbers the earth can support in the future, any more than those in the past could have guessed how many it would support to-day? O short-sighted dame! There is no wisdom in fear, and no knowledge in the counting of numbers. Learn therefore by a parable. In the days when the world was young and evolution yet in its infancy, the Gods chose Bonellia Viridis to be the first of living creatures to be endowed with a soul, and thus made like to themselves, and capable of carrying out their high purposes. After a while, the Devil, making mischief after his fashion, put it into the Bonellia's head that love is the highest good; whereupon he began to wallow in sex, declaring it to be the most beautiful and spiritual thing in the world, the mainspring of his noblest actions, his supreme mode of self-expression, and so forth, after your own fashion, mistress, till at length he became so besotted that his sole occupation, between couplings, was in running at the tail of his female, whining for more. In course of time he degenerated into a sort of tick attached to her rump, and so shrivelled away till now he is but a microscopic parasite dwelling entirely within her genital passage. Do you perceive the moral?'

'The moral' said Progressa 'is that you are more hidebound by repressions and narrow-minded dogmas than the most benighted of the churches. I will waste no more time on you.' She vanished forthwith.

'You take things too seriously, my lad' said Mr Jolliboy. 'Morbid. Introspective. Doesn't do. Have to compromise a bit in this life, you know. I don't agree with everything that lady says, but there's a lot in it all the same. Something in what you say, too, but you're too serious altogether. You must learn to cultivate a sense of humour, and, if the world doesn't quite come up to your ideals, just laugh at it. Cheerio. Be jolly.' With these words he skitted off to Elysium.

'By Priapus!' cried Bricriu. 'What a race of gelded machine-minders is this that so misuses the glorious horn of plenty, and must be taught how to enjoy itself out of text-books compounded of slush and science. Verily I think the gods have already scrapped them, and you waste your time in trying to rescue them.'

'Nevertheless I must perform the task I was sent for' said Cuanduine, drawing the Cruaidin

Cailidcheann to see whether it were rusting in its sheath.

Afterwards he told his boys very plainly the use and care of their parts, giving them only this counsel, that they should be the masters, not the slaves, of their appetites, and that they should rather forego all pleasure than do anything unseemly for the sake of it.

BOOK II

The Triumph of Cuanduine

CHAPTER I

How Queen Guzzelinda lost a treasure

ON a spring morning about this time King Goshawk and Queen Guzzelinda were awakened from slumber by the pealing of the alarum bell in the great tower of the royal castle.

'What the hell?' cried King Goshawk, sitting up in bed, and touching a bell-push.

A terrified lackey entered and prostrated himself before the presence.

'What's that goldarned row about?' demanded King Goshawk.

'So please your Majesty' said the trembling lackey, 'a blackbird has escaped from the royal aviary, and the garrison has turned out in pursuit.'

'Wal, darn my skin' said Goshawk, 'can't they do it without all that fuss? Tell 'em to stop that tarnation row and get on with the job.'

With that he fell asleep again, and the alarum bell was silenced. Later in the day, descending to the council chamber, he asked the seneschal whether the bird had been found.

'Not yet, your Majesty' replied the seneschal. 'They are still searching for it.'

'Wal, darn my giblets' said Goshawk, 'what's the sense of wasting all that energy over a goldarned bundle of feathers? Tell 'em to let the blamed thing alone.'

'As your Majesty commands' said the seneschal, bowing.

When Queen Guzzelinda heard of this decision of her lord, she was much distressed; for she loved her little birdlings and would not willingly part with one of them. Therefore, going into the King's private chamber, she remonstrated with him, saying: 'Say, big boy, what's the big idea? Are your soldiers such a pack of mutts that they can't find my lil bird?'

'Sweetie' replied King Goshawk, 'give it a miss. You gotta billion or two of them feathered squeakers, so one more or less ain't worth bothering about.'

'Ain't it, though?' said Guzzelinda. 'Suppose somebody catches the critter, my record's busted, and I ain't gonna stand for it.'

'Aw, quit' said Goshawk.

Seeing that her husband was not in the granting mood, Guzzelinda withdrew to her own apartments, and sent a minion to command the attendance of Mr Slawmy Cander; who, coming in his own good time, after kissing her fingers, said: 'What does your Majesty desire of your humble servant?'

Guzzelinda told him of her trouble, and proceeded: 'Now, big boy, I know you got a pull with the old man, and I want you to use it. I want that bird brought back to the aviary if it costs a million dollars.'

'It shall be done, your Majesty' said Mr Slawmy Cander, who cared not a thraneen for the Queen's pretty whims, but knew that the whole financial system would be upset if the people could have anything for nothing.

You must know that when Mr Slawmy Cander had arranged for the issue of the credits by which the original purchase of the birds had been effected, he had not been influenced at all by the poetic notions of the Queen, or by the high moral purpose of King Goshawk, since poetry and morality are entirely outside the purview of economics. His hope had been that by the removal of the birds from the fields the numerous maggots and insects on which they feed might increase in numbers, and, by destroying the crops, reduce that abundance of foodstuffs which had so discredited the financial system. Unfortunately his calculations had been upset by the ill-timed activities of certain scientists, who had discovered other means of conquering the pests, and the fertility of nature had continued its embarrassing course, with the results you have seen. But though there was no longer any positive economic advantage in keeping the birds shut up, Mr Cander felt that a dangerous precedent might be created if any of them were let loose. Therefore he issued orders to all the soldiers, officials, and other retainers of King Goshawk that the missing blackbird must be recovered at all costs; enlisting also the services of the Press, the Wireless, the Publicity Firms, and the Churches to make it known to the world how disastrous it was, both morally and socially, that the creature should be abroad.

CHAPTER II

The Beginning of the quarrel between Mr Slawmy Cander and the men of Eirinn

WHEN the blackbird had escaped from the royal aviary, it flew first to the tower of Notre Dame de Paris (which, as you know, was in the adjoining gardens), and sang a joyous song of liberty, likewise a supplication to Our Lady Saint Mary to preserve him from the snares of the enemy. But alas! the days are gone when the Blessed Mother could defend the humblest of her servants against the might of princes. The soldiers climbed the tower and had very nearly seized upon the songster in his ecstasy; but he saw them in time, and, spreading his wings, flew to the top of the Pyramid of Cheops hard by. Another regiment ran swiftly to scale its massive sides, and, after much scrambling and falling and barking of shins, and a most horrible expenditure of oaths and foul language, had nearly reached the summit when the bird took flight again and was lost in the woods. After that there was a hue and cry of vast dimensions. Incited by the offer of a huge reward, the whole population of America turned out to seize this opportunity of getting rich quick. The unemployed rushed from the breadlines, twenty million strong; the workers abandoned the factories; engine-drivers left their trains, and seamen their ships, to join in the pursuit. The office workers next absconded from their desks. In one day the cities found themselves stripped alike of police and criminals. As the reward offered was increased, the social status of the hunters improved. Judges leaped from the bench, professors from their desks, and rushed, butterfly nets in hand, into the Adirondacks. The legal and medical professions followed. Then the owners of speakeasies. At last only the really big men in the business and crime world remained out of the hunt. It was the vastest hue and cry that ever was raised in the world. Compared with it, the hunt of the Kalydonian Boar was but a game of hunt the slipper, and the great huntings of the men of the Fianna were only nursery romps. Every corner of the country was ransacked, from the orange groves of California to the cotton fields of the Carolinas, from the arid wastes of Nevada to the fertile farms of Massachusetts. Every tree in every forest was climbed, and every branch was shaken. Fleets of high-powered cars swept the land from end to end; swarms of planes and dirigibles combed the air. Gee, boys, it sure was some hunt: for they do things on a big scale in America.

But all the fuss was of no avail. It happened that the blackbird was of Irish descent, and long before the pursuit had got fully into its stride, it was winging its way eastward to the land from which its ancestors had been ravished. It alighted at last in a field in the County Clare, and, having had a good feed of snails, flew inland till it came to the Hill of Teamhair, where it perched on a thornbush and burst into song.

There were some children playing near at hand, who, hearing the song, were astonished, and thought it must be the voice of an angel; for they did not know that birds could sing, as this knowledge was not taught in the schools (being of no practical utility), and their parents had not bothered to tell them. The song was so sweet that they stopped their play to listen to it; and when they went home they told their parents, who whipped them soundly for telling lies, and sent them to bed without any supper.

Next day some men going to work in the fields heard the music, and, looking into the bush, they found that it was indeed a bird that was singing, as they remembered to have happened long ago. They rushed off and told their neighbours, and thus the news spread through the county and the province, and away to the four shores of Eirinn. Thereafter the people came running from all parts to hear the song of the bird, which poured forth the joy of its heart in fullthroated melody so that all the men of Eirinn were enchanted with it; and they forgot their sorrows and their hatreds, and mingled like brothers upon the green slopes of Royal Teamhair. Pressmen also came from Dublin, who reported the matter to the world; and from that came great trouble and strife, as you shall hear.

When the news came to Mr Slawmy Cander, he immediately sent out an airplane to recapture the bird. The machine accordingly flew to Teamhair, and, having landed close by, the crew marched towards the thornbush. At first the crowds made way for them, thinking they were come to listen to the song, and being naturally courteous to strangers. But when the men came close to the thornbush and began to spread their nets, the people became alarmed, and demanded to know their business.

The leader of the expedition said that they had come to recapture the bird for King Goshawk, whose property it was.

'Begob, you don't' said the people.

The airman tried to argue the matter, but, as the people would not listen to him, he ordered his men to press on and do their duty. At that, anger came upon the men of Eirinn, and, laying hands upon the men of Goshawk, they beat them soundly and sent them home to their master without their breeches.

At this defiance King Goshawk was thrown into a most appalling rage; his royal interior (which, as you know, was in a somewhat unhealthy condition) being put entirely out of gear for several days, so that his physicians at one time almost despaired of saving his life. When he was somewhat recovered, he swore a mighty oath that he would never let a day pass to the end of his life without doing some mischief to the men of Ireland; to which end, after the manner of King Darius in the ancient time, he appointed a minion to come to him every morning at breakfast and say: 'Master, remember the Irish.' Meanwhile, for the immediate vindication of his wrongs, he sent a note to the Irish Government, demanding apology, compensation, the restoration of the blackbird, and the handing over of the offenders for punishment. To these terms the Government was very willing to agree, knowing what powers the Great King wielded; but no sooner was the suggestion made than a mighty shout went up from the men of Eirinn that they would die rather than yield to the tyrant. Thereupon the Government, fearful of losing votes, reconsidered its decision, and replied to King Goshawk that it was impossible to comply with his request.

Such contumacy shocked the public conscience of the world; which, as you know, is very tender where the morality of small nations is concerned. All the governments, parliaments, newspapers, and public men began forthwith to lecture the Irish very unctuously upon their naughtiness; the French reminding them of the dishonesty of debt-repudiation, the English laying stress upon the sanctity of treaties, the Americans accusing them of graft and materialism, the Japanese of being greedy and unchristian, and so forth. Never was heard such a unanimous championship of truth and righteousness; yet the Irish obstinately refused to listen to reason, and began to prepare themselves for the war which they now perceived to be imminent. Mr Slawmy Cander thereupon appealed to the International Air Police to enforce his rights.

CHAPTER III

How Mr Slawmy Cander fostered the Spirit of Internationalism

I MUST now tell you what the International Air Police was, and how it came to be founded.

During the years of Cuanduine's retirement, the Public Conscience of the World had been so much shocked by the revelation of the horrors of the recent war, that an enormous outcry was raised for Something to be Done about Disarmament: the idea being that, if the nations had nothing to fight *with*, they would not fight, no matter what they might have to fight *about*. A Preliminary Conference to a Preparatory Conference to a Precursory Conference to a Prefatory Conference to an International Conference had, indeed, been sitting for about a hundred years; but though it had uttered several trillion words, and published several thousand tons of Official Reports, it had not yet agreed upon a basis of discussion sufficiently comprehensive to justify calling the Preparatory Conference. Irreconcilable differences of opinion still persisted, particularly in regard to the size and number of the guns with which the armies were in future to be allowed to slaughter each other. The British proposed that they should slaughter each other with 9⅜ inch guns, reduced in number according to a ratio proportioned to individual requirements. The Americans, on the other hand, contended that the number of the guns with which they slaughtered each other should be calculated on a yard-stick basis, and the calibre restricted to 9.387 inches. The French said that they should slaughter each other with 13.5 centimetre guns, unrestricted as to number, while the Germans insisted that the guns with which they slaughtered each other should be unlimited as to calibre, but restricted as to tonnage, numbers being calculated *pro rata* on a datum line. Further differences arose on the question of poison gases. All the nations agreed that their use in warfare should be prohibited; but when a Bulgarian delegate suggested that they should no longer be manufactured, the larger Powers objected that this was pushing an excellent principle to impracticable extremes. After much discussion it had been agreed to insert the words: 'as far as possible.' A proposal by the Russians that all armaments should be abolished at once was ruled out of order as it annoyed the others.

Another difficulty had been raised by the French, who would not agree to disarmament in any form without 'adequate guarantees of security' for themselves. There was once a time when France had been a very gallant nation, ready to take on the whole of Europe; *mais ils avaient changé tout cela: autres temps, autres mœurs, vous comprenez*. Pressed to define 'adequate guarantees', *la France*, in the language of diplomacy, *ne dit rien*. At length a Swiss delegate asked what security France would require if all the nations agreed to scrap ninety per cent of their armaments; whereupon the French delegate, M. Chauvinette, said that she would be prepared to accept this figure on condition that every male living within a thousand miles of any French frontier should have his right hand amputated. All the other delegates at once protested, as tactfully as possible, and with due regard for French susceptibilities, that this was rather unreasonable, but M. Chauvinette merely shrugged his shoulders. '*Il faut souffrir pour être sot*' he said with characteristic Gallic wit.

In the middle of these burblings came the thirteenth Trade Depression, bringing to the Governments the realisation that they would have to disarm or go bankrupt; and this was reinforced by a whisper in their ears from Mr Slawmy Cander that if something wasn't done about it in less than half no time, he would have everybody bankrupted all round. Not that Mr Slawmy Cander cared a brass farthing for International Peace. He had fish of his own to fry.

After that events moved rapidly. The Governments asked Mr Cander what he thought they ought to do, and instructed their delegates to act accordingly. The Conference at once decreed that all fleets and armies should be reduced by 90 per cent, and that a force of International Air Police should be raised to keep the small nations in order, these being the real menace to international peace, which has always been strictly maintained by the large nations and empires, except of course, when their honour and interests have compelled them to go to war. The control of this force was vested by general consent in the only truly international body in the world, that is to say, the guardians of High Finance, whose directing brain, though nobody knew it, was Mr Slawmy Cander.

To get away with this scheme, it was first necessary to tell the world what detestable things nations are, and to make them thoroughly unpopular with their own citizens. For this purpose Mr Cander had to his hand a huge fry of authors, bought by him body and soul: for the poor devils had to live, and in those days of universal penury, nobody could afford to buy books. Under his instructions these proceeded to spill out millions of penny pamphlets crying up World Unity, Big Ideas, Larger Interests, Wider Horizons, Broader Visions, and Windy Spaciousness in general; all of which were dutifully published by the League of Nations in the cause of Universal Brotherhood. I'll quote you a sweet passage from one of them:

'The history of Europe begins with the small city states of ancient Greece. Each went its own way regardless of the others, except when their quarrels led them into war. They had no desire to unite; they were unwilling to help one another towards a larger life and wider interests; they were slow to join forces when danger threatened from outside; and in the end they perished—in spite of their glorious achievements in philosophy, in literature and in art—because they would not learn to subordinate their private interests to the common good.

'So the glory that was Greece gave place to the grandeur that was Rome. Nearly all the known world came to belong to the Roman Empire, where all the peoples learned to live peacefully side by side.'

The slave would have been more accurate had he written '*were larned* to live peacefully'—by fellows like Sulla, who, when the Senate seemed perturbed by the groans of the Samnites he was butchering at their doors, told them to go on with their business—that he was only chastising some rebels; by fellows like Crassus, who crucified thirty thousand rebels along the Appian Way; by fellows like Cæsar (renowned for his clemency) who cut off the right hands of ten thousand Gaulish prisoners of war; and a hundred more of such civilisers and peacemakers. However, that is by the way. The well-informed public had no difficulty in appreciating how much Hellas lost by omitting to become a great power and conquer the world, by going in for philosophy and art instead of the 'larger life and wider interests' that we enjoy to-day, by experimenting in city democracies instead of co-operating in the magnificent dreams of World Unification of Darius and Xerxes. They realised, too, how much happier the world had been under the humane and enlightened rule of Tiberius, Caligula, Nero, Domitian, Elagabalus, and the rest than those parochial Athenians under the narrow tyranny of Pericles. Being thus well prepared to swallow something big—the poor sheep really did want to stop having to cut one another's throats if their betters would only show them how to do it—they hopefully acquiesced in the 'subordination of their private interests to the common good,' that is to say, to High Finance. The national armaments were all disbanded amid popular rejoicings, and the International Air Police was solemnly inaugurated.

It was to this force that Mr Cander now appealed; appealing from Cander naked to Cander armed, so to speak. Redress was readily promised; but Mr Cander stipulated that the Irish should be given a month's grace to reflect in, for he wanted time for his propaganda to work up the Conscience of the World into such a state of indignation that it would regard the obliteration of the Irish people with bombs and poison gas as an act of the highest virtue. He hoped also that in the meantime the courage of the men of Eirinn might give way, or that they might fall out among themselves. In this purpose he succeeded to the extent that the newspapers took alarm at the solidity of world opinion against the country, and counselled the people to surrender, on the grounds, firstly, that they were wrong in keeping the bird, and secondly, that they would be better off without it; which latter contention they proved by three arguments, namely: that it was demoralising to receive anything for nothing; that what was free was not valued; and that thousands of people were neglecting their work to hear the bird singing. By the influence of this potent reasoning, many of the better classes were induced to declare themselves in favour of compromise. The common people, however, remained obstinate, and declared that they would fight and be damned to it.

CHAPTER IV

The warlike preparations of the men of Eirinn

YOU may be sure that the turn of events was very welcome to the Philosopher, who had no fear of the issue, never doubting that Cuanduine would come home to the assistance of his countrymen. Meanwhile he wrote to the newspapers, replying to their arguments:

Firstly, that the Irish people were not in the wrong, for the original purchase of the birds was an immoral transaction; since the birds were by nature free, and the people had no right to sell them, nor King Goshawk to buy them; moreover, King Goshawk had never really paid for them, since the purchase money had been created out of nothing by Mr Slawmy Cander.

Secondly that if it was demoralising to receive something for nothing, they ought to take steps to cut off the sun's rays from the earth.

Thirdly, that if what was free was not valued, there was no danger of the people neglecting their work to hear the bird singing.

Fourthly, that if it was true that the world was suffering from overproduction, it would help matters considerably if the people stopped working for a time.

The papers unanimously suppressed this letter as being stupid and the work of an obvious crank. The people, however, took no notice of the papers anyway, and continued their preparations for resistance.

The strength of the International Air Force was five hundred planes, all equipped with the most modern weapons, of a frightfulness of which you will be told later on, and manned with a crew of the most desperate sort, men without a country, reckless devils who had never had a home or property anywhere, but had spent their lives wandering over the world in search of machines to mind: for, as they might be required to serve against any country at any time, and their master was Mammon himself, no other sort could join them.

Against this force the Irish, having scrapped all their war planes in obedience to Geneva, could only put a hundred civil planes hastily converted, and equipped with makeshift weapons, like the Carthaginians in their last war with the Romans. There arose in consequence two schools of strategy, which were represented not only in the high command, but in the rank and file, in Parliament, and among the people themselves. One party, known as the Slashers, was for staking everything on a pitched battle to prevent the enemy reaching Ireland: the other, nicknamed the Trimmers, propounded a Fabian policy of harrying the invaders in numerous skirmishes, thus wearing them down and preventing them from inflicting a decisive blow. For many weeks the whole nation did nothing else but discuss the two policies. The Trimmers declared that the policy of the Slashers must end in immediate and utter disaster, as the fleet would be destroyed in the first battle, and the country would then be helpless to defend itself further. The Slashers replied that there was at least a forlorn hope that the battle might not go against them, but that, if the Trimmers' policy were adopted, the fleet would be destroyed piecemeal, and all the time the country would be at the mercy of the International bombers. There was so much to be said on both sides that tremendous heat was engendered. Tempers were lost very early in the controversy. Reason and persuasion rapidly gave place to rancour and recrimination. At first the Trimmers had been content to describe the Slashers as rash and imprudent, and the Slashers to call the Trimmers overcautious and deficient in enterprise. But before long they took to more vigorous language, inveighing against each other in a degringolade of courtesy after this fashion:

Trimmers:	Slashers:
Over-confident enthusiasts	Faint-hearted compromisers
Audacious gamblers	Timid ineffectives
Reckless hot-heads	Spiritless slackers
Foolhardy jingoes	Pusillanimous defeatists
Brawling flag-waggers	Trembling white-flaggers
Mad swashbucklers	Frightened poltroons
Swashbuckling idiots	Skulking runaways
Truculent fools	Lily-livered cowards
Fire-eating nincompoops	Dirt-eating cravens
Senseless fanatics	Soulless dastards
Insensate furies	Worthless degenerates

Trimmers:	Slashers:
Raving maniacs	Cringing slaves
Criminal lunatics	Cowering lickspittles
Thoroughpaced scoundrels	Abject kiss-the-rods
Detestable ruffians	Sneaking rotters
Bloody-minded butchers	Fawning puppets
Sanguinary cut-throats	Contemptible wretches
Diabolical murderers	Grovelling serfs
Brutal savages	Snivelling curs
Inhuman monsters	Stinking reptiles
Incarnate fiends	Loathsome skunks
Spawn of Satan	Scum of the earth

Creatures unworthy of the name of Irishmen
Scurrilous calumniators
Foulmouthed slanderers
Unscrupulous liars
Traitors!

Such were the opinions which each half of the Irish people held of the other half. While they were expressing them, the preparations for national defence were somewhat neglected, and at last, about a week before the expiry of the ultimatum, were abandoned altogether, the country being on the verge of civil war.

All this was very distressing to the Philosopher, who knew from experience that no word of his would be of any avail in such a tumult. At last, however, being driven to despair by the imminence of disaster, he went down to College Green, and, climbing upon the pedestal of Grattan's statue, he addressed the raging mob as follows:

'Fellow citizens, there is much to be said both for and against both the policies which have been submitted to your judgment. For my own part, being a foolish and inexperienced old man, I cannot tell which is better—'

'Then hold your gob' shouted a man in the crowd.

'Shut your trap' yelled another.

'Mind your own business, y'ould fool' shrieked a woman.

'Hear me a moment, my brothers' said the Philosopher. 'Although as I have said, I cannot tell which plan is better, this much is certain: you would be wiser to adopt the worse one than to wrangle about the matter any longer.'

'Faith, there's something in that' said one of the people. 'You're not such a fool as you look, old skinamalink.'

''Tis the first word of sense I've heard yet' said another.

Then the whole multitude began to cheer and to shout encouragement to the Philosopher; and finally they carried him home in triumph on their shoulders. Nevertheless, nothing was done about the matter, for both sides held to their opinion as strongly as ever. Meanwhile the blackbird was snared by a private speculator, who returned it to Mr Slawmy Cander, who, in paying him the reward, commanded him to tell nobody.

CHAPTER V

The curse of Crom Cruach upon the men of Eirinn

THE cause of this quarrelling among the men of Eirinn was a curse that had been laid upon them in the olden time by the god, Crom Cruach. When the people were converted to the true faith by the blessed Patrick, they did what no other nation has ever done, before or since: they accepted the faith wholeheartedly, believing that Christ really meant what he said, and from thenceforward they renounced the devil with all his works and pomps, and devoted themselves entirely to the service of God. Their warriors no longer crossed the sea for plunder and conquest, they sought neither glory nor dominance, and strove to excel only in piety, learning, and hospitality. They gave their friendship to all strangers, especially to those that came in search of knowledge, whom they taught and housed for love. They took no thought for the morrow, neither were they solicitous for food and clothing, but, seeking only the kingdom of God and his glory, all things else were added to them.

For this reason the devil conceived a peculiar hatred against the people of Eirinn; for all the other peoples of the world, though they accepted the Word with joy, and carried it about upon their lips, yet in their actions they remained heathen as before, striving after power and riches, hating and killing one another, and in all ways serving the ends of Satan: so much so that historians commonly censure the Irish people for not retaining sufficient heathenism in their characters to found a Centralised State and Institutions conducive to Modern Progress, for lack of which, they say, we fell under the dominance of a more Efficient and Businesslike Civilisation.

The devil, being enraged as I have said, entered into the heart of Crom Cruach, and said to him: 'Behold, this people are turned altogether from thy service, and bend the knee to a strange God. Curse them, therefore, for the pleasure of thy heart.'

So Crom Cruach cursed the people of Eirinn; and the curse he laid upon them was this, that whenever an enemy should attack them, and their need of unity be greatest, then should division and hatred disrupt them. So he cursed them, and so it fell out: for from that day to this the people of Eirinn have never failed to quarrel in face of a foe.

CHAPTER VI

How Cuanduine girt on his armour

AT this time came Badb the War Goddess to Cuanduine as he lay in the sunshine in the Golden Valley. She is called Badb of the Hundred Shapes, because her appearance varies according to the disposition of the beholder: to the poet, an awful goddess meet to be sung in heroic verse; to the newspaper editor, a handsome wench to picnic with; to army contractors, a wealthy paymistress; to young girls, a romantic figure in shining armour. To a young man not yet blooded she appears glorious and terrible as an army with banners; but when he has had his bellyful of service and goes home to write about it, he sees her as an obscene old hag, full of filth and folly. Pacifists call her a whore, not to be touched on any account; but these old maids most certainly wrong her, for Liberty and Honour have sought her aid from time to time, not always in vain, and may yet have to seek it again. The great Powers also profess not to love her, but that is only the talk of disappointed suitors when their mistress denies them her favours, and you may believe it when they renounce the possessions they hold in fee of her.

To Cuanduine she appeared as a very fine woman after her fashion, though somewhat past her prime, and a little over-raddled with powder and cosmetics; her locks too much resembling vipers, after the manner of Medusa; and her breath noxious, with whiffs of chlorine in it. She wore a shrapnel helmet on her head, a gas-mask hung at her breast, and there were a number of hideous contraptions strung about her waist. A mephitic cloud enveloped her round about, obscuring the ill proportions of her figure.

Thus spoke the great goddess Badb, whom the Greeks called Eris, and the Romans Bellona: 'Rise, Cuanduine. The day is come for you to put forth your strength and to perform your hero-feats. For your own people, even the men of Eirinn, are in danger of destruction at the hands of their enemies, and none but you can save them.'

Then Badb told him all that had happened; and Cuanduine, having girt on his sword, the Cruaidin Caileadcheann, went to bid farewell to his wife and children. And he said to his wife: 'Now is the time come for me to do the work the gods have appointed. Therefore, look to my babes, and from this day be to them both mother and father.'

His wife kissed him, but she shed no tear, though she feared that he was going to his death. Then Cuanduine made ready to depart, and Badb laid geasa upon him as follows: not to kill a lion and spare a jackal; not to answer the questions of White on the lips of Black; not to contend with the Headless Men of the Woods. 'These are good counsels' said Cuanduine, 'if I could understand them.' But Badb would say no more, for it is the will of the Gods to be inscrutable.

So Cuanduine departed from the Golden Valley and travelled by passenger plane to Ireland, where he arrived in the seventh week of the seventh year of his exile.

CHAPTER VII

How Cuanduine made offer to serve his country

AS soon as he reached Dublin, Cuanduine betook himself to Stoneybatter, to the abode of the Philosopher, who embraced him joyfully, saying: 'You are come in the very nick and fulness of time, for our state is more parlous than when Cromwell was hammering at the gates of Drogheda. Come now. Sit down and write to the Minister of War that you have come to lead us to victory against the enemy.'

Cuanduine accordingly wrote as follows:

'Sir,

'I have come to Ireland by the command of Badb to deliver my countrymen out of the hands of their enemies. Give me therefore an airplane that I may proceed against them forthwith.'

Two days later he received this reply:

'Sir,

'I am directed by the Minister for War to reply to your communication of even date.

'The Minister instructs me to say that he is unaware who Badb is, and that personal influence is inadmissible in the consideration of applications for commissions.

'Commissions in the Air Force are obtainable by

competitive examination only. Forms of application may be obtained from the proper authority.

'I am, sir,
'Your obedient servant,
'A. Dedhead.'

'Tush!' said the philosopher on reading this. 'We had better write to the President himself.'

So Cuanduine wrote to the President in the same words.

'Another crank who thinks he can save the country' said the President's secretary as he went through the morning's correspondence. 'The usual form, I suppose?' But the President said: 'No. Maybe the cranks are right for once. The practical people haven't been much help anyway.'

'But this fellow's a lunatic' said the secretary. 'Listen to this. "By the command of Badb—"'

'Hold!' said the President. 'This is our man'—For Badb herself had appeared to him in a dream that night and told him that a deliverer was at hand—'Send a messenger at once to invite him to come to me.'

The secretary thought that the President must have lost his wits from over-work and anxiety; but he despatched the messenger, and Cuanduine appeared within the hour.

'Well, sir' said the President, who liked the looks of the young man, 'so you think you can save the country?'

'Nay, sir' said Cuanduine. 'By the counsel of the Gods, I know it.'

'What are your plans?' asked the President.

'Why, sir, if you will give me the means, to grapple with the enemy forthwith, and fight like the devil.'

'You are a brave lad' said the President, 'and for my part I would very willingly appoint you to a command. But it is not in my power to put you above officers who have regularly served their course——'

'Your pardon, sir' said Cuanduine. 'I desire no command. Give me a single plane, and that will content me.'

'But surely' said the President 'you cannot hope to defeat five hundred enemies single-handed?'

For answer Cuanduine drew forth the Cruaidin Cailidcheann and laid it on the table. 'See if you can lift that, Mr President' said he.

The President tried, but could not stir it, though he put both hands to the task: for the electrons of the steel were packed as tight in its atoms as in the Star of Van Maanen; and so vast was the substance thus crammed into it that, when the hero brandished it in battle, it could stretch itself out to touch the horizon, and still remain as tough as a blade of old Toledo.

'The man who can lift that blade' said Cuanduine 'is a match for an army;' and he twirled it about his head as easily as if it had been a bamboo cane.

'Your wish is granted' said the President. 'Come, we'll go to Baldonnell.'

They flew together to the aerodrome, where the hundred planes of the fleet lay waiting. 'Take your choice' said the President.

Cuanduine stepped into the first plane, and began shaking it, and stamping about in it, in order to test its strength, until he had reduced it to splinters and small fragments: at which the staff of the aerodrome were mightily astonished.

'This plane is no good, Mr President' said Cuanduine.

'Try another' said the President.

So Cuanduine mounted the second plane, and broke it in pieces in the same manner.

'I must speak to the contractors about this' said the President. 'Try again.'

Cuanduine tried the third plane, and smashed it up likewise.

'Leave off now' said the President, 'or we shall have no planes left. It is very evident that these are no machines for a hero. We must build a special one for you, if God will grant us the time.'

CHAPTER VIII

The building of the great airplane Poliorketes

THEREAFTER Badb appeared again to Cuanduine, and said: 'Foolish one, no plane made by these people can avail thee. Build thee a machine in the manner I will show thee.' So Cuanduine and the Philosopher sought out a desert place among the mountains, and set to work as the goddess commanded.

They made the framework of the plane out of the Bare Bones of Balscadden. These were the skeletons of two great sea monsters, the Púcamór and the Ecnamór, that fought each other for many years up and down the seas of the world, till at last they slew each other in Balscadden Bay, at the foot of Ben Edair, and their bodies were washed up on the strand, where their bones had remained ever since.

Now the story they tell of these monsters is this. In the ancient times the race of men were ruled by giants, who oppressed them in divers ways, exacting human sacrifice, allowing the strong to prey upon the weak, and governing by ban and prohibition: one forbidding them to kill cats, another to touch dogs, another to eat pork, and another to drink wine. At last there arose one giant who conquered all the others and reigned alone over men. The name of him was the Púcamór. He was as huge as a mountain, and he had three eyes, and a great horn in the middle of his forehead. His rule was milder than that of the other giants. He protected the weak against the strong, and to all who obeyed him he was just and generous; but those who disobeyed he punished with imprisonment and fire and torture. To secure himself in the kingship, he made a law forbidding people to think; and as this is an exercise not much beloved by the multitude, he was readily obeyed, and his reign was long. One day, however, there appeared from no one knew where another giant called the Ecnamór, with a hundred eyes, and steel knives for fingers, and he challenged the Púcamór to fight for the kingdom. So they fought for a whole day, and at the end of it the Ecnamór was defeated and fled into the wilderness. There he lay for a long time till he was recovered of his hurts. And when he was ready to fight again he went first to the Cyclopes in their dark workshops beneath Aetna, and commanded them to make him a horn like that of the Púcamór; giving them seventy of his hundred eyes in payment. Then he returned to earth to fight the Púcamór, and they fought up and down the world for many days, wounding each other horribly, but neither could kill the other, since they were both immortal. At last, when they were both exhausted, they called a truce; and afterwards they ruled in the kingdom side by side, each man choosing for himself which he would be governed by. Most of the people gave their allegiance to the Ecnamór, as he was younger, and was generally believed to have come off best in the battle; moreover it was hoped that his rule would be lighter than the Púcamór's. But in this the people soon found they were mistaken; for as soon as his throne was well established, he showed himself no less bloodthirsty than the earlier giants, and no less hostile to thought than the Púcamór. He began by torturing dogs and cats; then he took to poking his nose into the most private concerns of the people, forbidding marriage to one and children to another, separating children on various pretexts from their parents, and interfering with the weak and the poor in a thousand vexatious ways. He flung people into prison, inoculated them with diseases, mutilated them, and sterilised them, and whoever opposed him he put to silence one way or another. At last his rule became so intolerable that the people called on the Púcamór to drive him out, and a new battle between the giants was begun. They fought up and down the world for many days, and so great was their fury that it changed them into two dragons; in which form they went on fighting more savagely than ever till they rolled over a cliff into the sea. There they were metamorphosed into a pair of horrible sea monsters, and they fought each other from sea to sea, till at last they came to Balscadden Bay under Ben Edair, where they grappled in a final tussle under the very eyes of the men of Atha Cliath. So terrible was the fight that all the waters of the bay were threshed into a filthy foam of mud and blood, and seven great billows were hurled against the cliff, breaking the solid rock as if it had been a wall of lath, and deluging the country to the very top of Shielmartin. At length the two great monsters made one last desperate rush at each other, so that each drove his horn through the skull and into the brain of the other; and thus they perished, for, having taken animal form, they were no longer immortal.

Out of these bones, then, Cuanduine made the framework of his airplane. It was so huge that if I told you the measurements you would not believe me; yet its proportions were so perfect that the hero could both fly and fight it without assistance. Instead of planes covered with stretched canvas, it had wings covered with feathers cunningly woven out of silk by the women of the Sidhe, so that it could rise, swoop, and hover like an eagle, and could fly as well in a storm as on the calmest day in summer.

The engine was made by the artificers of the Sidhe, and neither hammer nor cutting instrument was used in the manufacture of it: for the metal shaped itself in the furnaces in obedience to the spells and incantations of the master mathematicians of the Tuatha Dé Danann. It was so perfectly made in all its parts that all friction was entirely eliminated; it was as silent in action as the beating of a man's heart; and it consumed every atom of its own fuel, leaving no exhaust, so that it could travel a thousand miles to the gallon.

Such was the great airplane of Cuanduine. It was one of the three great engines of destruction, the other two being the Wooden Horse of Troy and the Super-Dreadnaught. It was one of the three great helpers of man, the other two being the fire-bearing reed of Prometheus and the Kettle of Watt. It was one of the three perfect works of art, the other two being the Parthenon and the Ninth Symphony of Beethoven. It was one of the three great discomforters of fools, the other two being the Socratic Question and the works of Voltaire. Because it was to be a taker of cities, Cuanduine gave it the name of Poliorketes.

The original bearer of the name, that is, Demetrius of Macedon, when he was besieging the city of Rhodes, refrained from attacking the wall at its most vulnerable point lest he should injure Protogenes' picture of Ialysus, which hung in a building hard by. Civilisation has progressed since then.

CHAPTER IX

The first flight of the great airplane Poliorketes

WHILE the plane was building many of the people of Dublin came out to see the work, and to dispense advice, objection, criticism, discouragement, ridicule, dissuasion, contempt, and condemnation. The Universities, and in general all persons of responsibility and position with a stake in the country, declared unqualified disapproval of the project. Expert opinion testified to the essentially unpractical and unsound construction of the plane itself, which violated all the accepted principles of aerial technology. It was pointed out also that Cuanduine had never passed an examination of any sort, nor even taken out a pilot's certificate; and that the admitted fact of his having defeated the whole of the Wolfian forces single-handed was no true criterion of what was normally possible, since the achievement was probably attributable to favourable conditions the contingency of whose recurrence was incalculable. The press supported this view with all the emphasis at its command—polysyllables for the educated, and italics for the rest; and the public, which would have been sceptical enough without such assistance, felt its stout common sense properly fortified. However, there were not wanting ignorant and unlettered men who commended the hero's courage, saying: 'Isn't he an Irishman anyhow, and why wouldn't he be a match for any number of foreigners?' Many young women too, having seen his beauty, thought it too sweetly romantic of him to be ready to die in their defence.

Cuanduine did not bother his head about any of them, being chiefly concerned with getting the airplane finished in time to meet the foe. When it was completed he sang this song:

'O flaming Phœnix
From ashes risen
Of hopes deluded
And faiths decayed,

Of visions vanished,
Of virtues wasted,
Of knowledge darkened,
Of truth betrayed;

O Bird of Valour,
To battle bear me
For Eirinn's right
And the world's desire,

To break the bonds
And shatter the lie,
And kindle anew
The living fire.

For the truth that lives,
For the light of knowledge,
The strength of virtue,
The vision's glow,

In the faith that fails not,
And the hope that dies not,
To the last great fight
For the soul we go.

The Triumph of Cuanduine

I, the Hound, the Hound of Man,
  Go to meet the Hawk of Hell.
Thrice a hundred ships he hath,
  Thrice a thousand are his men.

Thirty hundred willing slaves,
  Fettered hard with chains of gold.
If the Hound of Man shall fail,
  Death shall deluge Eirinn's shores.

Death by fire and death by venom,
  Death by every devil's plan.
From the living God's own heaven
  Hell shall vomit hate on man.

Then, Bird of Valour,
To battle bear me
For Eirinn's right
And the world's desire,

To break the bonds
And shatter the lie,
And kindle anew
The living fire.'

When he had sung this song, Cuanduine turned to board the plane: and behold, Pallas Athene stood before him, looking fondly at him with her grey eyes. Said she: 'Cuanduine, goest thou forth to battle without seeking counsel of me?'

'Your pardon, great lady' replied Cuanduine. 'I had forgot.'

'Nevertheless, I have not forgotten thee. Thou knowest not what perils thou must encounter.'

'Lady, I know them well; and by this and by that'—here he touched the airplane and the Cruaidin Cailidcheann—'I mean to overcome them.'

'I doubt you not' said Athene. 'But what shall these avail against poison gas?'

'Why, lady, if they fail, we can but die.'

'Nay' said Pallas gravely, 'the gods have not willed it so.' Then she stripped the shining many-scaled aigis, adorned with the Gorgon's head, from her shoulders, and put it on Cuanduine, saying: 'This shall protect thee against all kinds of venom,' and, smiling upon him, she vanished from his sight.

Cuanduine then boarded the plane, and took it for a trial flight to show it off to the people. He made the round of the four provinces of Ireland, and then, circling above the city of Dublin, he performed his hundred feats of skill, and his hundred feats of daring, and his hundred feats of air-championship, while all the people stood in the streets and watched him.

As he was thus playing, behold, Badb appeared to him in the form of a black eagle, and she said: 'For shame, Cuanduine, to be showing off like this, and the enemy's fleet already in sight of the shores of Mumhan. Away, and be doing: for this day it is given to you to save mankind, and to win for yourself a name that will be glorious for ever.'

At that a red blush of shame blazed in the warrior's cheeks, and the great airplane Poliorketes bucked like Pegasus when he first smelt the breath of the Chimæra. Then Cuanduine drave him up in mighty circles into the empyrean, and flew in hot haste over the plains of Leinster, over the mountains of Tipperary, past Cashel of the Kings, over the teeming lands of Mumhan, till he heard the roaring of the Wave of Cliodhna, and saw the white manes of the horses of Manannan. Immediately thereafter appeared the array of the enemy, like a swarm of locusts, rushing up from the south.

CHAPTER X

The resources of Civilisation

THE fleet of the International was in this formation. In the van flew a squadron of scouting planes, very swift and light, armed with machine guns. Next came a hundred heavy-armed fighting planes, the biggest ever made by man, to combat the forces of the defence. Behind these came a hundred and fifty destroying planes; and in their flanks and rear were a hundred more fighting planes to protect them in their punitive work.

The destroying planes were equipped in the following manner. First came fifty planes carrying high explosive bombs to destroy the cities of the enemy. Next came fifty planes carrying gas bombs of the kinds hereunder set forth.

Mustard gas (dichloro-diethyl sulphide), after a dose of which, says the Medical Manual, 'the victim's eyes begin to smart, sneezing develops, followed by nausea and vomiting. Eye trouble increases, and inflammation of the skin commences on face, neck, under the arms, and inside the thighs. Intense itching sets up, which prevents sleep. The rash has now developed into blisters and open festering sores. At the end of twenty-four hours the victim is virtually blinded. Acute bronchitis now sets in with heart strain, death usually occurring on the third or fourth day.' The story is told that a drop of this gas in its liquid form once fell upon the chair of a certain Director of the British Chemical Warfare Department, who was unable to sit down for a week in consequence: yet even with his arse in this state of torment, the valiant fellow continued to work for the advancement of science. A right useful weapon this for gallant men to employ against crowded cities and countrysides, especially as it vaporises slowly, and lingers long in the atmosphere. It is claimed that people may carry it unknowingly on their clothing, and thus spread it among their fellows hours after the bombardment is over and the heroic attackers have gone home with the happy feeling of duty well done. One would think that this gas alone would have been sufficient for all warlike purposes, but the resources of science are inexhaustible, and there is nothing like variety. The bombers also carried

Lewisite, so called after the benefactor of humanity who invented it; also known poetically as the Dew of Death; scientifically, Chlorvinyldichlorarsine. This gas has tremendous killing powers. Three small drops on the belly of a rat killed it in less than two hours, during which time, no doubt, it enjoyed itself thoroughly, as all good vivisectionists will assure you. Whether it actually danced for joy and licked its benefactor's hand, I cannot say, but you can find out by writing to the Research Defence Association. Lewisite has the disadvantage of finishing off its victims rather speedily, which somewhat detracts from its punitive effect. It was therefore carried only as a sort of reserve, in case the resistance of the enemy fleets might render rapidity of action desirable.

Chlorine, an old-fashioned gas employed in twentieth-century warfare, but still very effective. As the British Government Manual says, the victim is horribly drowned in his own exudation—mucus and saliva—the lungs becoming water-logged.

Phosgene, considered by experts as perhaps the most satisfactory of all war gases. The eyes of the victim smart and water. Irritation of the respiratory tract causes constriction of the chest and a violent struggle for breath. The face goes blue, then purple. The eyes start from the head, and death in agony comes in about twenty-four hours.

Prussic acid, usually employed to clear rats from ships, but equally effective in clearing men off the earth. The symptoms are giddiness, confusion, headache, failure of vision, intense pains in the chest, convulsions, and death.

Various sensory irritants, the function of which is to force people to tear off their gas masks and thus expose themselves to the effects of other gases. According to one authority 'the symptoms are most curious. They cause victims to have terrific pains in the head. Soldiers poisoned by these substances have to be prevented from committing suicide.' It was calculated, however, that a sufficiently wide distribution of the gas would make such prevention impossible. Lastly there was—

Demonio-arsine, the new gas invented by Mac ui Rudai, which drove people mad and set them slaughtering one another. Ten planes carried nothing else but this gas.

The remaining fifty planes were laden with cases containing rats infected with typhus, cholera, bubonic plague, and other diseases, to be liberated among the offending population.

I am not unaware how factious critics have misrepresented the action of the International fleet in making use of such weapons. Enlightened opinion, however, recognising the terrible responsibilities involved, and the high interests at stake, while regretting the necessity, must unanimously approve the decision. It is true that the Nations had all signed a solemn agreement not to resort to gas warfare; but it was known that they were all busily engaged in manufacturing the gases, and it would therefore have been an act of criminal negligence on the part of the International to take no counter-measures. Moreover, it had always been the policy of civilised nations, when fighting against savages, to use weapons forbidden among themselves; and the International could rightly claim that the Irish had put themselves outside the pale of civilisation by their disobedience to the laws of sound finance. Finally, expert opinion declares that the use of these weapons is inevitable. (Experts are people who know all about a subject, and can be relied on to prove that nothing can be done about it.) Says one:

'Poisonous gases in the world war proved to be one of the most powerful weapons, and for that reason alone will never be abandoned.'

In other words, man possesses no will, and automatically does what is expedient, however wicked it may be.

Says another: 'It would be unsafe to trust to stipulations laid down between nations on gas warfare' (that is to say, there is no honour among nations); and again: 'Gas, in fact, is far too efficient a weapon to be resisted. Chemical warfare has come to stay.' In effect, Chemical Warfare has a will of its own, and man is its humble servant.

A third expert declares: 'I consider Chemical Warfare to be the warfare of the future;' which settles the matter finally. And let nobody imagine that those who have thus spoken are bitter and venomous satirists, 'gnashing imprecations against mankind,' as Thackeray said of Swift. They are simply scientific and military experts, with views on mankind as conceited as your own, and I would give you their names only that they are not euphonious enough for epic poetry.

On all counts, then, the International fleet is to be exonerated from blame in this matter; for they cannot truly be said to have employed Chemical Warfare: it was Chemical Warfare that employed them.

CHAPTER XI

The Battle of the Atlantic

AS soon as he caught sight of this tremendous armament, Cuanduine shouted his warcry, and the great airplane Poliorketes mounted the winds like an eagle so as to strike at the foe from above. The scouting planes of the enemy flew up to meet him, but, however they strove, they could not overreach him; for no air was too rarified for the engine of Badb or the lungs of the grandson of Lugh. From his immense altitude Cuanduine turned his machine gun on the scouts, and shot down each in turn.

Then a huge fighting plane detached itself from the main force, and strove upwards towards Poliorketes, humming like an angry hornet. 'A worthy foe!' cried Cuanduine, and swooped upon it. The two belched lead at each other, but there was no hitting Poliorketes in his lightning dart. The enemy plane reeled, and dropped shattered into the sea. Poliorketes soared again, and Cuanduine flung bombs right and left into the fleet below.

The commander of the enemy took counsel with his staff. 'This is indeed a doughty fighter' said he. 'Signal to A Squadron to bring him down.'

Five planes accordingly rose to the encounter, while the rest of the fleet held on its course. Cuanduine continued his flight upward, his pursuers labouring after him, till, one by one, they fell back in extremity of distress from the tenuity of the atmosphere. Then, swooping again, he caught them each in turn with his deadly stream of bullets, and dropped them like shot birds on the heaving waters.

During this skirmish the main body of the enemy had pressed onwards, leaving the combatants behind. Cuanduine now hastened after them, spraying the rear lines with his machine gun, so that many sturdy airmen walked with the shades. At this the enemy's commander swore a great oath. Hannibal Pyrrhus was his *nom de guerre*, for all members of the International Air Force were known by pseudonyms, so that their nationality might not be known to one another. 'The devil must be in that plane, by God' said he, being one of those religious warriors of the stern old school. 'At any rate' said he, 'none of ours can outfly her. But we've a shot in our locker yet.' Then he signalled to Squadron Z of the rear guard: 'Drop back and fly as low as you can. At all costs draw enemy down.'

Squadron Z promptly went about and, as soon as Poliorketes made for them, sank low till their wheels were wet with the spume of the waves. Cuanduine pounced upon them joyously, and made an end of three of them before he was aware of his mistake. For in the same instant Pyrrhus despatched Squadron Y to attack the hero from above. 'Now, God defend the right' said he piously as they rushed skyward. 'You've got the battalions to work with anyway.'

Cuanduine, perceiving his danger, abandoned the remains of Squadron Z, and drove Poliorketes southward on a steadily rising course, with the bullets of Squadron Y whistling about his ears. It was then that the engine of Badb showed its full mettle, for it left the enemy behind as a horse leaves a pack of starved wolves; then, turning, the great plane rose in narrowing circles till it hovered above them like a hawk over a flock of starlings; and at last it came down in a death stroke, and scattered their fragments in flaming destruction.

'What odds can avail against this champion?' cried Pyrrhus. 'Will five squadrons suffice thee, O God?' He gave the word immediately, and twenty-five planes wheeled round, and came raging and roaring to battle against the hero.

Cuanduine then put forth a third of his strength, and began to play his hero feats upon the fighters of the International. The great airplane Poliorketes darted hither and thither like a jack-snipe, so that their fire could not touch him, and at each dart he struck down an enemy, till the cold sea was littered with broken machines and the bodies of struggling men.

'What! Does the devil still conquer?' cried Pyrrhus, and he despatched the whole remainder of the rearguard—thirteen squadrons of them—to the rescue, thinking that before such overwhelming numbers the hero must surely fall.

Then Cuanduine put forth another third of his strength, and the great airplane Poliorketes shot through the air with the speed of a bullet. The vortex of his mighty propeller caught the sixty-five planes of the enemy like straws in a whirlwind, and sucked them after him thirty fathoms upward, and shook them, and tossed them, and flung them far and wide over the surface of the ocean.

At this despair came upon Hannibal Pyrrhus, and he was filled with shame that a single airplane should make such havoc of his expedition. Nevertheless he resolved to do his duty or perish in the attempt. Ordering the destroying planes to go forward and wreak the vengeance of King Goshawk upon the land, he himself led the whole of the vanguard, a hundred strong, to battle against Cuanduine. These then came rushing at the champion, pouring forth torrents of bullets from every gun, and before Cuanduine could reply—for he was resting after his labours—he received three hard wounds. Meanwhile Pyrrhus's own plane had mounted above Poliorketes, and, swooping, wounded him again.

Anger came upon Cuanduine at that, and the hero-light shone about his head, and the spirits of the air raised a clamour about him. Then he put forth his full strength, and the great airplane Poliorketes flew at its full speed, which was that of the wrath of the gods. And Cuanduine plied his greatest feats of Badb on the squadrons of the International. First he passed across the front of the fleet westward threading his way through the streams of bullets as a bird among the branches of a forest. Then he made a round of the host, raking them through and through with his machine gun. Crossing their right wing he brought down fifteen planes, sweeping by their rear he brought down ten, and returning across their left wing he brought down fifteen more, leaving the rest all huddled and muddled like a flock of frightened sheep.

Then was Pyrrhus seized with wrath at seeing so many of his machines destroyed; and, rising out of the hurly-burly, he drove his own plane straight at Poliorketes, intending that one or other should fall, if so he might save his honour. The two circled round each other for a moment. Then Poliorketes dashed in, and with a blow of his right wing broke the planes of Pyrrhus's machine, and sent it plunging to destruction.

At this the sixty remaining planes of the enemy came rushing at Poliorketes to avenge their fallen chief. Thereupon Cuanduine drew the Cruaidin Cailidcheann from its sheath, and, standing upon the prow of Poliorketes, he whirled it about his head until it was the length of a rainbow. And he played the music of Badb upon the hosts of the enemy, till one and all had heard his death knell, and the air was filled with the parts of shattered planes and the limbs of slaughtered men.

When he had made an end of them, Cuanduine did not stay, but, still in the heat of his anger, made after the squadrons of bombers.

CHAPTER XII

How Cuanduine made an end of the International Air Force

THESE meanwhile had begun the task for which they were sent, and they made havoc upon the coasts of Munster, and a red scar of pain and destruction from Youghal to Baltimore. Then indeed did Baltimore suffer horrors such as she had not known since the paynim corsairs landed there in the olden times; of which visitation the poet sang:

'Then flung the youth his naked hand against the
shearing sword;
Then sprung the mother on the brand with which
her son was gored;
Then sunk the grandsire on the floor, his grand-
babes clutching wild;
Then fled the maiden moaning faint, and nestled
with the child.'

But these Christian hordes did better by five centuries of progress, and the naked hand of the youth was flung up in vain against liquid fire, and mother and child shrieked in vain to a heaven without pity. All the pleasant land of Carbery was deluged with the green and brown and yellow clouds of deadly gases, and crowds of maddened people rushed from blazing villages and poisoned fields to drown their tortured bodies in sea or river. Gasping multitudes, racked, blinded, speechless, ran hither and thither, not knowing what they did. Some strove to bury themselves in the earth. Some cast themselves into wells and pits. The inhabitants of one village, flying from a hail of bombs, found themselves in a sea of chlorine, and rushed back to a more merciful death in their burning homes. Altogether it was a most efficient operation, and the Commander felt justified in sending to Headquarters the wireless message: 'Raid successful.'

He spoke too soon: for in that moment Cuanduine came up with the bombers in a red fury of anger. His distorting fit had come upon him, and he had no longer the appearance of a man, but the appearance of a god. The great airplane Poliorketes dropped from the sky like a thunderbolt, and the hero, standing on the prow, cast hand-grenades right and left among the enemy. Every grenade he threw found a mark, and each machine that he hit burst into fragments, while the poison gas they carried poured out in dense clouds, drenching their fellows and slaying their crews, so that many machines, filled with dead men, ran amok among the rest, colliding with them and dragging them down to destruction in the hell they had created below. Well it was for Cuanduine that he wore the aigis, for the fumes of phosgene and chlorine rose about him and enveloped him; yet, being thus protected, he took no harm, but flew to and fro above the disordered ranks of the bombers, pelting them with death.

At this sight terror took possession of the enemy, for now they knew that the champion was more than mortal. With one accord those that were left of them turned to fly from the battle southward; yet would not Cuanduine stay his hand, but, following after them, he again drew the Cruaidin Cailidcheann and played the music of Badb on them till he had made an end of them all. And he chanted this song:

> 'Here the end of Goshawk's host:
> Slaughtered are the slaughterers;
> Poisoned are the poisonous;
> Badb hath drunk her fill.
>
> Red my sword and red my body,
> Red my heart and red my soul.
> God of love and pity,
> Purge my wrath away.'

Not long afterwards the fleet of the men of Eirinn arrived on the scene, and right disappointed they were to find that by their squabblings they had missed the fight.

CHAPTER XIII

How the news was kept dark

WHEN word of these events was flashed to Manhattan, King Goshawk nearly withered away for fear, and Mr Slawmy Cander was considerably upset.

'This is certainly the work of Coondinner' said he.

'Sure' replied King Goshawk. 'That guy, Slick, musta double-crossed us. Let's have him up.'

Orders were despatched accordingly; but it transpired that Slick had been bumped off by some private enemy, so Goshawk had to content himself with commanding that his body should be dug out of its grave and impaled at the palace gates.

'We must now take steps to keep this business dark' said Mr Slawmy Cander. He therefore summoned King Pulpenbaum to his presence, and in less than an hour the newspapers of the world contained the following official report:

'The International punitive expedition against Ireland has carried out its task with complete success.

'The International Sanitary Department has issued an order forbidding ships to approach within ten miles of the Irish coast for fear of infection by the plagues now raging in the country.'

Immediately afterwards Mr Cander held conference with Scab Slughorn, the Crime King, himself; who promptly set out for Ireland with a crew of picked gunmen to bump off Cuanduine by hook or by crook.

CHAPTER XIV

The Scouring of Baile Atha Cliath

WHEN the battle was over, Cuanduine had not yet spent all his energy; therefore, to the end that he might drive it from him, and that his battle fury might be cooled, he flew three times around the four provinces of Ireland. When he had done this, and his war fever had left him, he flew low over the city of Dublin to receive the plaudits of the people.

Then a strange thing happened: for the propeller of the great airplane Poliorketes created so huge a draught and vortex behind it that it raised a great storm of dust in the streets of the city; and the dust was drawn into the vortex of the propeller, and all the filth of the streets along with it: all the soot and the smut and the grit and the grime; all the paper, and rags, and straw, and orange peel, and banana skins, and cigarette ends, and used matches, and tram tickets that lay about; all the foulness and muck that was in the place; all the dried consumptives' spittle, and tobacco-juice, and diseased skin peelings, and scurf; all the horsedung and cowdung and dogs' dung and cats' dung and pigdung and mandung; all the tin cans and old boots; all the sordes and lees and the sweepings and scourings and draff that flavour the air for human lungs, were whirled into the vortex at the tail of Poliorketes.

After these came the loose slates and bricks and

chimney pots from neglected roofs and walls, and bits of broken gates and palings, and wretched summerhouses and toolsheds, and crazy balconies, and garden seats, and cheap makeshifts of every kind; all the posters from the hoardings, and the hoardings themselves after them.

Finally the people in the streets felt their very clothes being stripped off them by the violence of the whirlwind: first their overcoats, then their coats and their shirts and their vests and chemises: no matter how desperately they might cling to them, no matter how they clutched and hugged themselves and tied themselves into knots, all these were torn off; and when they were gone, the rude blast threw them down and whipped off their nether garments as well. Then were beheld such sights as were never seen in any city before. Stout pillars of society stripped of their importance; prominent public figures shown up for what they were; people of influence left without a rag of self-confidence; proud people cringing in dark corners; bankers without a shred of credit; materialists crying for the moon; bullies and oppressors shrieking to heaven for protection; politicians running away from their seats; journalists afflicted with shame; publicity mongers looking for a hiding place; fine ladies in reduced circumstances; hard riders to hounds skulking to earth like foxes; the whole mass of humanity blushing for itself for the first time in history. It would have made Mrs Grundy laugh to see them all—all that vast modest miserable mob scurrying like rats from the sight of each others' eyes, and locking and bolting themselves into their homes, and burying themselves in their beds, where they lay wondering how they were ever going to face the world again.

Thus the whirlwind passed over the city, till it came to a place where Solomon Beetlebrow, ex-Minister of the Interior, was haranguing the multitude about his own importance. Here all happened as elsewhere. Every mother's son and daughter in the audience was stripped of the last stitch and stiver, and left standing there, not knowing what way to look, or what way to turn, or where on earth to go, or what the dickens to do, think, or say, excepting only Solomon Beetlebrow himself, high up on his platform, who, when everything else was gone, clung to his drawers with such tenacity that the devil himself could not have dispossessed him, let alone a whirlwind: for there is no getting to the bottom of a politician. Nevertheless this action lost him his seat in the end, as the people felt a grudge against him for getting away with it when nobody else did.

This episode did not much increase Cuanduine's popularity; for though people like to be saved from oppression and danger, they do not like to be shown up. A deputation was accordingly sent to the hero to thank him for his valiant defence of his country, and at the same time to request him to scrap Poliorketes and in his future operations to use an ordinary airplane like anybody else. The leader of the deputation was the Lord Mayor of Dublin, who addressed Cuanduine as follows:

'Illustrious preserver of our historic race: standing here to-day at the head of the most representative body of my fellow citizens ever assembled in this place, it is my painful duty to utter on their behalf a respectful protest against the unfortunate occurrences of yesterday afternoon. Our public life has been degraded, our most intimate secrets exposed to vulgar curiosity, the modesty of our womanhood—famous the whole world over—has been put to the blush and dragged in the mire, the innocence of our children, the scandalising of which, according to the holy Gospels, is worse than tying a millstone round your neck, has been brutally and prematurely illuminated, and the business of the city has been unwarrantably interrupted.

'Furthermore, the foulness and filth and pestiferous atmosphere raised by the aforesaid airplane has disgusted and nauseated us all, and left a bad taste in the mouths of every decent inhabitant of our ancient, historic, and singularly handsome city, which contains, as you are aware, the broadest street in Europe and other magnificent features too numerous to mention.

'Furthermore—'

'Never mind the furthermore' said Cuanduine. 'Come to the point.'

'The point, sir' said the Lord Mayor, whose eloquence was now a little unsettled, 'the point is, sir, that you mustn't do it again; and the sooner you get rid of that outrageous machine, the better we'll be pleased.'

'Hear, hear' said the Deputation.

Cuanduine thereupon made answer, and said:

'Gentlemen, there are few things I would not do for my country, but this is one of them. For consider. In the first place, Poliorketes is a gift of the gods, and therefore not to be rejected without ingratitude, or with impunity. In the second place, I cannot fight with ordinary planes or ordinary weapons, being no ordinary man; for which reason they would break in my hands. And in the third place, by this catharsis and excoriation that you complain of, I have not done you an injury, but a service: nay, even a greater service than by the destruction of your enemies. You know the precept that Bias of Priene gave to his disciples: *γνῶθι σεαυτόν*, that is, know thyself. For there is no injury that an enemy can inflict on a people so great as the injury they can inflict on themselves for lack of this knowledge. And now you know yourselves very thoroughly. Moreover you now breathe a purer air than the inhabitants of any other city, and are no longer plagued and deceived by the sight of advertisements. So God be with you; for I still have dragons to fight.'

The deputation did not like this answer very well, but, having nothing more to say, they withdrew.

This, then, is the Scouring of Dublin: and it is one of the three great Feats of Scavenging, the other two being the cleansing of the Augean Stables and the purging of Pantagruel.

CHAPTER XV

The slaying of Scab Slughorn

AFTER this Cuanduine made ready to do battle against King Goshawk in his own stronghold. When he was fully equipped and about to start, who should present himself once more but that indefatigable scribe Mr Robinson, with a request to be taken along. Cuanduine bade him step aboard, and at once took flight, driving the great airplane Poliorketes westward across the great Atlantic towards the land of America.

When he had gone about half a day's journey he perceived another plane coming eastward; and as it drew nearer he saw that it was filled with men of evil appearance, with low narrow foreheads over their hard cunning eyes, and mighty jaws chewing long cigars. These were Scab Slughorn and his picked gunmen, coming to make an end of Cuanduine if they could catch him unawares. The hero knew nothing of that; but his godlike soul felt the evil that was in them, and he said to himself: 'These men were better dead.' Accordingly he turned the head of Poliorketes towards them, and laid a bomb ready to his hand.

When Slughorn saw his change of course, and perceived the marvellous shape and size of the great airplane Poliorketes, he guessed at once who was in it. 'Boys' said he, 'this is Coondinner. We gotta make a gettaway, or our number's up.'

At these words the faces of the fifteen gunmen turned pale, and the cigars dropped from their nerveless jaws. The pilot dared not go about, for fear of losing distance, but he deflected his course north-eastward, hoping that in the chilly regions of Iceland they might find some cloud or fog to hide them. But there was no escaping the lightning rush of Poliorketes, or the bomb sped by the hand of Cuanduine. By a single cast the racket of Scab Slughorn was ended, and he and his men were bumped on the Atlantic waves. Mr Robinson adroitly took a snapshot of the event, which was afterwards published in the press.

CHAPTER XVI

The taking of Castle Goshawk: and how Cuanduine broke the first of his geasa

AT length Cuanduine sighted the shores of Manhattan and the skyscrapers sticking up above them like houses of cards. By the guidance of Badb he flew past them towards the Adirondacks; for King Goshawk and Mr Slawmy Cander, when they heard of his coming, had fled from the Palace of Manhattan and sought refuge in Castle Goshawk. Thither Cuanduine now pursued them, and circled round the great fortress, looking for a point of attack. Immediately there sallied forth from the castle a squadron of fighting planes, which assailed him on all sides. A sharp swift battle followed. With a bomb from each hand Cuanduine destroyed two of the enemy; with his machine gun he made an end of two more; the last he cleft in twain with a single stroke of the Cruaidin Cailidcheann. Then he turned once more to attack the castle.

Now while the battle was being fought, the noise of it was carried far and wide over the country. And the spirit of Badb passed into the men who were wandering hungry along the roads between the fields of full-eared corn, and by the great warehouses packed with unsaleable grain. And lo! a voice in the air: 'The people's champion is at the tyrant's gate. Why wait ye?'

Thereupon men came running from all parts, and they broke into the gunsmiths' shops, and, arming themselves, they marched to the attack on Goshawk's stronghold. As they reached the scene of action they saw the great airplane Poliorketes, like an avenging angel, poised above the castle, and Cuanduine making fine havoc of the defence with an unceasing storm of bombs. Already one tower was in flames, and the gateway a mass of shattered wreckage, in the midst of which lay heaps of men gasping in the swirl of their own poison gas. With right good will the armies of hungry men flung themselves into the fray. The outer defences were stormed; the inner walls; and the courtyard filled with a raging host that shot through windows, broke down doors, and swarmed through every opening into the keep.

At that Cuanduine left off his bombing, and, descending to the roof, went down into the Castle, sword in hand, to look for Goshawk. He found him very quickly in an upper room of the great tower, whither he had fled in terror to conceal himself from the raging mob below. As Cuanduine burst in, he gave a yell of mortal fear, and made a frantic effort to scramble up the chimney; but his belly hindered him, and he came down again in a cloud of soot.

'Turn round' roared Cuanduine, 'for I would not kill you from behind.'

Goshawk did not much wish to be killed from the front either; but there was no disobeying the compelling voice of the hero. As he stood there, shaking like a jelly, with his face miserably bewrayed with soot, Cuanduine wondered what to do with him; for the fellow was unfit to live, yet he was unwilling to soil his sword with such blood as his. However, he was spared the necessity. At the sight of the hero, with the light of battle blazing in his eyes, and the Cruaidin Cailidcheann gleaming in his hand, the heart of King Goshawk stopped in his breast, and he fell dead upon the floor.

At the same moment Cuanduine perceived a dark unobtrusive figure in a corner of the room.

'Who are you, sir?' he demanded.

'O sir, a nobody' said Mr Slawmy Cander. 'A mere secretary, unworthy of your steel. A very humble person. Besides, I never approved of his late Majesty's business methods. I often told him it would lead to this, but he wouldn't listen to me.'

'You may live' said Cuanduine.

'And if you will be so kind as to protect me from your followers—' said Mr Cander, 'I shall be eternally grateful.' For the roar of the mob could now be heard on the stairway.

'You are safe with me' said Cuanduine as the multitude poured into the room.

Thus Cuanduine broke the first of his geasa: namely, not to kill a lion and spare a jackal. For though Goshawk was but a mangy lion, Mr Slawmy Cander was a jackal of parts.

CHAPTER XVII

How King Pulpenbaum told the truth for the first time in his life

AFTERWARDS Cuanduine went through the Castle, and he found many kings and financial magnates skulking in various funk-holes: some in attics, some in cellars, some under bedsteads, and some in dustbins. These he made prisoners, and confined in the dungeons of the castle. As to Queen Guzzelinda, some say that she was suffocated in an ashpit where she had taken refuge; others claim that she escaped from the castle and afterwards choked herself accidentally with her own vest, being unable to undress without assistance. You can believe which story you like, for all I care.

Amongst the prisoners was King Pulpenbaum, whom Cuanduine addressed in this fashion: 'You mangy rat, was it not you that sent out the lying message that told the world that the men of Eirinn were defeated and their land lying waste? Come now to the microphone and undo your work.'

So presently all the television screens of the world projected the figure of King Pulpenbaum held by the neck by Cuanduine like a misbehaving kitten, his face all daubed with the garbage and offal of the dustbin, while he spoke these words:

'The message I sent out to the press of the world, like everything else it has ever printed, was a lie. The men of Eirinn were victorious, and the International fleet is destroyed. To-day Castle Goshawk has been taken, and Goshawk himself is dead from fear. The reign of the kings is ended, and mankind is as free as it dares to be.'

After that Cuanduine turned to liberate the birds from the Goshawk aviaries. But Mr Slawmy Cander said to him: 'Is this wise? These birds belong to many nations. If they are set free, they will hardly find their way home across the ocean, but will remain in America, or perish miserably.'

'True' said Cuanduine, and stayed his hand. Then he sent out a message to the nations that they should draw up lists of the birds that properly belonged to them, and make preparations to carry them away.

CHAPTER XVIII

The death of the Philosopher

WHEN the Philosopher, in his room in Stoneybatter, heard of Cuanduine's triumph, he said: 'Now the task I set myself is accomplished, and there is no need to borrow more years from usurious time: for indeed I have paid heavily in weariness for all I have taken beyond my allotted span. Now let me be scrapped, and pass into the crucible of the Button-Moulder, that the stuff of me may be recast in other and better forms.' With that he lay down on his bed, and the life went out of him.

BOOK III

The Passing of Cuanduine

CHAPTER I

How the news was received by the Public

THESE events caused much perturbation throughout the world. Governments everywhere issued a stream of official statements, proclamations, notes, remonstrances, *démarches*, protocols, and other documents, amounting to many millions of words, but meaning simply that they were in a funk. Political parties issued manifestoes claiming that a moderate release of birds had always been an essential feature of their programmes. The League of Nations declared that the Bird Question could now at last be treated as One Big World Problem, and solved to the complete satisfaction of all interests. The Pope issued the Encyclical *Quae Cum Ita Sint*, declaring that whereas the monopoly of all singing birds by one individual was a grave abuse, nevertheless human inequalities were decreed by divine law, and the doctrine that all private ownership of birds was itself wrong was contrary to the teaching of Holy Church. Other churches also spoke after their fashions, which were many.

The feelings of the upper classes are best represented by the leading article of *The Times:*

'Great as were the services rendered by the late KING GOSHAWK to humanity in promoting employment and reducing overproduction, the termination of his régime will not be regarded with entire disfavour by moderate men. While monopoly has been the source of many undoubted benefits to society, it will not be denied that it has not infrequently given occasion for abuses, which have exposed it, not altogether without justification, to the strictures of critics of our magnificent economic system. The monopoly of the birds is a case in point. The economic advantages which it produced were not sufficiently obvious to counterbalance the psychological effect of what was, to a superficial view, an act of personal aggrandisement. The determination of the Irish people to retain the bird which came into their possession was, in the circumstances, not unnatural; nor can King Goshawk's advisers be entirely acquitted of exercising undue severity in the methods employed to recover it. We may now look forward to an amicable settlement of the whole question, which, while securing a moderate supply of birds for popular enjoyment, will not prejudice the rights of future possessors of property in these commodities.'

The vulgar had their opinions formed for them by the penny press by such articles as this:

'King Goshawk has fallen. We write the words with unmitigated satisfaction. He abused his power.

'*It must not be supposed, however, that all millionaires are like him.* There are good millionaires and bad millionaires, just as there are good poets and bad poets. Most millionaires are good millionaires.

'*Millionaires are a necessity. Without them, none of us would have any employment.* In these hard times we need more millionaires than ever.

'*It would be a mistake therefore to do anything that would discourage millionaires.* Nobody would ever do his best to get on if he knew that as soon as he became a millionaire the elementary human right of listening to the songs of birds was to be taken from him.

'While, then, we agree that King Goshawk's monopoly of the birds cannot be defended, *we disapprove of any action which would prevent the legitimate accumulation of birds in the future.*'

The Socialist press, on the other hand, showed marked disapprobation of Cuanduine's action. To restore the birds to alleged freedom under national capitalist governments was, they said, merely to bolster up the existing state of things. Birds were confirmed individualists, and sang for their own enjoyment. They should therefore be kept under the control of an international bureau, and trained to sing for the enjoyment of the proletariat.

Of other papers I need only quote *The Rationalist*, which said: 'The belief in the presence of a celestial warrior on earth is not without precedent in world history. The intelligent Athenians of the sixth century were convinced that the shade of Theseus fought by their side at Marathon. The Americans of the nineteenth century imagined that the spirit of a certain John Brown, whose body they supposed to be mouldering in the grave, marched at the head of their armies. Even as late as the twentieth century, there was the tradition of the Angels of Mons. What makes the present occasion unique is the extraordinary ubiquity of the delusion. More extraordinary still is the fact that belief in it is accepted not only without plausible evidence, but in the teeth of convincing evidence to the contrary. The future historian, with the solid documentary evidence of the International Air Force's Report before him, will find it difficult to believe that credence was ever given to this fantastic legend.'

The American dailies decided that it would pay them to boost Cuanduine as the Man of the Day: which they did with marvellous pep and punch.

CHAPTER II

The Machinations of Mr Slawmy Cander

IT was one of the strong points of the character of Mr Slawmy Cander that he knew how to make the best of a bad job. It was another, that he cared not two pins what the world did so long as he had the management of it. He had created the credits by which King Goshawk had purchased the song-birds, and he was equally ready to create the credits by which they should be restored.

Now the power of Mr Slawmy Cander was founded in this manner: and may you all be sick of the mulligrubs with eating chopped hay, according to Master Rabelais' malediction, if you do not now listen with all your ears. This god-forsaken scrivener of Mammon, this joyless quill driver of Plutus, was not, as you might imagine, a direct creation of the Evil One, but was begotten by a father, Mr Sweedle Cander, and had likewise a grandfather, Mr Crawley Cander, and a great-grandfather, Mr Ikey Cander. This last, in the ancient times, having neither the will nor the ability to make anything worth making or do anything worth doing, joined him with seven others nearly as bad as himself, and set up a bank. To this institution came sundry honest men, makers of bread, boots, bricks, books, and other good things, to place their hard-earned money in its care. Between them they lodged, let us say, £1,000; ten of them depositing £100 each.

Now all these gentlemen had business with one another, and found it convenient to pay one another by cheque. This was even more convenient for Mr Cander; for he discovered presently that only one-tenth of his business was transacted in cash, the rest being merely clerical work: that is to say, a payment by Mr Green, a bootmaker, to Mr Brown, a tanner, was carried out simply by transferring a figure from one ledger to another. Mr Cander thus realised that most of his cash (or rather, theirs) would never be wanted by the depositors, and was free to play certain little tricks with it, by which, from their exceeding greenness, they were all to be done brown, as you shall see.

One day Mr Green received a large order for boots. To fulfil it he had to pay out, in wages and other expenses, more money than he had at command; so he approached Mr Cander with a request for an overdraft. Mr Cander graciously consented, and allowed him to draw £100 in addition to his own money, making £200 in all, on condition that he should repay £102 in three months' time. Mr Green fondly imagined that the money he was borrowing was a portion of that deposited with Mr Cander by his other clients: but Mr Cander clearly perceived that that would be a poor way of doing business. Knowing that Mr Green would pay out most of his overdraft in the form of a cheque to Mr Brown for leather, he opined that it was altogether unnecessary to lend him any real money at all. Nothing more was needed than to write down the figure £100 opposite his name in the ledger, and, when the cheque came in, to transfer it to the ledger of Mr Brown. By this process none of the other customers had his deposit reduced by a penny. Each of them was still credited with £100, which he was entitled to draw if he liked, though Mr Cander well knew he would not. Thus, instead of reducing his cash in hand to £900, Mr Cander increased his liabilities to £1,100. By a stroke of the pen he had created £100 out of nothing. In one moment this black-coated totter of figures had become a god.

No sooner was Mr Green granted his overdraft than he gave an order for leather to Mr Brown, who now found himself in need of accommodation in his turn. For you must note that at this time, owing to the inventions of men of science, the productivity of industry was increasing so rapidly that the supply of real money, based on sterile gold, could not keep pace with it. Mr Brown, therefore, was also driven to make application to Mr Cander, who created another £100 for him in the same way. In like manner he dealt with others of his clients, as the need arose, until discretion counselled him to stop.

Now open your ears wider still, and may you be tormented with wind from eating burnt wheat if you skip a line of what's coming. In order to repay this 'loan' and the £2 interest on it, Mr Green had to increase the price of his goods by £102, which in due course he handed over to Mr Cander, who, after putting the £2 in his pocket as profit, set the £100 of real money received from Mr Green against the £100 of sham money created three months ago, and cancelled both out. Thus there were now £100 worth of boots in the world which nobody, not even Mr Cander himself, had the money to buy; and when, in due course, the other loans were also called in, there were more shop-loads of bread and shirts and things in the same predicament.

In this way Mr Cander used poor Mr Green and the rest as so many sponges to suck up money both from their workers and the public, and then squeezed them dry; and that is the reason why none of us ever has enough money in his pockets to buy the good things that the shop-keepers are so anxious to sell. Do you understand it now, my friends?—the dismal science, ha! ha! Isn't it a rare joke to enjoy over the coffee you can't afford while they are burning it like weeds on the plantations?

But the cream of the jest is this. In order to fix a reasonable price for his boots, thus overloaded with costs, Mr Green has to keep down the wages of his workers as low as possible; and in order to buy the necessaries of life, whose prices are all forced up by other bankers in the same fashion, the workers must try to get as high wages as possible. There is therefore continual friction between them, leading to strikes and lock-outs. When matters come to this pass—listen still, my hearties: we'll come back to our story in a moment—both sides to the dispute have to borrow money from the Banker in order to carry on. The Banker—fairly splitting his black sides—creates it out of nothing as before; and when the strike is over, no matter who wins or loses, the poor devils have to scrape and cheesepare to pay it all back again, with interest, in hard-earned real cash. Is not this the greatest joke that ever was in the world? And the fellows that work it—instead of being sent to gaol like counterfeiters, who at least make their money ut of honest paper or metal that has cost them omething—are taken into the counsels of governments, and decide all questions affecting the public urse and our private pockets. Juvenal, Rabelais, 'oltaire, Swift, do your spirits slumber in Elysium, hat your laughter does not come rolling in thunder bout our ears?

Such is Finance: and when it is done on a large nough scale, it is High Finance. Mr Slawmy Cander inherited this fruitful mountain of debt from is ancestors, and developed it to world proportions. As his great-grandfather had financed Mr Green, o had he financed King Goshawk, and in the same ashion he proposed to finance Cuanduine. He herefore approached the hero with an air of nodesty and discretion, which well suited with is unobtrusive appearance, and besought him, f he could in any way make use of him, not o hesitate to do so, for that it would be his greatest appiness to place his knowledge and experience t his service, and, through him, at the service f the world. This suggestion was very welcome to Cuanduine, who was beginning to be a little bothered y the way things were going: for the children of ght are in many matters less wise than the children f this world. He therefore appointed Mr Cander to e his secretary, and kept him always close to his ear: step which the press of the world greeted with nqualified approval, saying that it was a most opeful augury that the policy of the new ruler ould be guided by sound financial principles.

CHAPTER III

How the liberation of the birds was found to be attended with some little difficulty

THE first difficulty that had arisen was with the many vested interests that had grown up around the Goshawk aviaries. The feeding and care of the birds gave employment to more than three thousand men. About a thousand more—gardeners, carpenters, metal workers, painters, and the like—were engaged in keeping the grounds and the cages in order, besides a couple of hundred gate-keepers and attendants. Then there were the owners of booths, refreshment rooms, side-shows, and conveyances, with their employees; not to mention a crowd of photographers, hawkers of matches, confectionery and picture postcards, fortune tellers, and others. All these would lose their means of livelihood if the aviaries were abolished. The shops and lodging houses of the neighbourhood would lose the greater part of their custom in consequence. Finally, the contractors who supplied the requirements of the institution would be deprived of lucrative orders and be compelled to dismiss large numbers of their employees. Angry remonstrances had come in from all quarters, the labourers in particular declaring that they would resist the closing of the aviaries by force.

'Tut-tut' said Mr Slawmy Cander. 'We cannot allow our noble and idealistic work for humanity to be held up by such selfish and parochial interests as these.

'True' said Cuanduine. 'Therefore I would have ·ou point out to these people, in such simple lan- ;uage as they can comprehend, that though their *neans* of livelihood must be taken from them, their ivelihood itself shall not.'

'I do not understand you, sir' said Mr Slawmy Cander. 'Do you mean to suggest that all these ›eople are to be paid in future for doing nothing?'

'Why, truly' said Cuanduine. 'For as the work hey are doing is not only useless but harmful, if it is eft undone, the world will be no poorer than before, f not richer. Therefore we can go on paying them vithout loss.'

'That sounds very well in theory' said Mr Cander, 'but I'm a practical man, and all I know is hat if people don't work, the only way you can pay hem is by taxing other people; and we can't do that ıow, because taxation is already so high that the mallest increase would mean a revolution.'

'My friend' said Cuanduine, 'I greatly fear that he Devil has put those words into your mouth. For if hey are not wickedness, they are folly, and though it s plain that you are not gifted with the wisdom of ıeaven, it is equally plain that you are no fool. Now ıone but a fool could imagine that in a world over- lowing with good things it is necessary to tax any- ›ody to provide for others: therefore I greatly fear hat the Devil has you by the ear.'

Mr Cander laughed. 'I did not think you would ›e so superstitious as to believe in the Devil' said he.

'Why then, Master Cander' said Cuanduine, 'you vill not be of much help to me in fighting him.' \nd he dismissed him from his service forthwith.

CHAPTER IV

How Cuanduine broke the second of his geasa

ANOTHER of Cuanduine's difficulties was this, that the world showed itself completely indifferent to the birds which he had been at such pains to deliver. One after another the Governments replied to his message that this was no time to bother about a lot of song-birds: that what the world really needed was the restoration of normal trading conditions; and in this attitude they were supported by the people, among whom the general opinion began to spread that though Cuanduine might be a good man at handling a fighting-plane, he was in other respects a bit of a crank and unfitted to manage practical affairs. 'A demi-god' said the popular press 'is no doubt valuable in stimulating the natural idealism of mankind, and idealism is an excellent thing in its proper place. The problem before the world, however, is essentially a practical one, and can only be solved by sane hard-headed men with practical experience.'

The Socialist press said more concisely: 'We have had enough of this demi-god with his bourgeois dilettantism and his callous disregard of the real needs of the workers. What the workers want is not birds, but work.'

The comic press said cleverly: 'Cuanduine offers us birds. We give him the bird.'

At this hostility Cuanduine was very much

astonished. Addressing the people through the microphone, he said: 'My friends, whether you mean anything in particular by normal trading conditions I cannot tell. I can only tell you that at all times the conditions under which you have traded have made your world a laughing stock in hell and a heartsore in heaven. Whether practical business men will get you out of your present mess is likewise problematical: seeing that it was they that got you into it. As to why you should be so voracious for work puzzles me entirely when so many good things can be produced with so little work. Do you think that man has no other purpose in life than to labour eternally at material production?'

At this, Mr Slawmy Cander, who had been awaiting his opportunity, sprang to his microphone, and cried out for all the world to hear him: 'Why, what other purpose can he have?'

'He might listen to the birds' said Cuanduine; and thereby he broke the second of his geasa, namely, not to answer the questions of White upon the lips of Black: for wisdom appears as folly to darkened understandings.

At his words the whole world burst into a roar of laughter, and the sound of it was as the laughter of damned souls. Mr Cander, pushing his advantage, spoke again.

'I do not profess to understand these metaphysical subtleties' said he. 'Will you give me a plain answer to a plain question? Have you or have you not any scheme to propose which will provide work for our starving millions?'

'Truly I have a score' replied Cuanduine. 'First

you might build a tower to reach heaven; but as that kingdom is somewhat remote, and I perceive that none of you wants this world to be dumped with the goods they produce there, you should stop a little short of the gates thereof and put up a strong customs barrier. In the lower storeys you could set parties of unemployed to fish for clouds and to catch whales. Secondly, you could dig several passage ways through the earth from various points on the surface to their antipodes, being careful to use no machinery in the process, nor even steel tools, but only mattocks of pine or other soft wood, that your toil may be as prolonged and as onerous as possible. Afterwards you should fill the passages up again, lest they should be of any use and thus add to the abundance of riches which has proved your undoing. Thirdly, you could melt the polar ice-caps with matches or candles; but on no account with electric heat or the oxyhydrogen flame. Fourthly, you could distil the seas to obtain drinking water, and use no salt but what you can abstract from the rivers. These tasks will suffice to begin with. I can set you more later on if you are in need of them.'

When Cuanduine had finished speaking, a vasty silence fell upon the world, the unfortunate people being so muddled in their heads by all they had been taught by their school-teachers, their professors, their novelist-philosophers, their publicists, their economists, their politicians, and their newspapers, that they were quite incapable of thinking to purpose for themselves. Presently Cuanduine, seeing them thus driven to a nonplus, and pitying them, said: 'Well, then, since these works seem too much for you, let us return to our birds, which you can have without any work at all. And hark ye, my friends, if you cannot agree among yourselves on this matter, I myself will solve the difficulty in the way of Alexander with the Gordian knot, even with the sword. For I swear by the gods my people swear by, that not for your sakes only did I come to liberate the birds, but for theirs; and the work of the Gods must be done whether your worships like it or not.'

CHAPTER V

Professor Banger demonstrates the economic impossibility of liberating the birds

NOW although it was generally felt that Cuanduine was something of an extremist on the bird question, there were many people who thought it would be a pleasant thing to have a moderate number of birds about the world. These complained that there had been too much shilly-shally about this question; that it was time it was settled once and for all; that they could see no reason why a compromise could not be effected by the exercise of a little goodwill on all sides, and a partial distribution be made at once; and in fact showed more annoyance than can safely be ignored in persons with votes and influence. There were also others who cared not a jot about birds, but thought it would be better to set them loose than to have an angry demi-god rampaging about the world in an invincible airplane.

These opinions coming to the ears of Mr Slawmy Cander, he took alarm lest the scheme he was maturing should be imperilled, and announced that a series of lectures explaining the situation would be delivered by the leading economists forthwith. He sent to the microphone accordingly Professor Banger, Professor Whipcord, Professor Juggins, Professor Swallowdown, Professor Darkness, Professor Stone, and Professor Gudgeon;

all good men of excellent parts and discretion, of whose soundness and orthodoxy he was fully assured. It is true that they did not entirely agree with one another, in so much that if what one said was correct, the others must of necessity be fools or liars: but in this subject of Economics, orthodoxy does not consist in a slavish uniformity either of first principles or of consequents, but in the recognition of the supremacy of Finance over humanity: only those who deny this are counted heretics.

The first lecture was delivered by Professor Banger, who spoke as follows:

'Ladies and gentlemen, the suggestion that the birds accumulated by the late King Goshawk should be redistributed would appear at first sight to be a most attractive one. Such Utopian ideals have, indeed, been advocated from time to time by some of the finest minds of our race, and have even exercised a certain fascination over large sections of mankind. We must not, however, confuse the desirable with the possible; and it will be my duty to-night—not altogether a pleasant duty, ladies and gentlemen—to demonstrate that this project does not come within the latter category. To put the unpleasant truth as plainly as possible, this project is simply another example of the human tendency—natural but unreasonable—to demand something for nothing. It is yet another case of trying to get a quart out of a pint bottle.

'The plain fact of the matter is that the number of birds is not infinite, but strictly limited. I have demonstrated on another occasion that if all the money in the world was equally divided, there would only be about four and sixpence a week for each person. It is obvious, therefore, that we cannot afford the expenditure necessary to liberate the birds, or to maintain them afterwards. It is true that many of them feed on things that are unfit for human consumption—such as worms, grubs, snails and caterpillars—though even these are not to be discounted as potential sources of nourishment in times like the present. But in addition they would, if set at liberty, consume thousands of pounds' worth of wheat and other grains which, under modern conditions, form such a useful source of fuel supply for locomotives and destructors.

'Another important point to which I wish to direct your attention is this. So long as our working classes believe that we can tax business profits indefinitely in order to provide subsidies and doles and other alleviations of that kind, so long must our present downward course continue. And the reason is obvious. Why are people employed, and how do they become employed? Simply because someone with money saved from personal consumption employs them to produce something which he can sell at a profit. If there were no incentive to such people to save and invest their money, there would be no employment for anybody. We should simply stand about with our hands in our pockets and starve. That was what actually happened in primitive times. There were no capitalists to employ the people, so they just sat down and died.

'Suppose a party of people were wrecked on a desert island, what do you think would be the first thing they'd do? Obviously they would look around for a man with money to employ them in gathering fruit. If there were no capitalist among them, or if he didn't see his way to make a profit out of the business, they would all remain unemployed and starve to death, no matter how fertile the island might be. If therefore we want to have plenty of employment, we must give every possible incentive to entrepreneurs—encouraging them to get as much of our money from us as they can, so that they can spend it on employing us to make more for them. The accumulation of the birds in the Goshawk aviaries illustrates this principle perfectly. Upwards of ten thousand people are employed in that magnificent industry, who would otherwise be condemned to perpetual destitution.

'You must realise, therefore, ladies and gentlemen, that, quite apart from ethical considerations, any attempt to increase the amenities of life for the majority by raiding the profits of the minority, must be quite ineffective. The remedy for our present troubles lies not in redistributing the cake that we have, but in increasing the size of the cake. We must work harder, consume less, and produce more. In that task the constant singing of innumerable birds would be a distraction and a hindrance. Let us therefore go on pinching and squeezing and cheeseparing for as long as is necessary to tide us over the present unfortunate depression and get back to normal trading conditions. Then, and not till then, we can have all the birds we want.'

When this speech was concluded, Cuanduine

gave out such a roar of laughter as nearly brought the castle tumbling about his ears. He rolled in his chair, holding his sides, and kicking the floor to pieces with his heels, while the thunder of his merriment shook heaven and earth. 'Twas such a laugh as had not been heard in the world since the mockery of Voltaire made oppressors turn pale in their council chambers, nor even before that if the truth were known. I think Master Rabelais must have laughed in the same fashion, all by himself, when he was writing his flim-flam stories: but the secret of such mirth is lost. His microphone was in the room with Cuanduine at the time, so that his jubilant bellowings were carried to every listening ear. But of the whole multitude there was not one to share the joke. They all sat there as solemn as gelded clerks.

CHAPTER VI

Why Economists are not generally considered funny

YOU are not to suppose that humour was altogether vanished from the earth in those days. Indeed, most people were careful to cultivate a sense of it, making to themselves a sweet little private garden to run and hide in when they were frightened of reality. They could all snigger very knowingly, and also smirk when convenient; many of the less cultivated could even cackle. I do assure you that if Professor Banger, in coming on to the platform, had tripped on the carpet and fallen on his face, they would have giggled right gleefully. Or if, on his rising to speak, they had observed a smut on his nose, they would have been nudging each other and tittering all through the evening. If in the course of his lecture, he had made a bright allusion to mothers-in-law or to Mrs Partington's mop, or so much as mentioned the word *beer*, he would have had an instant response of chuckles. And if, at the end, on sitting down, his chair had collapsed underneath him, there would have been such a squeal of high-pitched shrill-throated yauping and caterwauling as would have given you a headache for a week. After all, men are only human, and perhaps it is only the Gods that can relish the full flavour of a solemn fool learnedly proving that the way to get out of a mess is to stick to the way that led into it. All these good people thought Mr Banger's speech most learned and profound, and resented Cuanduine's laughter accordingly, deeming it to be in the worst possible taste, and a reflexion on their own discrimination to boot. Perceiving this, Mr Robinson hastened to his presence and besought him to moderate his glee, assuring him that it would do his reputation no good if he treated serious subjects so flippantly.

CHAPTER VII

Why Economists are so impressive: and why some have longer necks than others

'THAT speech will go down' said Mr Robinson to Cuanduine. 'I know the public. That sort of stuff impresses them no end.'

'I do not know the public' said Cuanduine, 'but I fear you are right, though why I cannot tell. An economist is not interesting, like a scientist, nor elevating, like an artist, nor stimulating, like an original thinker, nor informing, like a traveller, nor suggestive to those that read between the lines, like a politician, nor authoritative, like a priest; yet he impresses more than any of them. No matter what dull nonsense he talks, it is swallowed without straining. No matter how many of his prophecies have proved false, they are not remembered against him. 'Sdeath, but when I see one of these shallow pompous asses mouthing it on a platform, and mark his dreary ditherings of a sham science whose premisses anyone in whom common sense has not been destroyed by text-books and newspapers can see to be false, whose logic any first-year student could pick to pieces, and whose conclusions are not only what you might expect from such antecedents, but can be clearly seen to have landed the world in the filthy mess from which they have the impudence to pretend to be saving it, I marvel that such blitherers and such blitherings can be listened to without shrieks of derision.'

'Steady on, old chap' replied Mr Robinson. 'Aren't you drawing it a bit strong? I don't know what premisses are, I never learned any logic, and as for conclusions, I've got to draw the sort that Lord Cumbersome pays me to draw. So you see I'm not in a position to say whether these fellows are right or wrong; but if they're such fools as you say they are, how the deuce do they get away with it?'

'It can only be by this magic power of impressiveness that the Devil seems to have dowered them with' said Cuanduine. 'Tell me this, my friend. suppose I were to give a lecture on the art of growing cabbages, and to deliver myself in this fashion: "Gentlemen, the purpose of growing cabbages is to wear away the edges of spades. To begin with, therefore, you choose the hardest and stoniest ground you can find, and on the coldest day in midwinter you begin to dig. When the ground is fully prepared, you sow it, but not with cabbage seed, for this is an extremely scarce commodity, and, if placed in the ground, might rot, so that there would be danger of a future scarcity of cabbage seed, with a consequent danger of loss of opportunity to wear down spades. Instead you sow dandelions, and while living on this plain but wholesome fare, you proceed to wear away some more of your spade by preparing another bed for next year's crop." Who, if I were to speak thus, would be impressed?'

'None but a congenital idiot' said Mr Robinson.

'Therein lies the solution of the mystery' said Cuanduine. 'For the economists' stuff impresses idiots that are not congenital, but made so by education. This puts me in mind of a dinner to which I was invited when I was a lion in London; whereat an economist held forth after his usual fashion. Well, thought I to myself when he had finished, and the whole company sat agape at his learning, this fellow has neck enough for anything: which put it into my head to ask out loud: "Why have some people longer necks than others?"

' "I suppose" said a priest who was present, seeking to improve the occasion, "because God made us in what shape conforms in each case to his divine will."

'A scientist sitting opposite took him up, saying: "Does it not rather show that God—or the Life Force—like every other artificer, proceeds by the method of trial and error?"

' "Doesn't it mean" said another guest "that Nature, like a true artist, aims at variety?"

' "You are all wrong" declared the Economist. "The variations in the length of the neck are Nature's method for increasing employment. The purpose of the neck is evidently to give employment to collar-makers, and the more it varies in size, the greater the employment they get." '

CHAPTER VIII

Professor Whipcord explains the economic impossibility of liberating the birds

THE second lecture was given by Professor Whipcord, whose wisdom was carried through the boundless ether in this fashion:

'Ladies and Gentlemen, the immediate problem for which the world needs a solution to-day is different from the problem of a year ago, from that of two years ago, and from that of ten years ago. It is still more different from that of fifty years ago, that of a hundred years ago, and that of a thousand years ago. As for the problems of five, ten, and fifty thousand years ago, it can scarcely be said, with any pretence to scientific accuracy, to resemble them at all. There is no longer any real danger of mankind perishing of famine, or of suffering from a serious shortage of any useful commodity. This is not a crisis of scarcity, but a crisis of plenty. Our sufferings are due not to any parsimony on Nature's part, but to our own incompetence to make use of her gifts. Under such circumstances the voices that urge economy as the remedy are the voices of imbeciles and maniacs. Our duty to-day is to spend. We live by getting employment from one another, and by saving we throw one another out of work.

'Let us now consider the question of the birds in the light of these truths. It is obvious that there is no scarcity of birds: it is therefore unnecessary and undesirable to keep the whole race of them on a caged basis. On the other hand, to go to the other extreme and release them all indiscriminately, as Mr Coondinner suggests, would be an act of lunacy. Apart from the toll that would be levied by birds of prey, there would be an immediate rush by the unemployed to get employment in killing them, and before very long the whole of our feathered friends would find their last resting place within the abdominal viscera of our hungry fellow-men.

'We must, therefore, find some *via media* between the cast-iron rigidity of encagement and the chaos of unregulated manumission. This, in my opinion, is afforded by the policy of *controlled liberation*. By that I mean that a small and strictly limited number of birds should be released as soon as practicable; then, when these have been killed off, provided that their numbers have been replaced by the procreative efforts of the caged reserve, a second instalment could be excarcerated, and the process continued indefinitely on the same principles. In no other way can the enjoyment of avian melody be obtained by this generation without risking the ornithological reserves on which its enjoyment by subsequent generations is dependent.

'I am afraid that many of my hearers will regard this solution as altogether too sweeping and drastic. But in times like these we cannot afford to show timidity or reluctance to act boldly. Safety to-day can be won only by reckless daring.'

CHAPTER IX

How two Economists were confuted in a laughable manner

THIS speech was received with the same solemn respect as its predecessor. Even Cuanduine could not laugh, being rather smitten with despair at the invincible cloddishness and fatheadedness of man. He spent the night reading Bergson on Laughter, and next day locked himself into his room and was seen by nobody.

The same night Professor Juggins was billed to deliver the third lecture of the series. As his stately figure appeared on ten million television screens, his foot suddenly caught in some obstacle, and he fell flat on his face. Screams of amusement greeted this mishap, which became shriller when, as he struggled to rise, the seat of his pants (an oldish pair which he had specially dug out for the occasion as an example of economy) burst open with a loud crack. The learned man put the best face he could on the matter, and, as soon as he was on his feet began his oration with as much serenity as might be expected after such an unpropitious introduction. However, his trials were not over; for his nose had picked up a large smut from the carpet, and, feeling an itch, he scratched it with his finger, smearing it good and large over the whole organ; which occasioned so much merriment among the audience that they heard not a word of his lecture. As if this were not enough for the poor devil, just as he was in the act of insisting on the necessity for a stable currency, his braces suddenly snapped, and his trousers began to slip down about his middle. Thereafter he was compelled to keep his hands in his pockets, and to turn over his notes with his teeth; which was conducive neither to his own good temper nor to the dignity of his science. Being now thoroughly fed up, he skipped the main part of his discourse, gabbled a few bright words of hope in the future, and so made an end. Unfortunately, in backing away from the microphone (as the state of his breeches required) he fell over a chair and became firmly wedged in a waste-paper basket close behind it; which threw the world into such paroxysms of glee that you would have thought he had given them a solution of all their troubles, past, present, and to come.

Now this little contretemps had not fallen out by chance, as you might imagine; but was produced by the will-power of Cuanduine, acting upon information received from Bergson. That philosopher declares that laughter is the product of the sense of incongruity aroused by the spectacle of the rational creature, man, behaving like an automaton, as he does when he sits down after slipping on a banana skin or starts up after sitting on a pin. On the same principle it should be aroused by the spectacle of man automatically obeying economic laws invented by his own stupidity. But no matter. Professor Juggins had been brought to such a state of mindlessness in the course of getting mastered by his subject, that he fell completely under the dominion of Cuanduine's will, though exercised at a distance of above a hundred miles. When Cuanduine said 'trip' he tripped; when he told his braces to part, they parted. Thus, in one evening, all the good achieved by the two previous lectures was undone, and Mr Slawmy Cander's hopes were dashed in the dust. To prevent a recurrence of the disaster, he gave orders that the carpet at the studio should be well tacked down, that no chairs or waste-paper baskets be left about, and that the lecturers should be provided with brand new braces tested beforehand by himself.

Cuanduine, however, had another shot in his locker. When on the following night Professor Swallowdown appeared on the screen, the spectators were amazed to see that he was wearing a false nose, check trousers, a fawn coat with a huge sunflower in the buttonhole, a ginger-coloured wig, and an ancient bowler hat three sizes too small for him. He rushed on to the platform carrying an enormous green gamp, and shouting: 'Cheerio, boys and girls! Here we are again! Cheerio!' Then he pulled a concertina out of his coat tails, and, after a preliminary *pas seul*, struck up the following song:

'Sing a song of plenty,
  A planet full of fools:
Everybody starving
  By sound financial rules.
While the folk were starving
  The banks paid dividends.
What a pretty state of things
  To live among, my friends.'

At this point the manager of the station rushed in, and, catching Professor Swallowdown by the coat tails, tried to drag him from the studio.

'Naughty! Naughty!' said Professor Swallowdown playfully, slapping at him with his gamp. Then, as the manager still persisted in interrupting, he gave him a push in the face that sent him reeling throught the doorway, and the audience heard nineteen terrific bumps as he went headlong down the stairs, followed by a crash of broken glass. Professor Swallowdown, with a beaming smile of self-satisfaction, lifted his hat and resumed his song:

'The Banker in his counting-house
  Was counting out his money;
The land was overflowing
  With bread and milk and honey;
The shops were full of good things,
  The factories likewise:
The Banker shut his books and said:
  "We must economise."

'Nothing like economy, girls, eh, what?' said Professor Swallowdown, descending to patter. 'Keep the boys up to it, my dears. Why go to Woolworth's for the ring when you can get curtain-rings at any ironmonger's for a penny a dozen? Like my hat, boys? I borrowed it from the scarecrow to come out to-night, but I'll have to give it back in the morning, or the sparrows will be eating the groundsel.'

Here the Professor spun the hat skilfully on one finger, which suddenly went through the crown. 'Tch! Tch! Tch!' he ejaculated sadly. 'That's because I'm always talking through it. I'm an economist, you know. Professor Swahollowdown, the famous Ecohonomist.' He made a gesture as if to smooth down his Adam's apple, and said: 'Prosy stuff, economics—What! Perhaps you'd prefer to hear my little poem, The Oyster.

'The sun was shining brightly
  Upon the fields below:
He did his very best to make
  The corn and fruit to grow;
And that was wrong because it brings
  The prices down, you know.

The corn was ripening in the fields,
  The fruit upon the tree;
The shops were full, and laden ships
  Were sailing on the sea:
All things had a fictitious look
  Of fair prosperity;
And that was wrong because the world
  Was ruined utterly.

The Banker and Economist
  Were walking hand in hand.
They wept like anything to see
  Such plenty in the land.
"If this were only stopped" they said,
  "The prospect *would* be grand!"

"If seven pests or seven plagues
  Were loosened every year,
I think" said the Economist
  "That things would then be dear."
"I wonder" said the Banker,
  And wiped away a tear.

"Consumer, come and walk with us"
  They both did make request.
"The time has come to tell you what
  We think for you is best."
"O thank you" the Consumer said
  With lively interest.

"And first" said the Economist
  "It's needful to explain
The economic laws which prove
  That trade must wax and wane,
And why abundance is a curse,
  And scarcity a gain."

"But not to me" the man replied,
  Turning a little white.
"Such dismal scientific stuff
  Would stupefy me quite.
I'll take it all on trust because
  I know you must be right."

Two winking eyes behind the back
  Of that Consumer met,
As if to say: "This blessed boob
  Has asked for what he'll get."
"Old chap" said the Economist,
  "Your trust you won't regret.

"This gross abundance that you see
  Before your hungry eyes
Has ruined all the primary
  Producing industries:
And so, to set things right again,
  We must economise.

"And first we'll make a cut in costs
  By cutting down your screw,
And next we'll cut production down
  Till prices rise anew.
Then, though you'll have less goods to buy,
  More work you'll have to do."

"Right oh!" the good Consumer said
  (A sturdy Briton he),
And, smiling bravely, yielded up
  His share of L.S.D.
By such contraction wages show
  Their elasticity.

"It seems a shame" the Banker said
  "To play him such a prank."
With sobs and tears he cancelled out
  A credit at the bank:
And that was right, unless you are
  A monetary crank.

"Consumer" said that pleasant pair,
  "We've had a useful day.
Shall we be trotting home again?"
  But nothing did he say:
And that was right enough because
  He'd faded quite away.'

Mr Slawmy Cander, sitting over his coffee, was a little late in switching on the wireless, and so he plunged *in medias res* when Professor Swallowdown was at the second verse of his song. Straightway he was thrown into the most hideous rage that ever distorted a financial countenance. He let out a bellow of wrath, and dashed for the telephone, kicking and cuffing everybody who got in his way. By his orders a flying squadron of police was at once rushed to the studio, and the unfortunate Mr Swallowdown, in the midst of kissing hands to the audience at the conclusion of his recitation, was dragged out, bundled into a Black Maria, and hurried into the potentate's presence.

CHAPTER X

How Professor Swallowdown was hauled over the Coals: and how Cuanduine broke the third of his geasa

'WHAT the devil do you mean by it, sir?' yelled Mr Slawmy Cander.

'What do I mean by what?' asked the Professor innocently.

Instead of answering, Mr Cander propelled him in front of a mirror, shouting: 'Just look at yourself, you bleating goat. What the blazes do you mean by this tomfoolery?'

When Professor Swallowdown caught sight of his get up, his jaw dropped, and he blushed like a schoolgirl. 'What on earth have I been up to?' he cried.

'What indeed, you miserable buffoon! You and your hat, and your sparrows, and your groundsel!'

The Economist looked blank. 'Have I made a faux pas?' he asked.

'A faux pas!' screamed the Banker. 'A faux pas, you ineffable ass! You've given the whole show away.

'With sobs and tears he cancelled out
A credit at the bank—

'Yah! You zany.'

'Good heavens' gasped the Economist. 'You don't mean to say I've been reciting *poetry*?'

'Of the most touching kind' said the Banker.

'Not to mention song, *and* dance, *and* concertina obligato.'

The unhappy Economist here caught a second glance of himself in the mirror, and in a spasm of shame dashed his hat and wig on the floor, sank into a chair, and covered his face with his hands.

'I'm ruined' he said. 'I had a vague notion something was wrong. I had a headache, and wasn't quite conscious of what I was saying.'

'You must have been drunk' said the Banker.

'O no' protested the Economist. 'I had a glass of white wine with my dinner. Not a drop more of anything.'

'Then there's no excuse for you at all' said Mr Cander.

Professor Swallowdown groaned again. 'I cannot tell what came over me' he said. 'I had prepared a most beautiful, comforting, and constructive speech, proving that while unemployment on its present disastrous scale is a calamity which all men of goodwill must seek to remedy, nevertheless it would not do to abolish it altogether. A society in which everybody was absolutely certain that he would always have a job would be a society without change, a dead society. There would be no spice to life, no adventure, no excitement, nothing to relieve the intolerable monotony of existence. It would be a dull, dreary, miserable life of ineffable boredom—'

'There was no need to lay it on quite so thick as that' objected Mr Cander.

'Oh?' said the Professor timidly. 'Is that—is that a little—unorthodox?'

'No. But, as it happens, I've got a plan to abolish unemployment altogether.'

'I'm sorry' said the Professor.

'Never mind' said Mr Cander. 'That wasn't the speech you delivered anyway.'

The Professor blushed, and groaned again.

'Since you weren't drunk, and you aren't mad' said Mr Cander, 'I can only think of one explanation of your behaviour. Putting two and two together—that is, Juggins's collapse last night, and your tomfoolery just now—I guess there's some hanky-panky afoot, and that fellow Coondinner is at the bottom of it. Hypnotism: that's what it is.'

'That's right' said Professor Swallowdown. 'I felt hypnotised. I was conscious of some irresistible force dragging me on—'

'Well, we've got to see it doesn't happen again. I'll have the studio surrounded with insulating material to keep out psychic influences, and, to make sure, I'll have some police handy to carry our man off if he begins to say anything silly.'

This plan was carried out, and from thenceforward the lectures proceeded harmoniously. On the next night, Professor Darkness declared that the only possible solution of their difficulties was to treat all their problems as essentially One Big World Problem, to be solved by a Planned Economy. Within such a plan the birds would find their place; but any attempt to deal with them at the moment in piecemeal fashion, as if their distribution could be carried out without reference to other factors, would only add to the existing confusion.

Professor Darkness was followed by Professor tone, who declared that the liberation of the birds ould have disastrous repercussions on trade nd industry. 'Trade' said he 'is a delicately alanced process of exchange. Industrial activity epends on the maintenance of exchange: and we ave found to our cost that any large movements of oods in one direction without exchange checks hat activity and causes depression. The transference f the birds from America to the other countries vould have exactly the same effect as the payment f war debts and reparations. As it would promote o reciprocal industrial activity, it would disrganise the whole financial system.

'It may be good for individuals to receive somehing for nothing—ha! ha! but to nations it is uinous. Indeed the best way to destroy a hostile ountry is not to make war on it, but to flood it vith goods and take no payment whatever. In a very ew weeks millions of its people would be starving, nd the government would be compelled to sue for eace.

'To be quite serious' resumed the Professor, we must remember that *nations live by their exports*. The restoration of the normal export trade of the vorld, and the reduction of all imports, is therefore he first essential of stability. That rules out all question of liberating the birds. The only country vhich would gain anything would be the exporting country—America. All the others would have their lready unfavourable trade balances tilted still more recariously against them.'

Cuanduine had listened to these two lectures in

patience, though not without amazement at th shifts of argument to which men of intellect an learning could be driven by not knowing wha they were talking about. But at this crownin piece of folly his anger came upon him, and h leaped at his microphone as if it had been a hostil machine gun, and cried out to the people of th world:

'What devil hath twisted the minds of thes fellows that such utterances can come from them How in the name of Beelzebub can a country b enriched by what it gives away, and impoverishe by what it receives? O people, I think you must b bewitched if you can believe such things. But hark you now. What do you think you live for? Is it to toi with pick and spade, to serve in shops, to pul the levers of machines, and to sit on office stools Or is it rather to live comfortably or adventurously according to your choice, to laugh and to love to enjoy sunshine and flowers and the song o birds, and to give glory to your heavenly Father Then if these things can only be had in return fo work, well and good: do the work that lies to hanc to produce them. But if the work can be done by machines, better still: you will have more time t live.'

By this speech Cuanduine broke the third o his geasa, namely, not to contend with the Headles Men of the Wood: for the Economists were headles men, wandering in a dark forest of dead ideas and the only weapon that could avail against them was laughter. The wisdom of the Gods in laying this geis upon him was quickly shown. For the Devil entered into the heart of a comfortable fat fellow sitting in a drawing-room in Kensington, who went to his microphone and shouted:

'Who is to do the dirty-work in this Utopia of yours?'

Cuanduine answered: 'Well, sir, why not you?' Then, as silence followed, he continued: 'Are you not answered? Know then that I gave you that answer because you did not question me truly. For what you really meant by your question was: who *else* shall do the dirty work? only you dared not say it. Therefore, though there is a better answer, you shall not have it, but must rest content with that.'

Now since all the rest of the people knew that they would have asked the question in the same form, they held their peace: but they hated Cuanduine.

Then another listener spoke. It was no other than Mac ui Rudai, who had begun to make good once more. After leaving Cuanduine he had got a job addressing envelopes at a penny a thousand. Then he had taken to making confectionery at home, at which he could easily have earned five pounds a week in his sparetime if he could have got any customers. Then one day a friend had said to him: 'If you are disappointed with your position and prospects, why not be a Salesman? It's a pleasant job and a well-paid one.' Mac ui Rudai said 'Right Oh!' and the friend took him along to the Modern School of Selling. Afterwards he peddled tea from door to door for a year, then stockings and lingerie for another year, then vacuum cleaners, then wireless sets. He then came to the conclusion that selling was a wash-out, and set up in business as the Ultra-Modern School of Selling, which was making good, as I have said. He cried out now to his microphone in answer to Cuanduine:

'Sure, if we've nothing to do, we'll all go to the devil entirely.'

'What?' said Cuanduine. 'Are you all such a lot of besotted insensate fools as that? God knows I do not think any of you very wise or virtuous, but have you no common sense?'

'Not a grain' said the people, for now the devil had them all by the ear. 'We will do nothing but by compulsion. We are a very scurvy crowd, a very filthy crew.'

Then there was vouchsafed to Cuanduine a vision of the people of the world sitting listening to him and he saw them all as a wretched shambling crawling lot of counterparts of Mac ui Rudai. With that he gave a laugh, and cared not a whit what became of them.

The next morning he went early to Castle Goshawk, and with a stroke of the Cruaidin Cailidcheann he ripped open the great aviary, and said to the birds: 'Now, my beauties, you are free and my task in the world is done.' And he sang this song:

'Away! Away!
  Your wings spread wide.
On the winds of the world
  In freedom ride.

Field and forest
  And vale and hill,
Moor and meadow
  With music fill.

Freedom and joy
  And youth again
Awake ye now
  In the hearts of men.'

The birds, however, were so much accustomed to captivity that they would not stir, and pecked him viciously when he tried to shoo them forth.

CHAPTER XI

Professor Gudgeon propounds a Panacea

THAT same evening the world was all agog to hear the solution of its difficulties from the lips of Professor Gudgeon, who, promptly upon his hour, strutted to the microphone and spoke as follows:

'Ladies and gentlemen, there is one lesson which you will have gathered from all the lectures by those who have preceded me. That is the lesson, which cannot be too often repeated, that *a nation lives by its exports*. The nations, indeed, have learnt this lesson only too well, and interpreted it in an extreme sense which has defeated its own ends. They all want to export, and they all refuse tc import: the result being that none of them is now able to enrich itself by getting rid of its goods.

'In such circumstances what can we do? Th answer is that we must treat the difficulty not a a number of national problems, but as One Big World Problem. The world itself must find a export market. But where? That is the questio I propose to answer to-night.'

The lecturer paused to sip some water, while th world held its breath.

'Gentlemen' proceeded Mr Gudgeon, 'th market has been found. While cranks and dreamer and idealists have been content with destructiv criticism, and with putting forward proposal which were obviously impracticable, the plain business men, assisted by those economists whose orthodoxy has been such a source of derision to their opponents, have been working. That work has been crowned with success, and its results will now be put before you.'

Mr Gudgeon took another gulp of water, which unfortunately went the wrong way, so that a full minute went by before an expectant world could hear the message of salvation.

'The market, ladies and gentlemen' said Mr Gudgeon when he had recovered, 'is supplied by an old and valued ally of ours, our comrade in prosperity and adversity, one whose friendly face never fails to smile upon us in the darkest night. I refer, ladies and gentlemen, to the Moon.'

Mr Gudgeon paused dramatically, and went on:

'I have no doubt, ladies and gentlemen, that that announcement has taken you all by surprise. Some of you, indeed, will be incredulous. You have all been accustomed to believe that the moon is too far away to be reached, and that, even if reached, it is uninhabitable. That, however, is not true. The moon has actually been visited, and found to be not only habitable, but inhabited. The belief of astronomers that it could not sustain life arose from their failure to discover any atmosphere upon it. This, however, was due to the imperfection of their instruments, for we now know that the moon has an atmosphere, of no great depth it is true, and perhaps more rarified than ours, but sufficient for the needs of a population of beings very similar to ourselves.

'They are an extremely primitive people, though

by no means savages. That is to say, they live a very simple life, with few wants, and with no mechanical equipment of any kind; but so far as a hasty observation can judge, they are peaceable and inoffensive. I need hardly explain what ideal conditions of trading are possible with a people like that.' (Cheers).

'This discovery' went on Mr Gudgeon 'is the work of a man of whom our race may well feel proud. Step forward, Mr Aloysius O'Kennedy.'

CHAPTER XII

The Periplous of Mr Aloysius O'Kennedy

WHEN Mr Aloysius O'Kennedy's soul rejoined his body after its voyage among the stars, he found his reunited self without a job; for his manager, Mr Gallagher, would not believe a word of his story, and sacked him on the spot. In this exigency it occurred to him that he might put his adventures into a book, and so make his fortune. He therefore borrowed paper and money from the Philosopher, and asked his advice how to proceed.

'There is no better course for a young author' replied the Philosopher 'than that which was commended by the King of Hearts to the White Rabbit. Begin at the beginning, go on till you came to the end, and then stop.'

Mr O'Kennedy, taking this counsel, produced a very commendable book indeed: for in truth anybody can make a book who has something to say. Nevertheless it was not well received by the publishers, a dozen of whom rejected it either without comment, or with a note to the effect that it was too fantastic. The thirteenth, however, was of a more enterprising sort. Having invited Mr O'Kennedy to call on him, he said: 'Young man, I like your book. There's good stuff in it. But you don't know how to catch your public. They don't want a lot of blurb about manners and customs.

They want human interest—romance and adventure and that sort of thing, do you see?'

Mr O'Kennedy said: 'Yes.'

'Now I tell you what I'll do' said the publisher. 'Just you take this manuscript home with you, and cut out all the chapters about religion and science, politics, economics, law, education, and so on, and all the long descriptions. Then work up the love interest a bit more, and stick in a few more exciting adventures. If you do that, I'll publish it, and I wouldn't be surprised if it turns out a seller.'

Mr O'Kennedy did as he was asked; the sales went to more than a hundred thousand copies; and he found himself in possession of a handsome income, on which he lived right royally for a number of years. In time, however, his book was displaced in public favour by worse ones, and he found himself becoming hard up, and without a notion how to write another. In this difficulty he remembered a thing he had seen on his voyage. In passing the Moon, he had observed its inhabitants, and it now occurred to him that if he could go back there and capture some of them he could exhibit them on the halls and so make another fortune. Compared with the immense distance of Rathé, the journey to the Moon seemed but a trifle, and he thought it could be accomplished by airplane.

He broached the subject to a business acquaintance forthwith, but the latter only laughed at his story, and said that, even if it were true, it would be impossible to reach the Moon, as there was no air on the way. Mr O'Kennedy's hopes being thus dashed, he let the matter drop until the contest between Cuanduine and Mr Slawmy Cander put a new idea into his head. Flying to America, he sent a copy of his book to Mr Cander with an accompanying note saying that he had a plan against Cuanduine, and soliciting an interview.

Mr Cander, being a little unsure of himself at that stage of the contest, was ready to welcome assistance from any quarter, and graciously granted the young man's request.

'I had read your book before you sent it to me' he said after greeting him, 'and found it most entertaining.'

'Well, sir' said Mr O'Kennedy 'what I wanted to tell you was this. That book is a true book. I mean, it isn't a novel.'

'You don't mean to say that it really happened?' said Mr Cander, looking at him hard.

'That, sir, is just what I do mean' said Mr O'Kennedy, 'though I dare say you'll find it hard to believe it. I've actually been in Rathé.'

Now Mr Slawmy Cander was the shrewdest man in the world. It was clear to him that if the book was not true, it was the work of a very fertile imagination; and it was clearer still that Mr O'Kennedy was a man without a spark of imagination of any sort. So he said: 'Very well. Let us take that for granted. How does it affect the present situation?'

Mr O'Kennedy then told him of the men he had seen in the Moon, and suggested that the world would find in the satellite a useful export market, 'which I have no doubt' he said 'would be very profitable to us, as these primitive people will hardly know much about business.'

'Very true, my young friend' replied Mr Cander, 'but how do you imagine we are to get there?'

'Well, your worship' said Mr O'Kennedy 'this fellow Cuanduine has an airplane which is evidently magical. Couldn't we get hold of it, and so cook his goose and help ourselves at the same time?'

'I doubt if we could fly it' said Mr Cander. 'But I've thought of a better plan.—Mr Lickspit' said he, turning to a secretary at the other end of the room, 'do you remember a young engineer who used to be always pestering us to finance some invention of his for flying to the Moon? You might look him up if he's still alive?'

Searchers were accordingly sent out, and after a while the inventor was found dying in a workhouse infirmary. Mr Cander bought his patent, and next day set a factory to work on a fleet of machines. It was a smart piece of work altogether.

CHAPTER XIII

How they rounded the corner and came in sight of prosperity

MR O'KENNEDY delivered his speech to the multitude with such aggressiveness and self-confidence as carried immediate conviction: for in the interim he had attended a school of salesmanship, where he took an intensive course for the development of pep, punch, personality, persuasive talk, and methods of overcoming sales-resistance. He put the goods over all right, I tell you.

Afterwards Mr Gudgeon resumed his discourse, and told how a fleet of machines capable of flying to the Moon was already under construction and would be ready in the immediate future. 'A golden prospect now lies before us' he said. 'The primitive lunar population will provide a constant market for the sales of our manufactured goods, thus giving abundant and permanent employment to all our workers. In return we shall buy raw materials from the Selenites, the working up of which in our factories will give further employment. The lunar natives wear garments of a singularly beautiful fabric made from some native plant. We shall import this plant, spin the fabric, and manufacture the garments, and I have very little doubt that our more modern methods will soon drive the native manufacturers out of the market. We shall thus win for ourselves the whole of the enormous volume of employment required to clothe an entire world. Other fruitful sources of trade will, no doubt, follow, but this will suffice for the present. From this moment we can say with every confidence that prosperity is no longer round the corner, but actually in sight.'

Having thus spoken, Mr Gudgeon called for three cheers for High Finance, which were given right lustily. He then sat down rosy with triumph. From that moment the world fairly danced with optimism. Here was employment beyond its wildest dreams; enough to keep them toiling and moiling from morn to night to the end of their lives. Everybody went about beaming with smiles. Perfect strangers shook hands in the streets and slapped each other on the back. Girls gave away kisses to all comers. Men and women of all ages went frantic with joy, and cavorted around crying ecstatically: 'Work! Work! Work!' Economists were seized upon by enthusiastic mobs and carried shoulder high through the streets. Not till the end of a week of wild rejoicing did the routine of normal life return.

There was universal agreement that the lunar trade would inaugurate an era of unexampled prosperity. The only difference of opinion was on the question whether the development of the new field should be left to the free operation of private enterprise (as the capitalists required) or should be undertaken by a Government department (as the Socialists demanded). Both parties, however, were equally agreed that in the financial arrangements they must be guided by the skill, experience, and knowledge of Mr Slawmy Cander.

CHAPTER XIV

The further machinations of Mr Slawmy Cander

WHILE world affairs thus prospered, care still lay at the heart of Mr Slawmy Cander; for he could not believe that Cuanduine would submit tamely to his defeat, and feared that he might yet deal him some vengeful blow. Moreover he had been informed that, after his failure to liberate the birds, the hero had flown from Castle Goshawk in his airplane and had not been seen since; which, Mr Cander felt, boded some secret preparation.

As he thus pondered, there came to him young 'One-Eye' Slughorn, son of 'Scab,' who spoke as follows:

'Say, bo, I guess it ain't gonna suit your racket if this guy Coondinner goes rampaging round the world in his lil ole sky-broncho, eh? What you gonna do if he hangs around your trade routes holding up your moonships?'

'I have been considering that problem' replied Mr Cander.

'I guessed you was' said One-Eye. 'And now see here, bo. You and me's got one interest in this racket. You gotta save your business: I got it in for him for bumping off my dad. What you gotta say to that?'

'Let's get down to it' said Mr Slawmy Cander.

'You're the sorta guy I like' said One-Eye, seating himself. 'Now, what's your proposition?'

'What's yours?' said Mr Cander.

One-Eye laughed. 'Close as a clam' said he. 'Good. I like that. Now, here's what I say. This guy's gotta be bumped off, and it ain't easy work. I got forty planes, not real fighters, but light ones for rum-work. That ain't enough against Coondinner. He can beat five hundred—maybe more: say five-fifty for a safe margin. Now what do you say to putting up the extra four-ninety?'

'I haven't got them' said Mr Slawmy Cander. 'Of course I could build them in a few weeks, but the devil knows what he mightn't do in that time.'

'Wal, what's *your* proposition?' said One-Eye.

'I haven't had time to think of one yet' replied Mr Cander. 'But say: what do you think of this? The fellow has a wife and children living in a mountain valley somewhere in Europe. Suppose you slip over with a party of bombers and mop them up. He'll hear about it at once and go flying back for vengeance. Meanwhile you hide yourselves somewhere convenient. When he finds you've gone, he'll leave his plane to take a last look at his ruined home and the bodies of his dear ones. That's your chance, and if you don't get him you aren't fit to hunt butterflies.'

Thus spoke Mr Slawmy Cander: and if you will not believe that any responsible pillar of Finance could concoct so villainous a plot, I cannot help it. I can only say that Mr Cander would have been indeed squeamish to hesitate about blotting out one family with bombs, seeing that he had blotted out thousands in the course of his life by merely keeping money short. One-eye, for his part, thought the plan an excellent one, and said: 'O.K., Chief. I'll see it through.'

Afterwards Mr Cander went out for a stroll, first smilingly posing on his doorstep for a battalion of press photographers. There are three hateful things in the world, two that make the blood run cold, and one that makes it boil: the hiss of a snake, the snarl of a Tasmanian devil, and the smile of a banker.

CHAPTER XV

The youthful exploits of One-Eye Slughorn, and of his lieutenants

ONE-EYE Slughorn was but twenty-three years old at this time; yet he had killed more men than many a grizzled warrior twice his age. Trained to warfare from his earliest years under the watchful care of his father, he was reputed to be quicker on the draw than any guy in Chicago. He carried a gun in each of his hip pockets, another in each side pocket, two more in holsters at his jewelled belt, and a handgrenade in his breast pocket for emergencies. Up his sleeve was a very neat apparatus containing poison gas. He always wore a spotless white waistcoat with emerald buttons, and smoked a cigar two feet long. He had got his name because his left eye had been scratched out by one of his doxies in one of her tantrums.

The said One-Eye was by nature a man of quick wit, fertile in expedients, and audacious in executing them. He had acquired also, from the philosophical training of his excellent father, a serene and lofty contempt of human life, with its littleness and lack of meaning. Both these qualities he displayed from his earliest years. One day, when he was not yet fourteen, he sprayed a whole street of Chicago with poison gas in order to do in an enemy whom he believed to be walking there. When he was arrested a few days later, he escaped punishment by the following device. Asking permission to telephone to his lawyer, he rang up the Chief Justice of the state, and, declaring himself to be Kinch Bugbear (then Crime King) said: 'Now see here, Judge. A young follower of mine, One-Eye Slughorn, has just been copped for three hundred and sixty-nine murders in Ninety-ninth Street. I want him set free at once.' 'O.K., Chief' replied the Chief Justice, and that same evening One-Eye was restored to his anxious parents. Many such tales of his youthful wit and daring are told in other books.

His first lieutenant, 'Mug' Jenkins, was a much older man, who, starting his career under less favourable circumstances, had worked his way up from the ranks by sheer character and personality. The son of middle-class parents, he had been educated at one of the principal public schools in England, where his inability to master the elements of academic learning had earned him the name that stuck to him through life, as well as frequent thrashings from his teachers. The weight of his brain, indeed, was but twenty-six ounces, and his facial angle not above forty-five degrees, which, if you will perform the necessary measurements, you will find is somewhat less than your own. 'Twas impossible to get him to understand that *amo* means *I love* by any other method than the diligent hammering of his posterior, which, in the teeth of all cranks and sentimentalists, experienced pedagogues do rightly declare to be the true seat of learning. Likewise, it was only by frequent lambasting that the youngster could be convinced that rules are meant to be kept, or at least to act as if so convinced, which is the desired end of all authority.

Having thus gone through the whole curriculum, the youth left school with high hopes, having already observed that in the adult world there was much to do that involved no flagellatory penalty. Being then eighteen, he was seized one day with the heats of carnal lust, for the satisfaction of which it seemed to him but natural to ravish a girl in some obscure place and then take to his heels. By some mischance he was identified by his victim, and brought to trial. The magistrate, however, in consideration of his parents' position, his youthful age, and the fact that he was a first offender, treated him leniently, sentencing him to a brief imprisonment and a few strokes of the birch; which were afterwards supplemented by a vigorous fustigation from his father for the disgrace he had brought upon the family.

Not long afterwards his father went bankrupt in consequence of a trade depression, and blew out his brains. Young Jenkins, being thus thrown on the world without resources, could think of nothing else to do but to hold up and rob a bank messenger. Again he was brought to book, and sent to prison, from which he emerged with one fixed resolution, that never again would his victim have an opportunity to testify against him. His policy thenceforward was to attack his prey without warning, stunning him from behind with a sandbag or life-preserver, by which means he prospered exceedingly for a time. At length, however, his luck changed. He botched a job badly, was caught, convicted, and sentenced to seven years and a flogging. Having served his time, he resumed his interrupted career, but, being now well watched, was very quickly copped, flogged again, and imprisoned again.

His next spell of liberty was longer. His arm, well trained in the use of the pick, fell with unerring accuracy and power, sometimes killing his victims, but more often maiming them for life. His cunning too had been developed by the constant use of tricks to evade prison discipline, so that he left no traces, and none of these deeds was ever brought home to him. At last, however, a singular misfortune brought his career once more to a halt. In robbing a rural bank he had the ill luck to come up against a caretaker who was an ex-prizefighter. Grown careless by constant success, he foolishly attacked him in front, and his first wallop failed to knock the man out. He eventually succeeded in kicking him into insensibility, but not before the caretaker had gouged out his assailant's eye. Maddened with pain, Jenkins made no attempt to hide himself, and was easily captured.

The magistrate before whom he was brought was a retired colonel of the tough old school. 'Thomas Jenkins' he said, 'you are a man with a very bad record. You have spent nearly half your life in prison, and you have been flogged several times, yet it has not done you a scrap of good. I simply cannot understand it. There is nothing for it but to flog and imprison you again.'

This gentleman afterwards, in the evening of his days, wrote a book about crime and criminals, in which he said:

'If the "cat" were applied to a wider variety of offences, it would have a most salutary effect. There is a tendency to be squeamish over sentencing a man to be flogged, and not a few of the Justices spoil the effect by reducing the punishment to a minimum. Eighteen strokes is the really effective minimum; for it is those that come after the first sixteen or so that finally decide a man never to risk getting the "cat" again.'

In another part of the same book he said: 'I wish to make a protest against the soft, sloppy sentiment that is creeping into prison methods. There is much to be said for putting the fear of God into prisoners. In some ways it is a pity that the treadmill was abolished, for it was one of the things that made prisons unpleasant, instead of the comfortable homes from home that they now are—far more comfortable, indeed, than the houses of many honest working men.'

It is to be feared that the gallant colonel takes too one-sided a view, and leaves out of account the very important question whether we can really *afford* to discourage crime. Men like Mr Jenkins give employment to immense numbers of policemen, detectives, warders, narks, prison inspectors, floggers, receivers, solicitors, barristers, magistrates, and others, whose livelihood is entirely dependant on their activities: which is more than can be said for the honest men so naïvely pitied by the colonel, who so far from employing others, have much ado to get employment for themselves. They also provide a valuable market for numerous industries, such as the prison clothing trade, the skilly trade, the pick and shovel trade, the handcuff trade (an important consideration to the sorely depressed steel industry), the triangle manufacturers, the cat-o'-nine-tail manufacturers, and many others; not to mention the purveyors of jemmies and other articles of the burglars' kit. Crime, therefore, is an asset which cannot lightly be dispensed with in these difficult times; but the problem of how it can best be exploited in the general interest I must leave to the economists, as I have my story to tell.

Jenkins, having been duly flogged and incarcerated, after receiving some more floggings for sundry breaches of prison discipline, presently succeeded in murdering a warder and making his escape to America, where he joined Scab Slughorn's gang, and soon became his right-hand man.

Next to him in command was the Honourable Percy Popinjay (pronounced Ponjee), a man of somewhat different stamp. Of an ancient but decayed family, his parents had been unable to afford him a career in the Army, and he had no aptitude for business even if a job could have been found for him. Therefore, thinking with a certain knight of whom Froissart tells, that to rob and pill is a good life, or at least a better life than to be robbed and pilled, he sought service under Scab Slughorn, and soon rose rapidly in purse and reputation. He was a young fellow of pleasing address and knightly courtesy, insomuch that ladies declared it a pleasure to be held up by him. He killed, too, in a light-hearted fashion that was very agreeable to watch, an accomplishment that he had picked up on the moors in his youth, when he had spent many happy days slaughtering birds. His ordinary employment was in picking off young bridegrooms at church doors, and carrying off their wives for Slughorn's bed.

These were the men who led the expedition for the destruction of Cuanduine. They picked their crews very carefully. Every man they chose was the son and grandson of gunmen, and had at least seven killings to his credit. Before they started, One-Eye raised a golden catafalque to the memory of his father, and sacrificed a million-dollar bill on an altar before it.

CHAPTER XVI

How Cuanduine broke the gunmen at the knees

CUANDUINE meanwhile had gone apart into the Adirondacks to rest his spirit and to contemplate the heavens. There he abode many days, and his heart grew heavy, for he guessed that he had broken his geasa, and that the Gods had forsaken him. On the tenth day a cold fear entered into his soul, and the whisper of a thought that his wife and children were in danger. At that he strode to the great airplane Poliorketes, and, springing on board, he tried to set him going. But the engine was grown cold through long standing in the mountain air, and the oil congealed in the bearings, so that he refused to move.

'Alas, my plane' said Cuanduine, 'will you also fail me?' Then, as he went to examine the engine, he cut his hand against the casing, and he said: 'It seems that you are hanging back from the fight, Poliorketes, that you bite the hand that would drive you.'

At these words the great airplane Poliorketes shook with anger, so that with the heat he engendered his engine began to run, and he took the air like a bird that has been long caged, and headed for the Atlantic. Cuanduine noticed that his flight was not so speedy as of old, for he had neglected to look after him while he was arguing with the people; so he said: 'Alack, my plane, I fear we may be too late for what we seek to avert. On, my beauty.'

Poliorketes mended his pace after that, and sped across the ocean waves as he had done in their days of triumph. Midway a fog enveloped them, so that it seemed that evil spirits compassed them about to hold them back; but the great airplane put forth his strength and mounted above the choking vapours into the sunlight.

'On, on, my valiant steed' cried Cuanduine. 'Fail me not now, and afterwards you shall have rest for ever.'

At length they sighted the coasts of Europe. Blood-red lay its plains before them in the setting sun. 'On, on' cried Cuanduine again. 'They shall be redder before nightfall, for I smell villainy at hand.'

The great airplane Poliorketes bounded like a horse at the voice of his master, and rushed forward with such untiring energy that finally, to shorten the tale of a long hunt, he overhauled Slughorn's bloodthirsty flyers just as they were opening their cases of bombs in preparation for the coming sport. The thugs needed no second glance to tell them who was on their track; for the wings of the great airplane Poliorketes flashed in the sunrays, and the roar of his propeller was horrible to hear. At once there arose yells of terror and cries of 'treachery,' and many turned their guns on one another. From that instant the cut-throats had but one aim in life, namely, to find some deep dark hole in which to hide themselves from the wrath of Cuanduine. The fleet broke up like a crowd in a zoo when a lion is loose, and each plane made off as hard as individual enterprise could drive it. Slughorn himself, indeed, for the sake of his reputation, made some offer to bring his own plane into action; so also did the Honourable Percy Popinjay, remembering the family traditions; but their men mutinied and insisted on flying with the rest.

Cuanduine laughed when he saw them scatter. 'These foes are unworthy of death' said he, and, drawing the Cruaidin Cailidcheann, he brandished it about his head till the point of it stretched to the horizon. Then he whirled it in circles around the fleet so that each plane as it bolted was stopped short and driven back among its fellows like rats flying from the stack at a threshing. Not a solitary machine of them escaped, and at last they were all huddled together in a pitiful welter of confusion and terror beneath the dread shadow of the great airplane Poliorketes. 'Down to the ground with you now' called out Cuanduine, 'and await my commands.'

At once they made haste to obey, and, leaving their machines, they gathered together in a pale trembling flock, while the hero descended at his leisure.

'Now, you curs' said he, approaching them, 'I will teach you what fear is. For, though you have just had a taste of it, it is needful that you get your bellyful.' With that he raised the Cruaidin Cailidcheann, and gave a stroke above the heads of the crowd so as to shear off the hair of every man in it, from one ear to the other, yet without drawing a drop of blood: as we read that his father did to Etarcomal in the tale of the Táin. Then, while they were yet gasping, he gave a second stroke, whereby he cut away the sod from under the soles of their feet, so that they all fell flat on their backs.

'Rise up again, you scum of the earth' cried

Cuanduine at that, 'for I have not finished with you yet.' Then, when they had scrambled to their feet, he made play with the Cruaidin Cailidcheann about their heads, whirling it in and out among them till it flashed like lightning, and the steel sang a terrible song in their shuddering ears. They shivered till their knees knocked and their teeth clacked. Their faces went white as paper, their tongues as dry. Their blood turned to water, and their organs of manhood shrivelled up like little withered nuts in their sacs. At last they all fell in a heap, and lay flopping and gasping like a pile of landed fish.

Cuanduine thereupon left off his play, and said: 'Now, you spawn of hell, you know what fear is. Be off home with you, and tell Mr Cander what it feels like.'

It was some time before the thugs could rise to their feet and shamble off to find what shelter they could for the night. Cuanduine paid them no more attention; but it is recorded that their nerves were so wrecked from their experience that from thenceforward not a man of them could ever handle a gun, nor even so much as look at one without a scream of horror. Indeed it is said by some of good authority that it was many years before any of them could keep his hand steady enough to use a knife and fork. Slughorn himself, repenting of his sins, entered a monastery, from which he was soon expelled for excessive devotion. 'Mug' Jenkins went into the desert, where he died presently of self-flagellation. The Honourable Percy Popinjay founded a society for the Prevention of Cruelty to Vegetables, and took a solemn vow never again to eat food that had not died a natural death.

CHAPTER XVII

How Cuanduine went home

THE next day Cuanduine went home to the Golden Valley. As he crossed the rim of the hills he saw of a sudden that the appearance of the place was changed. The guardian Gods had departed: no nymphs played in the river, no dryads in the forest; the pipes of Pan were silent. Alighting from his plane, Cuanduine moved towards the house, and immediately his wife came running forth to greet him with a kiss.

'What has happened while I have been away?' said he. 'Who has disenchanted the valley? And where are my children?'

'Come and see' replied his wife. 'You will find them greatly changed.'

She led him towards the house that the artificers of the Sidhe had built for them, and lo! it was like a suburban villa, very aloof and prosperous. When they entered, they found the four children sprawling in armchairs before a fire. 'That you, dad?' they said without rising or looking round. 'How goes it, old thing?'

Cuanduine's anger kindled. 'Do you dare address your father like that? To your feet, young folk.'

'S'pose we'd better humour the ancient' said one of them, and they all rose languidly and draped themselves about various props.

Cuanduine opened his kingly eyes wide with

astonishment, for he could scarce recognise them or tell one from another. 'Which of you are men?' said he scornfully, 'and which girls?'

'Ho-ho-ho!' laughed one of the more painted pair. 'You *are* out of date, old thing. There are no men and women any longer. Only Moderns.'

'Equal and identical in everything' said another.

'Except that the feminine Modern uses more lipstick and has more right to a good time' said the third.

'Mind if we squat again, old bean?' said the fourth, and they all flopped back into their chairs.

'Wife' said Cuanduine, 'this is the hardest blow that life has dealt me. I came here hoping to find my sons ready to help in making a new world; and I find—this.'

The Moderns laughed.

'The jolly old world is good enough for us' said one.

'So long as it gives youth a chance' said another.

'And keeps up with the times' said the third.

'And provides opportunities to get on' said the fourth.

'I think we ought to tell you' said the first 'that we've all got jobs under the new Lunar Trading Company. I'm a salesman.'

'So am I' said the second.

'I'm an accountant' said the third.

'And I'm an insurance agent' said the fourth.

'Well, I wish you joy of it' said Cuanduine. 'Wife, let us go outside.'

'What is the meaning of this?' he asked as they walked down the valley. 'I cannot believe it is your training.'

'No more than yours, my love' replied she. 'By our own wisdom we left them free, and if we do not like the ways they have chosen, we must even lump them.'

'But why did they choose these ways?' asked Cuanduine.

'Truly, I cannot tell' replied his wife. 'But indeed the change began from the first day they left the valley to see what they called Life. When they came back they said they must move with the times, and moved as you have seen.'

'Alas!' said Cuanduine. 'I perceive very clearly that this is no world for you and me. Let us leave it.'

'Let us leave it indeed' replied his wife. 'And the sooner the better.'

'Then let us go at once' said Cuanduine.

They were now come to where the great airplane Poliorketes stood waiting. They went on board forthwith, and Cuanduine said: 'One more brave flight, my steed. We seek a new world among the stars.' Then he started the engine, and Poliorketes soared swiftly skywards. Some shepherds on the hills near by, watching his flight, saw him rise ever higher and higher till he dwindled to a speck that vanished in the blue. What became of the hero thereafter can never be told, for he was never seen again by mortal eye. Whether he found rest in Tir na nOg, or fresh fields for noble deeds in some corporeal world lit by some better sun, or whether he still rides through space in search of his heart's desire, nobody knows.

CHAPTER XVIII

The first expedition to the Moon

NOT long afterwards the Lunar Trading Company's fleet set sail for the Moon amid the acclamations of all mankind. It consisted of a hundred machines, but how they were constructed and by what power they were driven I cannot tell you; for though I have the full specification before me, I cannot make head or tail of it, no more than if it was written in Babylonic cuneiform, having had no education in these matters. The cargo, however, is more to the purpose. Of foodstuffs, they carried a vast store of wheat, oats, rice, barley, butter, eggs, cheese, frozen meat, sugar, tea, coffee, cocoa, preserved fruits, nuts, dried and salted fish, jam, honey, chocolate, and many other good things; with wines, beers, spirits, and a few soft drinks. Of clothing they brought ten million of every sort of garment; also the same number of boots and shoes, hats, and umbrellas. Of household goods, they brought furniture, kitchen utensils, cutlery, chinaware, glassware, carpets, linoleum, with bric-a-brac and whatnots. They brought also motor cars and motor cycles, with parts; airplanes; materials for railway construction; cinematographs; and the complete equipment to start a newspaper to be called The Lunar Daily Express.

After a prosperous journey of forty-two days they approached the surface of the Moon, only to find, to their intense dismay, not only that it was uninhabited, but that it was exactly such an arid inhospitable waste as astronomers had always declared. They cruised around for several days, but there was no change in the prospect: nothing but huge extinct volcanoes, dry rocky plains, and the salt-encrusted beds of long evaporated oceans. At last, however, they passed beyond the bounds of that hemisphere which is visible from the earth, and then came a miraculous transformation. The landscape, indeed, was not so pleasing as in our own world, but, compared with what they had just left, it was a very paradise. A vast plain covered with a soft carpet of moss spread itself as far as the eye could reach. A few tiny streams sparkled through it; and the whole surface was dotted with little wattled huts, the inhabitants of which came running out, without any sign of fear, to watch the landing of the fleet.

On this occasion it was not thought advisable to commence operations, after the customary manner of civilised pioneers, by massacring, enslaving, or plundering the natives: the necessity of obtaining work being regarded as paramount to all other considerations. The traders accordingly advanced with conciliatory gestures, and were kindly welcomed and accorded a suitable piece of ground to encamp on. A professional interpreter who had been sent with the expedition then went off with their hosts to learn the language of the place, which he succeeded in accomplishing, for practical commercial purposes, in a few days. He then proceeded to explain where the expedition had come from.

'No doubt you will find it difficult to believe me' he said, 'but we have come from another world.'

'We did not know there were other worlds' said one of the Selenites. 'But why do you think it would be difficult for us to believe you? Are you accustomed to tell lies?'

'O no. Not at all. I just thought it would be a bit of a stunner to you.'

'It certainly is' replied the Selenite, 'but we can believe you nevertheless, in spite of the mendacity you have confessed to, for it is obvious that you do not belong to this world.'

'Quite right. Well, now that I've broken the ice—'

'The ice broke at sunrise two hundred hours ago' said the Selenites severely.

'I dare say' said the interpreter. 'You needn't pull me up so sharp. I was only speaking metaphorically.'

'Are you a poet?' asked a Selenite.

'O lord, no. But let's be getting on. I mean to say, now we understand each other—'

'But we don't understand each other' objected the Selenites. 'You said you had broken the ice, which is the second lie you have told in half a minute. We shall never understand you at this rate.'

'I didn't mean anything about the ice up here' said the interpreter irritably. 'It was just a manner of speaking.'

'Well, you had better try some other manner. What world have you come from?'

The interpreter became expansive. 'From your constant companion in space, your elder brother world, so to speak, which you can see shining at night from the other side of the moon.'

'We cannot see it' said the Selenites, 'for we never go to the other side.'

'What? Never? None of you?'

'So we have said.'

'How unenterprising' said the interpreter. 'We have explored every inch of our world, no matter how dangerous or inaccessible.'

'We do not think it necessary to give ourselves so much trouble' replied the Selenites.

'Well, if you did' said the interpreter, 'you'd get a magnificent view of our Earth shining like a silver plate.'

'Where?' asked the Selenites.

'Up in the sky, of course.'

'Then what prevents it falling on us?'

The interpreter very nearly burst out laughing.

'Here' he said. 'I'd better give you fellows a lesson in astronomy. The Earth is a round body like an orange, revolving in space——'

'What is an orange?' asked the Selenites.

The interpreter produced one from his pocket, and the Selenites looked at it curiously. 'Like that?' they said. 'I am not surprised you have left it.'

'O, it's not exactly like that' said the interpreter. 'It's bigger, you know—bigger than the Moon in fact—with land and water on it, and all that sort of thing.'

'Then why did you say it was like this thing?' said one of the Selenites severely.

'I meant the shape' said the interpreter as patiently as he could.

'You must try and say what you mean in future' said the Selenite, 'or we shall find it too much trouble to try and understand you.'

'Well, the Earth goes round the sun, you see' proceeded the interpreter, 'and the Moon, if you don't mind my saying so, goes round the Earth.'

'Why should we mind your saying so?' asked the Selenites, 'if it is true—as we are much inclined to doubt after your remark about the orange. As far as we can see, the Moon is the centre of the universe, and everything revolves around us. What makes you think otherwise?'

'Our astronomers have discovered all this by—er—telescopes and things, which I don't suppose you'd understand.'

'On the contrary, we understand very well. We have invented telescopes ourselves, but we have never taken the trouble to make one. If you have made one, you probably know more about these matters than we do: that is, if your senses are trustworthy, and you are capable of interpreting their impressions accurately: which this business of the orange leaves open to doubt. However, granting your contention to avoid argument, what have you come here for?'

'Well—er—in the first place, to establish friendly relations——'

'In that case you had better have stayed away: for the perfect indifference consequent upon our ignorance of your existence can hardly be improved by an acquaintance which has been inaugurated by a ridiculous piece of deception about an orange.'

'I wish you'd forget about that orange' said the

nterpreter testily. 'It was an illustration, nothing more. An attempt to enlighten, not to deceive.'

'We will take your word for that' said the Selenites 'until we have further evidence to the contrary. Now what is the second object of your visit?'

'An object which I hope will be of mutual benefit o both of us. We want to trade with you?'

'For our part' replied the Selenites, 'we are only concerned to benefit ourselves. What have you got o sell?'

'Ah, now we're talking' said the interpreter, and proceeded to business.

Negotiations having been concluded to the satisfaction of both sides, the Selenites came swarming from all parts to buy, tendering notes of very artistic design made of the same silken material as their garments. Of these they apparently had a plentiful supply; everybody seemed to be extremely well off; and soon the whole population of the locality were swaggering about in European attire. Their houses were too small to hold all the furniture they were ready to buy; but the Commander of the expedition promised to return with material and labour to build bigger ones, and in the meantime the stock was warehoused under canvas. With part of the receipts the company bought a huge consignment of the plant—known as *klis*—from which the Selenites ordinarily make their clothing. The rest they expended on and for the railway. They then advertised for labour o commence operations, but found that none was forthcoming, even when they offered double, and finally treble, the wages paid for such work on earth: he Selenites politely explaining that such toil would be far too heavy for them, no matter how well it might be paid, and that they would sooner go without a railway than put themselves to so much trouble. They even suggested that labourers should be brought from Earth to do the job, to the great satisfaction of the Commander, who had been afraid to mention such an idea himself, lest the Selenites should resent having the work taken out of their hands. The matter being thus amicably arranged, and the whole cargo sold, the expedition took its departure with many cordial expressions of goodwill on both sides.

CHAPTER XIX

The manners and customs of the Selenites

THIS account of the inhabitants of the Moon was written by a journalist who accompanied the expedition.

'The Selenites are of about the same average height as human beings, but are of much slighter build. They have bigger heads, smaller bellies, thinner legs and arms, smaller ears, and longer noses. They have six fingers on each hand (which is good news for glovers) and seven toes on each foot. Their teeth are small and of a delicate coral colour. Their eyes are invariably green, and their skins dark brown.

'The Moon is not divided into nations. The whole satellite is governed by a committee of twenty-five, chosen annually by lot. The one check on them is a law that if anything goes wrong with the administration, they shall all be put to death at the close of their term of office. Nothing ever goes wrong.

'There is no law on the Moon except this: that if anyone is found to be disagreeable, he is put to death. The people are too lazy to do anything really disagreeable, and so this seldom happens. They consider ambition disagreeable, and so nobody tries to get on. The Selenites are indeed the laziest people in the universe. They do nothing but sing, dance, bathe, play games, write poetry, and design buildings which they never take the trouble to erect. Their wattle huts can be put together in a few hours; their clothing is a simple tunic; their food consists of wild berries and a sort of edible fungus that grows in great profusion among the moss which covers the greater portion of their territory. They say that it is far better to do without things than have the bother of making them: which is a good thing for us, as there is no danger of their starting industries of their own and so depriving us of employment.

'All the work of this extraordinary world is done by a comparatively small number of people, who command very high wages in consequence. A fungus gatherer can earn as much as thirty *blobs* (about fifteen pounds) a week; a tailor charges twenty-four *blobs* for making a tunic; and a builder gets from two to three hundred *blobs* for putting up one of the wretched little shacks they live in. The remainder of the population seem to have small private incomes, but from what source they obtain them I have not succeeded in discovering. These idlers look upon the workers with a certain good-natured contempt, as abnormal people who are too stupid to understand that money is not worth having if it costs any trouble. However, they admit that it is convenient that there are such people, since otherwise they would be driven by sheer necessity to do something themselves. The workers, of course, are not all equally industrious. Many of them are content to earn a small wage and idle the rest of the time. Only a few take the trouble to earn more than forty *blobs* a week. The really ambitious fellows, therefore, have tremendous scope and unlimited opportunities to make their fortunes. These buy themselves large states, on which they build fairly comfortable omes. As there are no cinemas, motors, or other ivilised amusements on the Moon, they spend the est of their money on personal adornment. A really ard worker can be recognised at a glance by the load f jewellery he wears all over him. As I write I can see a uilder starting work on a new house. He is literally blaze with diamonds. He has a diamond tiara on his ead, a rope of moonstones round his neck, emerald arrings in his ears, several diamond bracelets on each vrist, and diamond rings on most of his fingers. His elt is studded with jewels, and his tunic is fastened vith an emerald brooch. The amenities we have rought will be a godsend to these fellows. All our notor cars and expensive furniture have been bought y labourers. The leisured classes can't afford them.

'The Selenites have no religion. They worship themelves, which, they say, is a very agreeable occupation, nd saves them endless worry, as they can always be ertain what their deity wants, and how best he can be leased. Their ideas of morality are what might be expected from such a state of things, marriage being imply a civil contract terminable at will by either party. must admit, however, that changes of partners are infrequent: it is regarded as inconsiderate and disagreeable to marry without due deliberation, and ridiculous nd fussy to separate without grave reason. They simply letest a fuss: for they say that nothing under the sun s of such importance that they should disturb the erenity of their souls on account of it.

'A day on the Moon is as long as fifteen of ours, nd so are the nights, which, moreover, are frightully dark and cold. The Selenites, however, have become perfectly adapted to this unnatural arrangement. When night approaches they wrap themselves up warmly in innumerable shawls of *klis*, and retire into holes, snugly lined with dry moss, under the floors of their houses, where they sleep like dormice until the sun rises again. They say that people like us, who go to sleep fifteen times a day, have no right to accuse them of being lazy.

'The queer ideas of these people are well illustrated by their attitude to the civilised clothing we have brought them. Nothing we can say can persuade them that there is any necessity to distinguish between the attire of the sexes: they say that they have an infallible instinct which tells them at once what sex they and their neighbours belong to. They also refuse to make any distinction between outer garments and underwear. Each person wears what he fancies. After a period of experiment, the elder people of both sexes have adopted our male garb, the sobriety of which makes a strong appeal to them. The favourite attire of the young men is a chemise, a slip, or a pair of cami-knickers. The girls have unanimously fallen for woven combinations, which, they say, show off the curves of their figures to perfection. They prance about in these in shameless delight, gleefully calling the attention of their friends and sweethearts to their only too obvious charms. It is a most shocking sight, but a good augury for future trading prospects. There is one article of attire which nobody here will touch at any price: that is the bowler hat, which, for some reason or other, moves all the silly Selenites to uncontrollable laughter. The whole consignment of ten million remains a dead loss on our hands.'

CHAPTER XX

A Moon-struck World

FROM this date a new era of prosperity dawned upon the world. The population of the Moon was close upon four hundred millions, all fine lusty folk who would eat, drink, wear, and otherwise consume whatever was dumped upon them with the greatest goodwill in the universe. So from morning to night steam hammers were banging, factories clanging, furnaces roaring, coal drills boring, engines shrieking, pulleys creaking, shuttles shooting, sirens hooting, chimneys smoking, stokers stoking, heavers heaving, dockers docking, as the whole human race toiled and moiled, stretched and strained, to pour out goods for the Selenites. Mr Cander's promises were thus amply fulfilled. There was work for everybody, and even a slight increase in wages. It is true that there was a general rise in prices as well (since wages go into costs, and the huge drain of exports caused a certain scarcity of goods in the home market) but that was hardly noticed in the tremendous hum of production. At any rate, with employment so good, it was generally felt that it would be churlish to grumble. People even began again to have children, now that there were plenty of machine handles for them to pull.

On the Moon itself, gangs of terrestrial labourers set to work on the construction of roads and railways, while the idle good-for-nothing Selenites (little guessing how they were being duped) stood about and watched them. The work seemed to afford endless amusement to these flippant creatures. As the sturdy navvies sweated and strained hour after hour under the broiling sun, peals of laughter burst from the lines of spectators, lolling luxuriously on the moss; and when any particularly difficult task was accomplished, the shallow fools would fairly roll about the ground with merriment. They showed equally bad taste in their attitude to the big business men who came to start enterprises in their midst. Learning that Mr Hamridge, who had opened a lunar branch of his famous store, was already worth several million pounds, they used to point him out to one another when he walked abroad, rudely tapping their heads, and showing various signs of suppressed amusement.

Such little incidents as this, however, had no effect on the flow of commerce between the two worlds, which proceeded smoothly from the beginning. As to the *balance* of trade (for, as you know, exports are paid for by imports) that arranged itself very simply. At first the imports of *klis* and other raw materials, such as selenium and moonstones, were sufficient for the purpose. Later, as trade increased, it was found necessary to import large quantities of the berries (*nachrof*) and edible fungus (*oomshruf*) which had formerly been the staple diet of the Selenites, but had now been entirely displaced by earthly provender. These cheap and wholesome, though not very interesting, foodstuffs found a ready market among terrestrial workers, who could no longer afford the high prices of bread, butter, and meat consequent upon the enormous demands of the Selenites for those commodities. Thus does the free operation of a sound commercial and financial system, unhampered by vexatious governmental interference, arrange all things to a perfect harmony.

Now according to the wonderful laws devised by our brilliant and ingenious economists, the people of the Moon should have been utterly ruined by this flood of imports, which deprived them of what little employment their own primitive social system provided for them. Strange to say, however, this was not the case. The Selenites were too backward and ignorant to produce any economists; and as to entrusting the management of their affairs to some functionary analogous to Mr Slawmy Cander, such an idea never entered the Lunatic intelligence. They went on prospering in the most perverse manner. Not a man, woman or child went hungry in the whole length and breadth of the satellite. In fact, everybody grew richer every day.

The way they worked it was this. The economic affairs of the Moon were entrusted to five master mathematicians, who calculated from time to time the total production of goods by the various industries, and the total amount of wealth consumed in producing them. By dividing the latter figure by the former they arrived at a fraction (normally about $\frac{3}{4}$) which they called the Price Factor; and this fraction of the financial cost price of any article was known as its True Price. When a man bought an article in a shop, he paid its full price, and afterwards brought the receipt to the local clerk of the Mathematicians, who refunded him the difference between that and the True Price.

Having calculated the Price Factor, the Mathematicians next printed money exactly equivalent to the total cash prices of all the goods available. This was issued to the people in two parts. The first was the refund, already mentioned, to every purchaser of commodities. The second and larger portion, called the *Nid*, was divided equally among the whole population, workers and idlers alike. Thus the people as a whole always had enough money to buy all the goods on the market; everybody had a decent income whether his work was required or not; and those who did work had their wages and salaries in addition.

If this is not clear to you—involving as it does some knowledge of that 'dismal science' which your teachers have been so careful to keep you from learning—do not be discouraged. I confess that for a long time I could not understand it myself, and therefore submitted the theorem to a Mathematician of my acquaintance, who assured me that it was perfectly correct. Yet even after his explanation, which he delivered with great care and courtesy, I was still bothered.

'What is your difficulty?' said he at length.

'Well' said I, 'no juggling with figures will ever convince me that a people can go on selling their goods below cost price without coming to rack and ruin.'

'It is very simple' said the Mathematician. 'You know that all commodities are produced by the labour of men, assisted by the free gifts of Nature (such as sunlight, air, rain, and so forth) and the accumulated inheritance of the race (skill, knowledge, and capital equipment). You also know that all money comes into circulation as wages and dividends.'

'So far, so good' said I.

'Well, then' said the Mathematician. 'Nature and the Race Heritage do their share of the work without wages, and there is therefore no corresponding issue of money to purchase the increment attributable to them. The result in our world is that if there is a large increment of production (consequent upon a generous harvest, or the extensive use of machinery) no money is available to buy it: so that producers are ruined, goods are wasted, and consumers go hungry. What the Selenites do, then, is to issue the wages due to Nature and the Race Heritage as purchasing power to the consumers; or, in other words, they create the money-equivalent to the real wealth produced by these two sources, and issue it as purchasing power to enable the people to buy it.'

'It is not clear to me yet' said I.

'Well, then, suppose that *all* the work of the world could be done by one man turning a crank. As there would be no wages issued to anyone else, how could you get the goods bought?'

'I suppose' I said reluctantly, 'by issuing free money.'

'There would be no other way, except to give the goods for nothing, which is the same thing. What the Selenites do is to issue *some* wages and *some* free money, accurately calculated.'

'All the same' I said, 'I don't see how you can make a profit if you sell your goods at a loss.'

'Why, you fat-headed owl' said he—for you know that Mathematicians are characterised by a certain acerbity of temper when dealing with their inferiors—'can you not *see*——?' and here he went over his explanation again, but I couldn't understand it yet.

'I fear I cannot see it' said I.

'You addle-pated noodle' cried he, 'you thick-skulled ninny, listen again—' and he went over the whole ground once more.

'I'm afraid it's too complicated for me' said I.

'O you drivelling nincompoop' cried the Mathematician in a rage. 'You miserable shallow looney, you ass, you dunderhead, you silly gaby, you dolt, you imbecile, you Boeotian bullcalf, you sawney, you gowk, you vacuous mooncalf, you concentrated essence of bovine inanity, you unteachable mule, you fatuous gaping Tomnoddy, you blockhead, you jobbernowl, listen, and I'll explain once more—'

'No' said I. 'Better leave it at that, or you may begin to think me stupid.'

Therefore, my friend, lest you fall under the same accusation, if you cannot work out the sum, you had better take it on faith. After all, the proof of the pudding is in the eating, and this crazy-seeming plan worked. The Selenites were not in the least inconvenienced by the flood of extra-lunar goods that inundated them. For as fast as they came on the market, money was issued to buy them; and the less labour required to produce them, the lower fell the Price Factor. The native industries all rapidly closed down, but that mattered not a whit to the workers, for their loss in wages was more than compensated by the increase of the *Nid* and the fall in the True Price. Soon the Selenites had nothing to do but enjoy themselves, while the Earth sweated and stinted itself to supply them with good things.

It was a sight to make the Gods laugh; and you, sweet reader (if you have any sense), may well ask why the poor silly terrestrials went on with such foolery: to which I answer, that if they had stopped supplying the goods, they would have been all thrown out of employment again, while the Selenites would not have cared two hoots, for if their new luxuries had been cut off they would have gone back to their former simple mode of living with the best goodwill in the world: such is the equable nature of their character.

After a time, indeed, the stream of goods began to diminish, because the imports of Selenite material could not keep pace with it. Unemployment at once began to rear its unwelcome head again on earth; but Mr Cander was not to be defeated so easily. He arranged that in future the surplus profits should be invested in new enterprises on the spot: in other words, terrestrial-owned industries were to be started on lunar territory. This solved the difficulty for a time, giving much-needed employment to the 'heavy' industries; but after a while the competition of the lunar factories began to be felt, prices fell, and many terrestrial businesses were ruined. Only one course now remained: to conquer the Moon, and bring it within the ambit of the Earth's financial system. As the Economists put it, the economic problem was One Big Two-World Problem which could not be solved on narrow one-world lines.

The British were first in the field with this proposal. They claimed that their legitimate interests in the Moon were now so large that it was virtually their property; that these interests were imperilled by the absence of any really responsible government on the Moon; that it was their sacred duty to put down the abominable religion of the Selenites and introduce a few hundred true religions; and that a British conquest would be in the best interests of the Selenites themselves, as the prosperity of the two worlds was interdependent: moreover, the British Empire was the mother of freedom, and no true freedom could exist outside it.

The Americans promptly replied with a not less plausible claim, and both countries began to equip expeditionary forces. The Japanese did likewise. The other nations protested in vain. The League of Nations made no protest at all, as the Moon was outside its jurisdiction, and the Powers concerned were large ones, which could be trusted to go to war only when their legitimate interests were at stake. Finally the three armaments set sail almost simultaneously; each planted its flag on lunar territory, and executed as rebels all Selenites who resisted their authority; then they went for one another, and in a brief but murderous war they practically wiped each other out.

The Selenites, who had watched these proceedings with astonishment, now bestirred themselves, and, having rounded up the survivors of the three armies, packed them into a ship and sent them back to the Earth with a stern intimation to the inhabitants of that planet that they desired no further intercourse with them. On the receipt of this insolent message, the three Powers patched up an agreement, under the mediation of Mr Slawmy Cander, to partition the Moon between them, and sent a joint expedition to recapture it and inflict condign punishment on the rebels. In the meanwhile, however, the Selenites had roused themselves from their apathy and taken measures for defence. What weapon they improvised can never now be known. All that has been recorded is that when the terrestrial fleet approached the surface of the satellite, it was assailed by a succession of violent electric shocks, which destroyed most of the ships. A few crippled survivors turned and fled, but only one succeeded in returning to Earth. A second expedition met with a similar fate; and after that all hope of reducing the Moon was abandoned.

The effect on the Earth was immediate and tragic. Deprived of the only available market, industry after industry went smash, and the world sank into the blackest trade depression it had ever known.

CHAPTER XXI

The Wilderness

YOUNG JOHNNY SMITH sat on the parapet of the bridge, fishing. Old John Smith sat on the grass-grown railway track, smoking. Young Johnny's rod was a stout ash-plant, his line was the stem of a creeper, his hook was a fish-bone, his bait was a worm. Old John's tobacco was coltsfoot, dried in the sun, and when it went out, as it frequently did, he relighted it laboriously with two flints and a wisp of straw. Young Johnny was twelve years of age; Old John, his grandfather, was ninety-two.

Old John looked mournfully over the thickening landscape. The vegetation seemed to grow thicker and ranker every day. Not so long ago he had been able to see the ruins of Weybridge from where he sat. Now it was hidden by a growing jungle of willows and sally that shot up rapidly from the swampy soil between. Everywhere he turned, the prospect was the same: forests of young trees, tangled brakes of exuberant bushes and monstrous weeds, varied only by the desolate marshy tracts on the margins of the river. The very roads were distinguishable only as green trails through the jungle.

Young Johnny pulled in his line, and landed a fine bream. 'Good' said Old John. 'Now let's have supper.' He gutted the fish, split it in two, and laid it on the hot stones of the fire he had prepared. After the meal he lit his pipe, and the two sat silent for a while. Presently Johnny, fiddling in the grass, pulled out a sliver of rusting iron.

'That'll be a bit of railway line, I reckon' said Old John. 'Eh, lad, you should have seen them in the old days—long straight shining rails running all the way from London to Southampton. Straight as your fishing rod, all the way, and all shining bright.'

Johnny, who had heard this before, wriggled impatiently.

'And the trains, lad. You should have seen them' went on his grandfather. 'Thundering through, all day and all night. Great big iron engines, belching out fire and smoke, with fifty carriages full of people behind them, thundering along at seventy or eighty mile an hour.'

The old man shook his head sadly. 'Dozens of them went by every day' he said. 'Thundering through. Thundering through.'

A wild cat appeared on the edge of the jungle. The boy threw a stone at it, and it vanished. 'Must have smelt the roasting fish' said the old man.

He fell into reminiscence again. 'Then there were the flying machines, flying about like great birds, all full of people going to foreign parts. And that road there, so crowded with motor cars that it wasn't safe to walk across it. That's how my father got killed: just walking across that road. And the noise they made. You could hardly hear yourself think sometimes. Night and day, nothing but noise. And the lights. That road used to be lighted up at night so that it was like daylight, and the cars went shrieking along at all hours.

'It all seemed so natural in those days' he said. 'You wouldn't have thought it ever could stop. And now it's all gone, like the smoke of yesterday's fire.'

'How did it go?' asked the boy.

'It was all along of what they called Progress' said the old man. 'They invented machines, and more machines, and every machine did the work of a score of men, you see, so the men weren't wanted. In those days you didn't catch fish and things for yourself. You got money for working in a factory, and then you went to a shop and paid the money for whatever you wanted. But if you hadn't any work to do, you didn't get any money—or only a little bit, just enough to keep you alive—so you had to go hungry. Well, it went on like that for a long time, and at last there were so many people out of work that there weren't enough people with money to buy the stuff that was made by the machines, so the machines were put out of employment in their turn. People got poorer and poorer, and the whole place was chock-a-block with goods that couldn't be sold—'

'Why didn't they take them without paying?' demanded the boy.

'Some did' replied his grandfather. 'Thousands of desperate men took to killing and robbing as the only way to live. But most people kept on hoping for a change for the better. They tried every sort of way—the Government, I mean—to set things right, but they only made them worse. I suppose they didn't know any better. Factories went on closing down, land went out of cultivation, ships no longer sailed the seas. Nobody dared to have children, and the people began to die out. Then the war came—'

'What was it about?' asked the boy.

'I never knew' said the old man. 'I only remember the terror of it. There were bombs from the air, and poison gas, and liquid fire, and plague, and when it was all over there was nobody left alive in this part of the country but me and your father. He was only a boy then, younger than you are now. We didn't meet your mother till long afterwards, way up north, where we went hunting.'

The boy remained silent. His grandfather had often told him how his mother had died in giving him birth, and how his father had been killed on a hunting expedition by falling into an old quarry.

'You'd never have believed it could ever have ended' said the old man again, musing over the rusted flake of steel. 'It all seemed so natural, and like as if it always had been. If anyone had told me it would come to this, I wouldn't have believed him.

'Well, well' he said with a sigh. 'It's time we were getting home, lad.'

Thus do old habits of speech survive. They had a hundred empty houses to choose from and camped in whichever suited them best.

CHAPTER XXII

And the meek shall inherit the Earth

M. HENRI COQUIN came to himself slowly, and with many relapses into unconsciousness. When at last he opened his eyes, fully awake, it was too dark to see anything. An infinite weakness was upon him, and his head swam.

For a while he lay still. Then a sense of being in unfamiliar surroundings came to him. Moving his hands, he found that he was lying on a rubber mattress of extreme resiliency—evidently a water-bed. Then he perceived that he was naked, and covered with a single sheet, silky to the touch. Puzzled, he tried to rise, only to sink back, dazed and exhausted.

He wondered where he might be. Certainly not in his own bed. Then suddenly he recognised his sensations. He must have been seized with one of those cataleptic fits of his, and carried to a hospital. Satisfied by this explanation, he lay still, waiting for his strength to return and the day to dawn. Already, far above him, a dim grey light was beginning to infiltrate the gloom. As he watched it, his blood began to flow more warmly, and gradually memory returned. Yesterday—it must have been yesterday—he had been out in the streets when the air-raid began. He had made for the Underground at once—the station on the Place de la Concorde. He had become wedged in a fighting mob of people, while the noise of the bombardment came nearer and nearer. After that all was blank.

As the light grew stronger, he looked about him curiously. With surprise he saw that he was not in a hospital after all. He was lying in an oblong glass case, raised well above the floor, and the room he was in was—could it be a museum? There could be no doubt it was. He had visited it himself only a few days before. It was the Louvre.

Incredible, but true. Had his fit lasted so long that he had been exhibited here as a public curiosity? That seemed the only possible explanation, and he boiled with rage at the thought. Strengthened, he sat up, and, wrapping the silken coverlet round his arm, broke the glass roof that confined him, and then fell back coughing in a cloud of dust that had accumulated on top of it.

Recovering, he looked about him again, and now, in the clearer light, he noticed that the room was terribly dilapidated. Most of the pictures were gone from the walls, and the few that remained were but rotten canvas. A huge vase that had stood near one of the doors, lay in fragments on the floor. Dust lay thick on everything. Then, looking up, he saw a large hole in the roof. Utterly bewildered, he descended gingerly from his couch, and stood gazing at an inscription on a brass plate affixed to it.

Henri Coquin
Aged 53
Who fell into a trance during
the bombardment of
Paris.

A date followed—yesterday's in Coquin's recollection—but the plate was corroded with the verdigris of innumerable years.

'It seems that I have slept a long time' said M. Coquin to himself, 'and they have grown tired of watching me.'

He tottered weakly to a seat, covered with dust and cobwebs, which fell to pieces as soon as he put his weight on it. A stone sarcophagus, five thousand years older, offered a securer resting place, and there he sat in a state of futile wonderment, while he collected his energies for a further effort. He soon realised that he was desperately hungry, so, wrapping himself in the coverlet as in a mantle, he made for the doorway of the gallery, and descended the nearest staircase, clinging close to the balustrade, till he reached the main hall. The great doors hung loose from their hinges, and collapsed the moment he put his hand on them, revealing a view that, for all the preparation he had had for a shock, nearly made him cry out with surprise. The Place du Louvre was a green field studded with trees and bushes, and the Mairie and other buildings opposite were a heap of weed-grown ruins.

Coquin reeled out into the open air, and turned into the Rue de Rivoli; but instead of a street he found a grassy lane, sparkling with dew in the morning sun. Here and there a tangle of briars choked its course. Most of the buildings that had lined it had disappeared. A few stood, gaunt and silent, their façades blotched with growths of weeds and moss, or completely covered with ivy. Nowhere was there sign or sound of human life.

Scarcely knowing what hè did, Coquin advanced owards the Place du Palais Royal. Then, with lmost a yelp of delight, he saw that the brambles vere covered with ripe blackberries. Heedless of ricks and gashes, he gathered them ravenously, and tayed to some degree his gnawing hunger. Then he ushed on, past the ruins of the Palais Royal and he Ministry of Finance, past the silent shops that ıad once glittered with jewellery and fine clothes, ast the Jardins des Tuileries, now a dense forest f stunted trees, till at last he emerged where the lace de la Concorde ought to have been. In its stead vas a vast crater filled with stagnant water and rank ıorrible weeds. Looking to right and left he saw wo broken pillars where the Madeleine had been, nd a grassy hill, crowned with young trees, on the ite of the Chambre des Députés. Far ahead, above he green woods that grew all over the Champs lysées, stood the Arc de Triomphe.

He decided that he must push on. He must get way from this city of death. In the country outside ıe must surely find living men. Skirting the noisome rater, he struggled through the dense undergrowth f the Elysée towards the Etoile, took a long raught at a fountain there, ate some more berries, nd then, with fresh vigour, strode along the Avénue e la Grande Armée, through the Porte de Neuilly nd the suburb beyond. Everywhere was the same esolation: grass-grown streets, shell holes, ruined nd deserted houses.

Further fortified with some apples he had athered in a garden at Neuilly, Coquin reached the pen country as the day was declining, and then, tired out with his exertions, lay down in the shelter of a hawthorn bush, and fell asleep.

When he awoke next morning the sun was high. Looking about the once familiar landscape, he found it almost unrecognisable. On every side, fields, farms, and villages had disappeared, drowned in a rising sea of forest. There was nothing for it, however, but to go ahead; so, having eaten the last of his apples, he plunged into it with such courage as a bad swimmer puts on in jumping out of a sinking boat. He was soon hopelessly lost in the tangle of trees, and for the next two days blundered along aimlessly, till at last, after adventures that would be as tedious to tell as they were to endure, he saw light in front of him, and presently found himself on the edge of a clearing. Before him lay a good-sized plain covered with short grass like a lawn, very suggestive of human occupancy. Full of hope he stepped out from among the trees, and promptly stopped short before the queerest sight he had yet seen.

Not a hundred yards from where he stood was what looked like a pigmy town. The little houses, barely knee high, were built neatly of sods, and arranged in straight streets around a larger central building of the same material. The streets were crowded, and one glance revealed to him who were the inhabitants of this singular city. They were rabbits.

They were not scurrying about in the manner of the rabbits he was accustomed to. They were walking at ease, some singly, some in couples, and he noticed that these looked at one another every now and then like men conversing. Several parties came out presently into the surrounding plain, ate a leisurely meal of grass, and afterwards either returned to the town or walked off as if to some business.

Very slowly and quietly Coquin approached the town. Instantly a rabbit on the tower of the central building uttered a squeak of alarm, and a second later the whole population had scampered to the other end of the plain. Coquin was a kind-hearted fellow, and felt, moreover, that to eat such rabbits as these, supposing he could catch one, would be a sort of cannibalism; so he quietly walked back to the woods. When he turned round again, he saw that the rabbits had already reoccupied their town and were carrying on their previous businesses as if nothing had happened.

Full of amazement, he worked his way round the plain, keeping himself hidden within the fringe of the wood, and so obtained an excellent view of the rabbits at work. In one place a party was engaged in cutting sods, which they managed very dexterously with their forepaws, or else with some instrument held in these—at the distance he could not decide which. Others, in teams of four, were drawing the sods by means of some sort of harness towards a new town which was being erected near by. In another place a large party was busy nibbling down the seedlings by means of which the forest threatened to encroach upon the plain. He observed that perfect harmony and complete understanding existed between all the members engaged in these occupations, and that, while everything was done with exactness and expedition, there was no bustling nor hustling nor business efficiency. Each individual appeared to be working because the job pleased him, and to be more concerned with doing it to his own satisfaction than with getting it finished.

Moving on a little further, he perceived other groups amusing themselves at racing, tag, leap-frog, and such-like games; and again others, in a more secluded spot, amorously engaged in increasing the rabbit population. All these sports and occupations he watched with a kindly eye, wishing that his own life had been so happily spent. At the same time the saddening thought occurred to him that the existence of this peaceful community would have been impossible if man still lived upon the earth; and thus it came home to M. Henri Coquin that the human race had been superseded.

CHAPTER XXIII

The last word

TWO of the Gods, playing (by the grace of *'Ανάγκη*) with the stuff of worlds to come, observed a dim star among the drifting millions flash suddenly, and go out. Where the twain were situated is not easily described: for it depends on whether the Universe is of the homely old shape, straight and infinite, described by Newton, or curved and finite, after the bizarre pattern of Einstein. For my part I cannot understand why it should not be spiral, or zig-zag, or annular, or cruciform, or even higgledy-piggledy, provided it be large enough: in which case we poor midges could neither know what shape it is, nor be any wiser if we did. There was an astronomer fellow once wrote a marvellous fine book about this Mysterious Universe, very confident in all its measurements both of time and space (though perhaps a little doubtful whether its age were 5,000,000,000,000,000,000,000 or 6,000,000,000,000,000,000,000 years, which is a very trifling margin of error, as you will agree)—wherein he stepped aside for a moment from these momentous calculations to observe that social reformers are a little too apt to try and get a quart out of a pint pot: having been too busy waggling his telescope at infinity to have ever heard of over-production. From this we should learn to be humble in such speculations: nevertheless I cannot help putting forward a theory of my own, to wit, that the Universe is hour-glass shaped, and held about the waist by the grip of Ἀνάγκη: hence the number of fools it contains. A straight, or even a moderately curved, universe would surely have room for a little more wisdom.

To quit such abstruse matters and finish our story, the two Gods having observed the extinction of the star, one of them remarked to the other: 'There ends another of my experiments.'

'A successful one?' asked the second God.

'Nay, a miserable failure, though at one time it gave good promise. That star gave birth to a number of planets, on one of which I evolved, after much thought and toil, a strange creature called Man. At first he was truly interesting, but he reached his zenith too quickly, and then rapidly declined. During his last few hundred years, when he was already far gone in decay, he achieved a mastery of natural forces that was marvellous in a race so stupid, but his wickedness and folly were such that it did him more harm than good. In the end I superseded him by a somewhat lower creature called rabbit; but this had no great potentialities either for good or evil, and so nothing came of it. A few million years ago the planet fell back into its parent sun, which has now itself come to an end.'

'Did these Men that you have mentioned achieve nothing of lasting worth?' asked the other God.

'Almost nothing' replied the first. 'A few of them did occasionally show some glimmerings of divine wisdom, to which their fellows paid no heed. That, and some trifles of tolerable music, is their only memorial. If you listen you may catch some echo of the latter still moving among the spheres.'

The Gods were silent; and the ghost of the Ninth Symphony came stealing through the ether.

LONDON, *November* 1931
BYFLEET, *October* 1932